S.J. WEST

WOLF KINGS OF TWILIGHT

UNWAVERING

Contents

WOLF KINGS OF TWILIGHT

COPYRIGHTS

Proof Reader: Janelle Leonard.
Cover Design: Coversbyjuan.com
Interior Design & Formatting: Stephany Wallace @ S.W. Creative Publishing co, all rights reserved.

Published by Watchers Publishing Jun 30th, 2022.
www.Sjwest.com

WOLF KINGS OF TWILIGHT

BOOKS IN THE WATCHER SERIES

<u>The Watchers Trilogy</u>
Cursed
Blessed
Forgiven

<u>The Watcher Chronicles</u>
Broken
Kindred
Oblivion
Ascension

<u>Caylin's Story</u>
Timeless
Devoted
Aiden's Story

<u>The Alternate Earth Series</u>
Cataclysm
Uprising
Judgment

<u>The Redemption Series</u>
Malcolm
Anna
Lucifer

Redemption

The Dominion Series
Awakening
Reckoning
Enduring

The Everlasting Fire Series
War Angel
Between Worlds
Shattered Souls

Lucifer and Amalie's Story
Surrendering the Dark
Descending into the Abyss

Guardians of the Void
Restoration
Atonement
Exodus

War Angel Academy
Harbinger
Nemesis
Champion

OTHER BOOKS BY S.J. WEST

The Harvester of Light Trilogy
Harvester
Hope

Dawn

<u>The Vankara Saga</u>
Vankara
Dragon Alliance
War of Atonement

<u>Vampire Conclave Series</u>
Moonshade
Sentinel
Conclave
Requiem

<u>Circle of the Rose Chronicles</u>
Cin D'Rella and the Water of Life
Cin D'Rella and the Golden Apple
Cin D'Rella and the Lonely Tower.
Cin d'Rella and the Messengers of Death.

<u>Pandora's Legacy</u>
Pandora's Gift

<u>Wolf Kings of Twilight</u>
Untouchable
Unwavering

MULTI-AUTHOR ANTHOLOGIES

<u>The Monster Ball Year 3:</u>
A Paranormal Romance Anthology
Second Chances

ACKNOWLEDGMENTS

I would like to express my gratitude to the many people who were with me throughout this creative process; to all those who provided support, talked things over, read, wrote, offered comments, allowed me to quote their remarks and assisted in the editing, proofreading and design.

I would like to thank Misti Monen, Andie Ryder, Nicoll Edwards, Erica Croyle, Barb Todaro, Lisa Fejeran, my beta readers, for helping me in the process with invaluable feedback.

Thanks to Janelle Leonard, my editor for helping me find typos, correct commas and tweak the little details that have help this book become my perfect vision.

Thank you to Stephany Wallace for creating the beautiful Interior Design for my books and formatting them.
Last but not least, I want to thank my family, who supported and encouraged me in this journey.

I apologize to those who have been with me over the course of the years and whose names I have failed to mention.

CHAPTER I

Boris has always been a wise man. I should have realized he was right when he said living out the rest of our lives on a boat was an unrealistic notion on my part. I poked fun at him at the time, but after three days of sailing on Alek's ship, I realize he was right. The endless motion of the boat on the open sea is something my stomach wasn't trained to endure. Not only does it constantly sway from left to right, but it also bobs up and down. The nonstop movement has made it almost impossible for me to keep any food in my stomach, and I ruined my dress the very first day when I failed to reach a nearby bucket quickly enough. I was forced to change into the leather outfit Alek laid out for me, but at least it was easier to clean up the second time I lost the contents of my stomach. Not eating became preferable, but this just seemed to worry my captor.

"You've got to eat, Ivy," Alek says, staring at me, clearly concerned for my welfare.

"Like you care what happens to me," I groan, tightly clasping my arms around my belly as the motion of the ship continues to wreck its havoc on my body. "If you did, you wouldn't have kidnapped me in the first place."

Alek sighs and shakes his head in dismay. "If I've told you once, I've told you a thousand times already that I'm sorry it came to this, but my people need you. If we're going to maintain our humanity, we need your help. It's the same reason Damon and Simon want you. Why is that so hard for you to accept?"

I sit down on the bed in Alek's quarters in a vain attempt to steady myself.

"Everything you said about leaving the life of a pirate behind to start a horse stable in Midnight, was it all a lie?"

"Of course, it was a lie," he scoffs. "What was I going to say? That I planned to kidnap you myself the first chance I got? Damon would have had me tied and quartered if he'd known that was my plan. In fact, I'm surprised he even let me take part in the tournament. He gave us all false hope that we would be able to win you for our people, but it's obvious now that he never intended for anyone else to have you but himself. I have to say, he played his hand well, but I should have known he would never willingly let you go. He would have been a fool to do that, and after spending some time with him, I quickly learned that Damon is no fool."

"You know when he finds you he'll make you pay for what you've done," I say smugly.

Alek's lips stretch into a cocky grin. "Which is exactly why we're going somewhere he'll never find us. At least not until you have my child growing inside your belly."

"Fat chance of that happening, you son of a bitch! Unless you want me to slice off what manhood you have left, I would advise you stay as far away from me as possible."

Alek begins to chuckle which only fans the flames of my anger even further.

"I wholeheartedly believe you would do that too, if given the opportunity," he says, looking amused by my threat of bodily harm. "But if you give me a chance, I think you might find me more than able to satisfy your needs."

"What I need is for you to take me back home."

Alek tilts his head as he considers my words. "And where is that exactly? Dawn? As soon as you step foot in Simon's territory, he'll lock you back up inside that tower of his. Or maybe you think Midnight is your home now? Damon will never let anyone else have you, and he'll be forced into a fight to the death with Simon. It seems to me that I'm the only one giving you a genuine chance at a real life. You may not be able to see it now, but with me, you can have the freedom to do *what* you want *when* you want. I won't even force you to live with me and our children if you would rather not."

"Are you nuts?" I practically shout. "Like I would let any child of mine become a low-life pirate like you."

Alek's face contorts into a mask of rage. It's the first time since I woke up on this boat that he's shown an ounce of anger toward me.

"At least I work for what I have," he thunders, eyes blazing with fury. "I'm not like your precious kings. I've never lived in a fancy castle surrounded by servants who would wipe my ass if I ordered them to. Our children will understand what it means to work and earn an honest living."

"Pfft," I scoff. "You earn a living by taking what other people have worked hard for. You may think you're different, but you're just like Damon and Simon. They tax their people for money. You just steal it. Tell me, oh wise one, how is that any different?"

Alek's scowl deepens, but he doesn't reply. He can't. He knows I'm right.

"Get out of here," I say, turning my head away from him in disgust. "The sight of you and your hypocrisy is making me even sicker to my stomach than I already am."

The metallic sound of Alek turning the doorknob fills the uncomfortable silence between us.

"We'll be arriving at the island I told you about in less than an hour. Maybe your attitude will change once you're onshore." He opens the door and steps out, leaving me all alone yet again. All I can hear is the sound of rain hitting the glass of the windows and the creaking of the ship as the turbulent sea pounds against the hull.

An hour. That's all I have to endure before I can find respite from my nausea. The stench of my own vomit in the bucket beside the bed does nothing but intensify my queasiness.

I lie back on the bed and close my eyes wishing I was anywhere but here.

For three long days, all I've been able to do is worry about Boris and wonder what Damon must be thinking right now. Is Boris even still alive? When I left him, he had lost a great deal of blood, and Margaret was tending to his wounds from the intruder. The castle's "ghost" wasn't a spirit at all but a man dressed in an odd-looking white outfit. Who was he and why was he so intent on killing me?

Whoever my attacker was, he's dead now. Boris and I made sure of that. Unfortunately, all of his secrets died along with him. Is that for the best? I'm not sure, but at least Damon knows for certain that his father wasn't the one haunting the corridors of his castle.

Damon . . .

What is he doing right now? Is he trying to find me? Does he even know who abducted me this time?

I'm getting sick and tired of the men in my life pulling me this way and that like a toy just so they can ensure the legacy of their people. All of them, even Damon, seem to view me as a pawn they can trifle with, but I'm no one's plaything.

Well, that's not entirely true. I don't mind the way Damon plays with me. In fact, I find it quite pleasurable, but that's beside the point. I should be able to decide my own destiny, but I fear the only way that will be possible is if we go into the Barrens like we discussed and find more of the serum Margaret used to cure the wolf pups in Midnight. If we can do that, maybe . . . just maybe I can reclaim my life and live where I want to.

But where is that?

Do I want to stay on the path of my original plan? Do I really want to live out my days with Boris in the woods? Or do I want to stay with Damon and possibly build a life together? With Margaret's cure, I can have a family of my own with children who would always know a mother's love. It was something I never had a chance to experience. Boris did his best while raising me, but I missed the touch of my mother. It's something I can't adequately explain to anyone else. In all honesty, it's a little hard for me to understand it myself, but I've always felt like a piece of me was missing without her in my life.

I was never given the opportunity to meet my parents. In fact, I don't even know who they were or why they left me with Grandma Mable. Were they ashamed of my humanity? Were they sickened by the mere sight of me? Maybe I was better off not knowing who they were if that's the case.

Yet, deep within my soul, there's still a scared little girl who yearns for the love of those who gave her life. A girl who desperately wants answers to her questions, but who also knows she will probably never get them. I don't even know if my parents are still alive, and worse yet, if they are, they've never presented themselves to claim me as their own.

When I open my eyes, warm tears slide down my face. They're tears I've cried a thousand times, and I know they won't be the last ones shed for the shadows lurking in my past.

Almost an hour later, I hear the crew of the ship shouting to one another on the deck. I assume it means we're approaching this secret island Alek has been referring to for the past three days as his home. I mostly tuned him out during his visits because I didn't want him to assume any attention he gained from me was because of interest in getting to know him better. I have absolutely no desire in learning more about his life as a pirate, and considering the fact that he never once asked me about my own past, I have to assume he has no real interest in getting to know me for who I am either.

That's fine by me. He's nothing but a heartless kidnapper who stole me away when I was at my lowest, and I'm not sure I'll ever be able to forgive him for taking me away from Boris when he needed me the most. Part of that blame falls on Margaret's shoulders because she ordered me out of the room and told Alek to take me for a walk, but I don't have it in me to be mad at her for that. She had no way of knowing what Alek's true intentions were. Her primary focus was on Boris, and I pray she was able to save his life.

When I hear the sound of running footsteps outside my door, I quickly stand up from the bed.

Alek slams the door open. The look of horror on his face instantly tells me that something is very wrong.

He stuffs his right hand into his pants pocket and pulls out a small silver key as he rushes over to me.

He drops to his knees by the bedpost that my chain is wrapped around and unlocks the padlock that's kept me prisoner during my time aboard his ship.

"I need your help," he says in a rush of words as he stands back up. "We're being attacked."

"Attacked?" Surely, he's joking. "Aren't you the pirate here? Shouldn't *you* be the one doing the attacking?"

"We're not being attacked by people." He grabs me roughly by the wrist and proceeds to drag me out the door.

I wrench my arm out of his grasp.

"If we're not being attacked by people, what exactly is attacking us?" I demand to know.

Alek grabs me by the arm again but this time he squeezes harder to make sure I don't escape him a second time.

"I'll tell you, but you still won't know what it is," he reasons before proceeding to drag me up the stairs toward the deck. "It's an octopus."

I hate to admit it, but he's completely right. I have no idea what kind of creature that is.

The closer we get to the deck, the louder the screams coming from Alek's crew are. Rain pours down the steps, but we're partially protected from the brunt of it by the wooden planks over our heads. An unnaturally loud clicking sound fills the air as thunder booms and lightning crackles in the sky.

Alek stops us just short of coming eye level with the deck.

"Your poison," he shouts over the cacophony of sound surrounding us, "it can kill animals too, right?"

"As far as I know," I answer, just as loudly. "Why?"

"We need you to touch the octopus and kill it! This ship wasn't built to fight one!"

"Then why in the world did you sail it out here?"

"We've only ever encountered them in this part of the ocean at night. They never come this close to the surface during the day, but the storm seems to have emboldened this one. The bastard has us wrapped up in its tentacles. All you have to do is reach out and touch it before it drags us down to the bottom of the ocean."

"That's all?" I scream derisively over the bedlam happening on the deck. I duck as the tip of one of the monster's red tentacles flicks into the stairwell over our heads. Before it disappears, I see rows of white suction cups on the underside of its appendage. Fear, like I've never known before, overtakes me. "I'm not going out there!"

Alek grabs me roughly by the arms and squeezes tightly. The desperation on his face tells me before his words do that our situation is dire, and I'm the only hope the ship and its crew has for survival.

"We're all going to die if you don't at least try."

I believe him, but all I want to do is run back into my room and lock the door. Unfortunately, that option would be a sure death sentence.

"Look out!" one of the crew shouts.

Alek and I look up just in time to see the monster use one of its tentacles to break the ship's main mast like a twig. The pole falls through the sky heading straight for the stairwell. Alek pushes me down toward the steps as he places himself between me and the pole, as if his body is enough to shield me from the debris. Luckily for us, the tumbling pole lands tip first on the first stair and falls over us instead of directly onto us.

You can do this . . . you can do this . . . you can do this . . .

You have *to do this.*

I say these words to myself to strengthen my courage and weaken my fear. It sort of works, and I know if I don't try to save us now I never will.

I look up at Alek who is still using his body to shield me. "Help me get on deck!"

He nods. A look of relief removes the worry lines from his face. I almost caution him not to look so relieved just yet. We're going to need a miracle for his plan to work.

Alek reaches out and takes one of my hands with his.

"Try to stay away from its tentacles. If it grabs you, you're dead. It'll either squeeze you to death, eat you, or drown you, understand?"

Awesome. I have one of three gruesome deaths to look forward to if I fail. It's not exactly the pep talk I was hoping for.

"Then where am I supposed to touch it?" I scream over the roar of the creature as it seems to squeeze the ship tighter considering the sound of creaking wood surrounding us.

"You'll need to touch its head." Even as Alek says these words, there is a sea of doubt swimming in his eyes that I can get the job done.

I take in a deep breath.

"Let's go!"

I fear if Alek tells me anything else about this suicide mission, I might lose my nerve.

I've been responsible for enough deaths. I won't live with the guilt of the ship's crew losing their lives because I was too frightened to use my curse to save them. Maybe in this one instance, I'll be able to use it to prevent deaths instead of cause them.

With Alek still holding my hand, we quickly make our way up the stairwell, past the fallen mast, and onto the deck. The sky is filled with dark clouds looming overhead like harbingers of doom. In the stairwell, we were partially protected by the rain, but up here on deck, it lashes us from every direction.

I raise my hand to shield my eyes from the pelting rain. It's not hard to figure out where the body of the octopus is. It's large, bulbous head towers over the bow of the ship. The creature seems to be the source of the loud clicking noise, but I can't tell how it's making the sound.

Just as one of the massive tentacles swings toward us, Alek pushes me down onto the wooden deck before either of us can be swept overboard. With my back pressed against the hardwood, I watch in horror as the creature's appendage catches two unsuspecting crewmen from behind. Each man becomes glued to the suckers on the underside of the tentacle. Their screams of terror mingle with the thunder until they're dragged over the side of the boat, never to be heard from again.

I have no desire to know what happens to them after that, and I pray I'm never forced to personally find out.

"Come on!" Alek yanks me off the deck.

I barely have time to wipe the rain from my eyes before he pulls me across the main deck to a set of stairs leading up to the bow of the ship. Once we reach the top, my breath is snatched out of my lungs by fear.

Staring back at me is the massive bulging milky gray eye of the creature. In the center, is a black, soulless horizontal pupil that's a thin black line at first but soon widens as if it wants a better look at me. While its attention has been drawn by our sudden appearance, I know I only have a few seconds to reach out and touch the octopus before it uses one of its massive tentacles to sweep us out of its way. If circumstances were different, I could see myself marveling at the sheer size and power of the monster before me, but time is not on my side.

I dart across the deck as quickly as I can, but that turns out to be a mistake on my part. The wood is so slick with rain that I begin to slide across the planks uncontrollably. Nevertheless, the result ends up being the same. I fall inelegantly onto the side of the octopus near its eye. As I touch its wet, rubbery skin, I realize the tables have finally turned in our favor. Now, I'm the bringer of death and my victim realizes this fact almost immediately.

In its death throes, the octopus lashes out. Before I can peel myself off its slick skin, the creature releases its hold on the boat and jerks its body back toward the churning ocean. Losing my support, I end up falling headfirst off the deck, following my victim into the murky depths below.

I faintly hear Alek scream my name, but there's no way he can offer me any help. If the monster doesn't drag me down with him in his wake, the turbulent sea will more than likely finish me off.

After I plunge past the surface of the water, I barely feel the cold. As swiftly as possible, I swim toward the faint light of day pointing me toward the surface, even though the ocean keeps trying to drag me down farther into its depths. At one point, a strong current spins me in a circle, and I find myself facing away from the surface. I faintly see the octopus use its tentacles to propel itself toward the ocean floor and expel some sort of dark liquid from its body. Being directly in its line of fire turns out to be unfortunate.

I lose my sense of up and down in the darkness. Without the outside world to point me in the right direction. All I can do is choose a path and hope it's the correct one before what little air I have left in my lungs runs out.

I make my decision and swim as hard as I can to what I hope is the surface.

A small glint of light tells me I chose wisely, but it's so far away I know I'll never make it there before I run out of air.

This is it. This is how my life will end.

Will Boris be waiting for me in the afterlife? If Margaret was unable to save him, his face is the one I want to see when I crossover. I hope he isn't upset with me. I hope he knows I tried my best to hold onto life.

As my lungs use what's left of the air in them, they begin to burn for more. Craving air, my body betrays me and automatically breathes in the salt water surrounding me. It feels like molten lava as it travels up my nostrils and down my throat to fill my lungs.

In that instance, I have a moment of euphoria where I imagine Damon swimming through a shaft of light piercing the darkness. As my lungs feel like they're about to explode, I close my eyes and pray for a quick end.

THREE DAYS EARLIER

***

IN MIDNIGHT

CHAPTER 2

(Damon's Point of View)

"You stupid son of a bitch," the idiot in the bathroom mirror stares back at me with complete self-loathing. "Why did you leave her behind?"

I punch my reflection in the face, but all it does is shatter the glass. Pieces fly across the room leaving a black hole in its place, a perfect representation of my mood.

"Although I can be rather moody," my mother says loftily from the doorway, "I don't believe I warrant the moniker of being called a bitch, Damon."

With a heavy sigh, I turn to face her iron visage. For whatever reason, she's worn her gray hair in the same tight bun at the nape of her neck since my father died. When I was a child, I remember her wearing it down around her shoulders. It was so wavy and long she would cover my face with it as a toddler and play a game of peek-a-boo. Those stolen moments in my past were when my father was absent and unable to spoil our time together.

"Sorry," I step back from the sink to face her. "You know I wasn't actually calling you that. I was cursing myself for not protecting Ivy better. If I had simply taken her to Dawn with me, she wouldn't be in the hands of that bastard Alek." I shake my head. "He fooled me, which is hard to do. I thought he was actually trying to change his life, but obviously, I was wrong."

"Don't be so hard on yourself." My mother looks away as she crosses her arms over her chest. "I'm the one who told him to take her for a walk while I tended to Boris. If I hadn't, she would still be here."

"You couldn't have known he would take advantage of the situation like that."

She looks me straight in the eyes. "Neither of us could have known, so don't wallow in should haves when we have work to do."

"I'm just grateful we didn't lose the whole day waiting on that shoreline after Castor sunk the Dawn ferry. What made you think to send out our ferry to get us? You couldn't have known about our situation."

"I sent it because I needed you here," she says in exasperation. "Ivy had been kidnapped. Boris was on the edge of death, and we have the corpse of who knows what lying dead in Ivy's room. I may give off the impression that I'm made of stone, but I assure you even I can break if bent too far."

"I'm sorry you had to deal with all of that without me." I stand taller, knowing my mother and my people need me to show strength and solve the problems that awaited me when I returned home. "Why don't you show me our ghost first? We can finally put an end to the rumors that this castle is haunted."

My mother drops her arms back down by her sides. "Can we though? It's obvious these people have been watching us for a very long time. Rumors of ghosts roaming the halls of this castle have been around since the days my grandparents were still alive. Why do you think these people were watching us? What information did they hope to gain? Considering the fact this man had something that was able to make him invisible, either their magic or technology is far more advanced than ours."

My mother and I have had quite a few arguments about the true existence of magic. I've never seen a witch actually do anything magical, but my mother has always believed there are forces greater than we know in the world. Her whole argument is based on the supposed magic that transforms us into wolves.

Whatever. One unexplainable occurrence doesn't make me a true believer.

If someone can magically send me to wherever Alek has taken Ivy, then I'll become a devout supporter of the magical arts. Until that time comes, I'll remain a doubter where conjuring things out of thin air are concerned.

"Come on." I readjust my brown leather vest as I exit the bathroom. "Show me the man who attacked Ivy."

As my mother and I stroll through the castle to Ivy's room, she remains conspicuously quiet.

"Why haven't you asked me anything about the fae we brought back?" I ask her. "I thought you would be busting at the seams with questions."

She shrugs. "I assumed if there was anything of importance to say about him you would have said it already."

I shake my head at her lack of curiosity. "Leave it to you to be so logical. We didn't really get to speak to him for very long in Dawn before we left to come back here, so I suppose there isn't much to tell. After we look at the body of the assassin, we can go speak to Vamir together."

"And what about finding Ivy?" She looks at me with a lifted eyebrow. "I thought that would be your highest priority. Her being the future of the pack and all," she snickers.

"Why did you say it like that?"

She rolls her eyes. "I know she means more to you than you'll admit to me. I knew it the moment you brought her into my cottage. Do you think I don't know about the daily reports you got about Ivy's movements in Dawn before you brought her to our side of the river?"

I feel slightly taken aback. "I wasn't aware you knew about that. Who told you?"

"I have my spies too, Damon," she says with an air of mystery. "And I'll never give them up. Just rest assured, there isn't much in this castle that I don't know about, especially when it concerns you."

"I guess I should have assumed that already, but when you left, it seemed like you didn't want anything to do with any of us, not even me."

My mother stops and looks curiously at the large empty wall ahead of the turn to Ivy's room.

"You know," she says with a tilt of her head as she considers the blank space. "Ivy is right. This castle is definitely stark." She turns to face me. "You should give her the duty of sprucing up the castle when she becomes your queen. I have a feeling she would excel in it and make you a real home you would feel comfortable in for once in your life."

"I like things the way they are." My gruff tone only makes my mother snicker again.

"Please, Damon. The only reason you haven't done it yourself is because you're afraid of doing anything your father did. He may have been a tyrant and a bully, but he did have good taste. Personally, I wouldn't mind seeing what Ivy can accomplish here. I might even move back in if the two of you give me some grandchildren."

"I think you're getting a little ahead of yourself." I suddenly feel ill at ease talking about this subject with my mother. "There's a lot that needs to be done before children can enter the picture. As you pointed out, I have to find Ivy first."

My mother's lips part, and I wait for her to say something, but they close again without a word passing over them.

"What is it?" I ask. "What were you about to say?"

"I, uh, well." She clears her throat, looking uncomfortable. "I have no doubt you will find Ivy, but what if Alek has already impregnated her with his child? What will you do then?"

The thought of that bastard laying a hand on Ivy instantly ignites my anger.

"I'll kill him and then bring her home," I state. "Anything he's done to her will have been against her will. Murder and rape are two things that I will never stand idly by and let happen to *anyone*, much less someone I care about."

My mother nods her approval. "Good. I'm glad to see we're on the same page about that."

As we walk down the hallway, my mother veers off toward Boris's room.

"I'll only be a moment," she says. "I want to check on Boris to make sure he hasn't done anything stupid to his bandages while he's still in wolf form. It's getting close to the twilight hour. Hopefully, he'll wake up and let me know how he feels. Go on to Ivy's room. Edmond should be in there."

When I walk into Ivy's bedroom, I'm met by a scene I didn't expect.

"Who the hell did this to all of Ivy's clothes?" I demand to know. Every piece of clothing Ivy had made by the seamstress in town is now lying in shreds all across her room.

Edmond, Oliver's father and one of my most trusted advisors, turns from the window he was staring out to answer me.

"We suspect it was Anya." He too surveys the damage done by jealous hands. "But who knows? It could have been our intruder looking for something."

"Anya seems the likelier suspect," I'm sad to say. "I'll deal with her later."

Edmond and I converge on the dead body in the room. The man is dressed in a white leather outfit from head to toe with a translucent mask over his face allowing us to see his features. His head lolls to the side at an odd angle.

"Alek broke his neck to get him off of Ivy," Edmond says. "At least the slimy bastard did one thing right before he betrayed our trust."

I drop to one knee beside our intruder to study his outfit a little closer. With an index finger, I tap the clear mask covering his face.

"What kind of material is this?" I ask, tapping it again. "It's not glass. It feels . . . hollower."

"I don't have a clue." Edmond strolls over to stand beside me. "I haven't touched the thing since we got back."

Along with the ferry, my mother sent Edmond along to retrieve me from Dawn. The moment I saw him standing on the deck of the boat, I knew only trouble would welcome me home.

"Why haven't you taken that thing off his head yet?" my mother questions brusquely as she enters the room.

"Just waiting on you," I say, looking for a way to remove the man's head piece. I don't readily see one. "What do you think this mask is made of?" I tap it twice in quick succession so she can hear the sound it makes. To my surprise, the mask and the headpiece vanish, giving us a clear view of the man.

He's bald and has pointy ears.

"Oh dear," my mother says as she stares at the man. "Another fae?"

I jump to my feet and look at Edmond. "Where is the fae I brought from Dawn?"

When we arrived back home, I asked Oliver to take care of Vamir while I went to take a shower. At the time, I didn't think the fae was a danger to anyone in the castle, but now I know differently.

"Oliver said he was going to take him out back. Something about getting some sun."

"You two stay here." I take long strides to the door. "We'll see if our new ally is actually a friend or a foe to us."

It doesn't take me long to reach the back courtyard. I find Oliver sitting on the steps leading down from the veranda with our guest lying completely nude out on the grassy lawn with his arms and legs stretched out.

"What's he doing?" I ask Oliver while I walk down the steps.

Oliver stands and chuckles softly. "He said he wanted to get some sun. I had no idea he was going to strip off all his clothes to do it, but it's definitely made people keep their distance from us."

"Come with me. Our sun loving fae needs to give us some answers."

Without question, Oliver follows me to the patch of ground Vamir has claimed with his body.

"Get up," I order brusquely.

Vamir opens his eyes to look up at me while shading them from the sun with a hand.

"You sound angry," he says, stating the obvious. "Why?"

"I need to show you something and then I need you to explain to me why it's in my home."

Vamir considers my request for a few seconds before standing and dressing himself in the raggedy clothes I found him wearing in Simon's dungeon.

"I thought my clothes would dry in the sun faster if I wasn't wearing them," he explains. "But in all honesty, I also wanted to feel the grass against my skin again. It's been a long time."

I don't say anything. I don't really care why he was lying out here naked. What I want is for him to explain to me why one of his people has been spying on my family for so many years.

Once he's dressed, I turn back to the castle.

"Follow me," I order.

Both Vamir and Oliver follow in my footsteps as we make our way up to Ivy's room. Along the way we garner odd glances from those still at court, but I pay them no mind. I'll have them all out of my house soon enough. The last thing I need is for the gossipers to start spreading misinformation among my people.

When we reach Ivy's room, both my mother and Edmond back away from the corpse.

"Vamir, this is my mother, Margaret," I introduce.

Vamir respectfully nods his bald head in her direction, but his eyes are drawn to the dead fae in the room.

"Do you know who he is?" I ask, watching the other man's reactions closely.

Vamir walks farther into the room until he's standing at the other fae's feet.

"I don't recognize him," he says, "but it has been quite some time since I was last with my people."

"And do your people live in the Barrens?" my mother asks. "I saw one of your kind traveling there a few years ago."

"Some live there." Vamir looks up at my mother. "Some do not."

"This one," I say, "has been spying on us. He also tried to kill someone in my court. Do you have any idea why he would do that?"

Vamir appears confused. "Who did he try to kill?"

"The woman I plan to marry. Ivy."

"The same Ivy that the pirate captain's son kidnapped?" Vamir asks.

"Yes," I say.

Vamir shrugs. "I have no idea why he would want to kill your fiancée. Was there anything particularly dangerous about her?"

"Only that she's a pure human," Edmond says before I have a chance to stop him.

I hadn't planned on sharing that much information with the fae just yet, but the cat's out of the bag now and there's no putting it back in.

"Human?" Vamir asks with a raised eyebrow. "What leads you to believe that?"

"She doesn't change into a wolf at night or at daybreak," my mother says. "She always remains in her human form no matter what time of the day it is."

Vamir returns his gaze to the corpse of the fae.

"Do you know anything about her parents?" Vamir asks. "Were they also human?"

"We have no idea," I say. "As far as I know, Ivy never knew who her parents were. The only relative we know anything about is her grandmother, but she died when Ivy was just a baby. Her adoptive father raised her."

"And where is he?" Vamir asks.

"Down the hallway recovering from wounds this assassin inflicted on him," my mother answers tersely. "He'll live, but it will take some time for him to fully recover."

"I'm truly sorry about that." Vamir meets my gaze. "Our people have a long history of mistrust, and Ivy's humanity would have been seen as a threat by some fae."

"Why is that?" I ask.

Vamir looks at all of us apprehensively. It's obvious he doesn't want to answer my question, but he also seems smart enough to know that I won't let him leave this room without an explanation.

"My people are the reason why all of you transform into wolves."

This is something I've never heard before. That possibly no one has ever heard before now.

"What do you mean by that?" I ask. "Explain."

Vamir takes in a deep breath. "A long time ago your people and mine were at war with one another. We were looking for a planet to call home and this one had everything we could possibly need, but your people were robbing Earth of its natural resources. When we first arrived, we came in peace and did our best to show you a new way to live, not by ravaging your world but by nurturing it. Some people took this the wrong way. They thought we were threatening to take away your way of life but all we wanted to do was share what was here. Eventually your rulers and ours came to an impasse and a vicious war followed."

"Hogwash," Edmond says, looking and sounding convinced Vamir is lying.

"Oh hush, Edmond," my mother says, appearing intrigued by the tale Vamir is weaving. "I want to hear what happened. It's not exactly like you know truth from fiction. None of us do."

"I assure you what I'm telling you is what happened," Vamir says. "My mother was alive to see it all unfold, and she told me what transpired when I came of age."

"How?" I ask. "That had to have been over five hundred years ago."

"My people can live to be three thousand years old. It's one of the reasons we had to leave our own planet. It couldn't sustain all of us because of our ability to live for so long."

"So what?" Edmond asks, eyeing our guest with even more suspicion. "You drained your own planet dry so you decided to search out other planets to pillage?"

"We had hoped to share our technology and our magic to help your ancestors prolong the life of this planet, but neither of our people would budge. My people..." Vamir casts his eyes to the floor as if he can't meet any of ours while he finishes his story. "My people decided that if humans were going to act like animals they might as well live like them too."

"So you turned us into wolves?" I ask as pieces from humanity's shared past seem to fall together.

"We tried." Vamir lifts his gaze to meet mine. "But the spell didn't quite work like it was supposed to. Our spellcasters didn't take into consideration how strong your human spirits were. That's why you live half your lives as wolves and half as humans."

"But why the difference between day and night?" my mother asks.

"We could only conclude that it depended on your bodies natural circadian rhythms. Some humans were more active at night and some during the daylight hours."

"And this war that broke between our people," I say, "how did it end?"

"Badly." Vamir's ominous tone warns me that his story only gets worse from here. "We were all fools. Your people for using the weapons they had to destroy our ships and my people for thinking they could change you. We were left with a planet that could only sustain life in a small area."

"So the Barrens were made as a result of this war?" my mother asks.

Vamir nods. "After the planet was nearly destroyed, my people did what they could to provide what was left of humanity a place to start over."

"Did the fae wipe our ancestor's memories too?" I ask.

"We thought it was the most humane thing to do at the time," he says without an ounce of remorse. "We hoped that a fresh start would allow you all to live your lives to the fullest for what time you had left."

"What do you mean by that?" I ask. "You make it sound like we're all about to die or something."

"Humanity would die, but your counterpart would live on and return to nature."

"Are you saying your people have simply been biding their time and waiting for us all to lose our humanity?" My anger quickly rises to the surface. "Why are they waiting for that to happen?"

"We're not murderers," Vamir states, "and time is on our side more than it is yours."

"He was certainly a murderer," I say, pointing to the dead fae on the floor.

Vamir doesn't say a word. He simply looks away from the man who tried to kill Ivy and who almost did kill Boris.

"Like I said before, I can only assume he saw Ivy as a threat because of her humanity," he says.

"How many fae live in the Barrens?" I ask.

"I'm not sure. It's been years since I saw any of them, but I do know that almost half of the fae left this world to find another planet to live on."

"You mean another planet to kill," Edmond scoffs.

"That was not our intention," Vamir argues. "We were refugees looking for a home and your people are the ones who bombed us out of the sky."

My mother holds up her hands in each man's direction. "Gentleman, I suggest we not quarrel about something that happened hundreds of years ago. Right now we need to focus on finding Ivy."

"Ivy . . ." a strained voice says behind us.

I turn to find a naked Boris leaned up against the doorway. His face is as white as a sheet and the bandage around his neck is filled with blood.

"Oh, you fool!" my mother chastises as she walks over to him. "What are you doing out of bed?"

"Where is Ivy?" Boris demands to know. Even in his weakened state all he can think about is the welfare of his daughter.

"Help me get him back into bed, Damon," my mother orders as she tries to help Boris remain on his feet.

I grab one of his arms, slinging it over my shoulders as I wrap an arm around his thick waist. Slowly, the three of us start to walk down the hall back to Boris's room.

"Alek has kidnapped Ivy," I tell Boris. "We're not sure where he's taken her."

Boris grimaces but I'm not sure if it's from the physical pain he's in or from the bad news I just delivered. More than likely both.

"Damn pirates," Boris curses.

Once we reach his room, I lay him back down on the bed. Before I can stand straight again, Boris grabs a handful of my shirt.

"You have to go after her," he practically begs.

"I would if I knew where to start looking," I tell him.

Boris slowly lets go of my shirt. "I know someone you can ask for help. Castor and his boy aren't the only pirates that roam the Issip River or the oceans, you know."

Hope reignites in my heart.

"Where can I find this person?" I ask, desperate to be on my way.

Boris closes his eyes from tiredness. I fear he'll pass out before he can answer my question but his lips part and he tells me where to find his friend.

"Just make sure you take a lot of gold before you go there," Boris advises me. "Her help won't come cheap."

Boris's head lolls to the side, and he starts to snore softly.

My mother's hand rests on the middle of my back.

"Take the ferry and go get our girl," she urges me. "I'll take care of things here while you're away."

"Thank you." With quick strides, I leave the room to prepare for my trip. I make a silent vow to Boris that I won't return home without Ivy.

Neither of us can live without her, and any future I may want solely depends on bringing her home alive.

CHAPTER 3

"This was a horrible idea!" Oliver shouts above the whistling wind of the sea storm as another ten-foot wave crashes onto the deck of the ship.

The wild, almost gleeful, cackles of our captain can be heard coming from above us as she attempts to steer her vessel through the hurricane to keep us on course. As we stand next to her beside the wheel, I have no idea how she can see anything through the pelting rain, but from her whoops and maniacal laughter, it sounds like she's having a grand time navigating her vessel through the chaos.

"We can't lose them now!" I tell Oliver. "Their ship is within sight!"

"What are we going to do when we catch up to it?" Oliver sputters as he tightens his grip on the leather tarp we're using as a shield against the storm. "Alek isn't going to stop just because we ask him to." Oliver wipes the water from his eyes. Our makeshift protection against the storm is doing very little to keep the sea water and rain from drenching us to our bones.

"We'll ram his damn ship if we have to," I declare.

"You're not using my ship to ram anything," Captain Nahla Wade asserts. Her long dreadlocks have soaked up the rainwater like a sponge, and her dark blue eyes match the anger of the storm as it tries to knock us off course from our goal. "What does that wench have to make you and Alek fight for her? Gold between her legs?"

The captain throws her head back in laughter, finding amusement in her own joke.

"I'll build you a better ship," I vow. I point ahead to Alek's vessel off the port bow. "Just get us to that one!"

A particularly savage gust of wind tears the tarp from mine and Oliver's grips and lifts it to the heavens, never to be seen again. It's just as well. It wasn't lending us much in the way of protection anyway.

"Captain!" A buxom blonde climbs up onto the foredeck, holding her tricorn hat on her head with one hand. Her white shirt and pants are soaking wet and clinging to her frame like a second skin. All of Captain Nahla's crew are women and just as crazy, or perhaps its brave, as their captain.

"What is it, Penny?" The captain yells above the storm as she continues to grip the wheel with steady hands.

Penny struggles to maintain her footing as she comes to stand by her captain. She points to Alek's ship.

"Octopus straight ahead! A big one!" she warns.

I use my hands to shield my eyes from the rain to better see Alek's ship. I've heard tales of monsters in the ocean, but this is the first time I've ever seen one in the flesh. It doesn't disappoint. The red-orange creature is massive and has its tentacles wrapped around the other vessel in a grip that will surely lead to the death of everyone on board. I watch in horror as it tightens its hold on the ship like a child with a new toy, bringing it almost to a dead stop.

"Get us over there now!" I shout to Nahla.

"Have you lost your mind?" She peers at me angrily from underneath her tricorn hat that stubbornly refuses to budge no matter how hard the wind blows. "If we get any closer, she's liable to take us down too."

I growl in frustration and return my gaze to the other ship as the creature begins to swing its tentacles around. Members of Alek's crew go flying through the air, attached to the underside of the monster's arms, and dragged overboard into the turbulent sea's embrace.

The sea and wind join forces against Captain Nahla by propelling her schooner toward the other ship. Even though she's spinning the wheel hard to stern, nature takes my side in this battle of wills and continues to propel us toward my target. Since the octopus has brought Alek's ship to a virtual standstill, we're slowly catching up to it. Impulsively, I jump over the railing to the main deck and almost lose my footing when I land on the slippery wood.

"Damon!" Oliver shouts. "What the hell are you doing?"

I don't waste my breath to answer his question. The wind would rip it into shreds before it rose to Oliver's ears.

Turning my gaze to Alek's boat, I realize my rash decision to jump down to the main deck was driven by my desire to do something no matter how crazy that something might be.

I'm waiting.

At some point, I'll have to make a spur of the moment decision to either jump overboard and swim to the other ship or let Ivy slip through my fingers. There's no way I'll leave her fate in Alek's hands. No way in hell.

As the boat sways from side to side and climbs waves as high as my castle, I struggle to maintain my footing as I yank my boots off and toss them onto the deck. Swimming under these conditions will be hard enough. I don't need the added weight of the boots dragging me down.

Captain Nahla's boat wasn't built to take this much strain from the elements. It was built for speed, which is how we were able to catch up to Alek even though he had a substantial head start on us. Whether her boat survives this storm isn't my highest priority. I need to get on Alek's ship if I'm going to have any chance of rescuing Ivy.

For the last three days, all I've done is imagine the worst things happening to her. I haven't been able to sleep, and I've barely been able to keep any food down. I worry that Ivy's stubborn brashness may have tested the limits of Alek's patience with her. I thought I knew the man, but after learning he took advantage of Ivy when she was at her weakest has made me rethink his character.

I've cursed him. I've beat him to a pulp in endless scenarios inside my mind, but the only thing that will satisfy my need for vengeance is placing my hands around the other man's throat and squeezing every ounce of life out of him.

He'll pay for what he's done, and I'll be his judge, jury, and executioner once I have him in my custody.

"Creature dead ahead, Captain!" one of Nahla's crewmates shouts in terror as she points to Alek's ship. The hull of the boat is being gripped tightly by the octopus's mammoth tentacles. Even at a distance of a quarter of a mile, you can clearly hear the snapping of wood as boards in the hull are being stressed beyond their limits. It's only a matter of time before the ship sinks. Alek has to know this. Why isn't he abandoning his boat and getting everyone off board before the beast takes the ship and all of its passengers to the bottom of the sea. What the hell is he waiting on?

"Hard to starboard!" Captain Nahla warns as she attempts, yet again, to turn our ship away from the other one, but the sea has other plans. Every wave nudges us to the left, inching us so close to the other ship I imagine I can see Ivy's red hair blowing in the wind.

Wait.

I wipe the rain and sea water from my eyes and look again.

I do see Ivy! But . . .

What the hell? Why is she heading straight for the creature's head? What madness has led her to do such a stupid and foolhardy thing?

Anger swells inside my chest, matching the raging storm's ferocity.

That bastard! He's using her curse to save his own hide and his ship.

"You son of a bitch! I'm going to rip you apart and tear your damn heart out and make you eat it!" I know Alek can't hear my vow to tear him limb from limb, but at least it made me feel a little bit better.

In horror, I watch as Ivy slides across the bow of the ship and lands right next to the creature's giant eye. With her body pressed against it, her poison seeps through its skin. It seems to immediately loosen its grip on the ship. Since all of her weight is being held up by the octopus, Ivy loses her balance when the octopus falls back into the ocean and gravity pulls her into the water after it.

"Ivy!" I stretch out my arm in a vain attempt to stop her from tumbling head first into the turbulent ocean.

Without thinking, I leap over the railing of the schooner and jump into the frigid waters of the open sea. Thankfully, we were only fifty feet away from the other boat by this time, but the storm has caused rip currents to form underneath the water's surface, making it almost impossible to see where I'm going. The only thing I can do is keep my mind focused and search for Ivy's red hair like a beacon in the dark.

A dark cloud of some substance appears straight ahead of me. It's blackness acts like a backdrop to everything in front of it, and I see Ivy's hair and pale face stand out. Swimming for all I'm worth, I head straight for her like an arrow being let loose from a bow.

In horror, I witness her body jerk as she runs out of breath. She's drowning. I kick harder. I stretch my arms out so far every muscle I have screams for restraint, but there's no time for delay. The one woman in this world who can not only save my people but also protect the small flame of hope I have in my heart for a brighter future is slipping away from me, and I'll be damned if I let that happen.

After what seems like minutes but in actuality is only seconds, I reach Ivy. Her body is limp in my arms. I want to scream. I want to kill the person who did this to her, but a small, more reasonable voice in my head shouts louder. I have to swim us both to the surface. If Ivy has any chance of survival, she has to have air.

I wrap my right arm around her and use my left one to pull us through the water and up out of its clenches. It fights me every inch of the way and my own lungs burn for air. I don't give in to the pain or my body's natural desire to pull in the water around me. If I give in, we're both dead.

Finally, I breach the surface and drag in enough air to fill both my lungs.

"Damon!"

I look up to see Oliver on the deck of Captain Nahla's ship. He throws a round life preserver into the water in front of me. I loop my arm through it and let him pull us in toward the ship. Once we're close enough, one of the crew lowers a rope ladder down the side. It takes all the strength I have left to lift both me and Ivy up to the railing. Once there, Oliver attempts to grab Ivy to relieve me of her weight.

"Get back!" I order, too tired to remind him about her poison and how close he was to death.

My body is weak from the fight against the ocean, but my willpower is stronger than ever. I manage to pull us both over the railing and lay Ivy down onto the deck before me.

"Is she dead?" Oliver asks, kneeling beside me with a look of worry.

"Oy! Get out of the way, land lover!" Captain Nahla rushes to Ivy's side while I continue to catch my breath. "You've gotta get the water out of her lungs, you fool."

"Tell me what to do!"

Nahla gives me a few brief instructions. I tilt Ivy's head back and cover her mouth with my own. To anyone else, it might look like a passionate kiss. Instead, it's a desperate attempt to bring her back to life.

I blow two quick breaths into Ivy's body before placing the heel of one hand over her chest and using my other hand to help press down firmly. Water begins to dribble out of Ivy's mouth and on the thirtieth compression she begins to cough.

"Roll her onto her side," Nahla orders.

As soon as Ivy is on her side, she expels the remaining sea water from her lungs. The moment I hear her take her first ragged breath, I feel the heaviness in my heart lift as hope returns to fill the void her death would have caused.

Ivy's eyelids flutter open. She looks straight at me and a faint smile tugs at the corners of her lips.

"What took you so long?" she whispers before closing her eyes again and passing out from what must be exhaustion.

I begin to laugh as I sit back against the railing. Relief floods my veins and removes the tension in my muscles but my joy is short lived.

"Captain!"

One of Nahla's crew runs over to her as the captain stands.

"What is it now?" Nahla asks irritably.

"The other ship is going down and what's left of the crew is jumping overboard," the woman announces. "Should we rescue them?"

Nahla lowers her head slightly as she considers her options. Then, she looks to me.

"What say you, King Damon? Should we help them or not?" She eyes me with an air of judgment, as if my answer will tell her a little something about the state of my soul.

I consider leaving Alek and his crew to the mercy of the ocean. If Nahla had asked me that same question only a few minutes ago, I might have told her to let them all drown or meet their demise to the creatures who roam these waters. Instead, I find myself in a mood to mete out justice.

I regain my footing on the deck of the ship. The rain has all but stopped now and the ocean seems to be mirroring my mood.

"Rescue them," I say as I gently pick Ivy up and cradle her in my arms. The feel of her weight against me brings me calm. "But make sure lock them down in the hold, or they're liable to try and take your ship."

"Aye," she agrees with a curt nod. "You can rest assured that none of them will be roaming around my ship freely."

"Good." I start to walk across the deck to find a quiet moment in my quarters below, but then I think of something and turn to face Nahla again. "Oh, and Captain, if Alek survived this mess, make sure you separate him from his men. In fact, cage him up here by the main mast so I'll know where to find him later."

"As you wish," she says with a smirk, as if she can guess my plans for the other captain.

Nahla begins to shout orders to her crew while I continue to make my way to my quarters.

"Do you need me to do anything?" Oliver says, following close behind me.

"Yes." I don't miss a step as I continue to make my way to my room. "Help the others and let me know how things go after the other crew is on board."

"Will do." Out of my periphery vision, I see Oliver walk over to the port side where Alek's doomed voyage has come to an end.

Serves the bastard right to lose his ship. He should have lost his life too, but I have a feeling I won't get that lucky. No good ever comes from an evil deed and kidnapping Ivy is an unforgiveable act in my eyes. I have no idea what he did to her in the three days she was with him, but I hope to God I can repair the damage his savage hands have wrecked on her body and soul.

I hug Ivy closer to my chest, silently promising her that she'll never have to go through anything like this again. I'll die protecting her if it comes to that because without her, my life would lose all meaning. With her, I have a chance to become whole and live a life I've always wanted but could never quite put into words.

Before I descend the stairs to go below deck, I look at her face and plant a gentle kiss on her forehead. Warmth infuses my heart, cracking the hard cold shell I didn't even realize it had protecting it until now.

Ivy is my world, and God help anyone who ever attempts to lay a hand on her again.

CHAPTER 4

(Ivy's Point of View)

The sound of seagulls wakes me from a slumber so deep I have a hard time telling if they're real or merely part of a dream. As my eyelids lift, they feel like sandpaper scraping against my eyeballs. I'm still not sure if I'm awake because I see Damon standing shirtless by a large paned glass window at the back of a ship, but it's not Alek's ship. This room is smaller with a narrower bed.

I give myself the gift of a silent moment to study Damon. His skin adopts the soft glow of the setting sun, and his profile is as regal as any king I've ever seen. The long strands of his dark hair are curlier than usual today, softening his face and making him appear more approachable. He must sense me studying him because he turns his head and looks my way. A smile filled with relief stretches his lips. The warmth in his eyes as he looks at me is new. It's almost as if our separation has made him realize I'm not only important to the welfare of his people but also to him on a more personal level.

He walks over on bare feet and sits on the edge of the bed beside me.

"I was hoping you would awaken before I change," he says, reaching out a hand to gently pull away a wayward strand of hair from my face. His fingertips linger against my cheek longer than they need to as if he needs to touch me to prove to himself that I'm real.

I try to speak but I find my throat sore. It's hard to swallow much less say anything.

"Hold on." Damon reaches for a glass and a pitcher of water on the nightstand beside the bed. After he fills the glass, he slides one hand behind my head to help me lift it and places the rim of the glass to my parched lips. I take a few slow sips. The coolness of the water helps relieve the dryness of my throat.

I pull away after downing half of the glass's contents. Damon releases his hold on my head and places the glass back on the table.

Memories of everything that's happened in the past few days come rushing back to me. I grab Damon's arm.

"Boris," I say, my throat so raw my father's name only comes out as loud as a whisper.

Even before Damon answers my plea, my eyes begin to well with tears. Their salt causes a burning sensation that practically blinds me.

"He's recovering from his injuries," Damon quickly assures me after seeing my distress. "He'll be fine."

I sob out of intense relief. I haven't lost my father. He's alive. He's safe.

Damon crawls into bed beside me and enfolds me in his arms providing a safe harbor for me to rest and release my pent-up emotions.

"I swear he's all right," he promises, kissing my forehead and cradling me even closer to him. "All he needs is for you to come home."

Home. Where is that now? My heart tells me it's anywhere Damon is, but does he feel the same way? I've had three long days to think about my future, and in every scenario, I've always pictured Damon playing the most important role in it. Husband. Lover. Equal.

"Thank you for saving me," I whisper, burying my head against his chest and finding not only warmth but comfort there.

Damon sighs heavily. It's a troubled sound, not one of relief like I would have expected.

"You never should have needed saving." His tone sounds furious, but I'm not sure who he's angry at. "I should have taken you with me to Dawn. If I had, none of this would have happened. You wouldn't have been kidnapped by that bastard or almost killed by the fae."

I pull back slightly to look into his beautiful eyes, one blue . . . one brown. The eyes of a man so unique I know I'll never tire looking into their depths and finding my place in this world.

"Fae? What are you talking about? What's a fae?"

Damon takes a few minutes to tell me everything that's happened to him since traveling to Dawn to meet the fae Simon had locked up in his dungeon. When he tells me everything that he learned from Vamir about our past, I'm practically speechless.

"A war that almost destroyed the world? That's insane!" I shake my head in disbelief against Damon's arm.

"I know." Two wrinkles appear across his forehead. His troubled look worries me.

"What's wrong? Do you think Vamir lied to you?"

"No," he says confidently. "I believe he's telling me the truth even if it does sound a bit crazy. The problem is that I'm not so sure his people will help us considering they're the ones who turned us into shifters in the first place. It sounds like they've simply been biding their time, waiting for us to devolve into animals so they can rule what's left of our world. Why would they help us now that they're so close to their goal?"

"What's left of humanity isn't the same as when they first came to our planet," I say. "If they've been watching us, maybe they see that. Considering how powerful they are, they could have wiped us out at any time. It sounds like they don't really want to do that. Maybe the fae who remained here have been waiting for us to change our ways and become our allies."

"If that's true, why did their spy attack you? Vamir thinks he tried to kill you because your humanity would have thwarted our final conversion into wolves. That's not something a potential ally would do."

I can't argue against Damon's conclusion.

"Then what are we going to do?" I ask. "Are we still going to search for the fae in the Barrens now that we know what they're capable of?"

"I don't think we have any choice but to go and see if they'll help us. It's either that or slowly watch our people lose their ability to shift. Even with any children you're able to have, the loss of our humanity will happen to the majority of the population. We would only be delaying the inevitable by a few years."

I know he's right, but a flicker of light still burns inside my heart whispering that all isn't lost. There is a way forward that will be beneficial to everyone. We simply have to find it.

As we lay together in pleasant silence, I realize something. I lift up the sheet and cover on top of me to discover that I'm completely naked underneath.

"What happened to my clothes?" I ask, lowering my covering before looking at Damon again.

A roguish smile plays across his lips.

"You were soaked to the bone and as cold as ice," he says. "I took both of our clothes off and held you under the covers until you stopped shivering. It's not like I haven't already seen you naked, Ivy. I've touched you in places that make us more than mere acquaintances."

"You don't have to convince me that you did the right thing." I snuggle my head even closer and feel him rest his on top of mine. "I just wanted to know where my clothes were. If nothing else, my little adventure taught me that I like wearing leather."

Damon doesn't make a response right away, but from the way his body suddenly tenses, I know he wants to ask me something.

"Did that bastard hurt you? Did he . . . touch you?" He tightens his hold on me as if he's bracing himself for the worst, and I instantly know he's been torturing himself with visions of Alek doing the unthinkable while he held me as his captive.

"He didn't touch me. Besides kidnapping me, he was the perfect gentleman while I was on his ship."

"Truly?" His voice is strained.

"Truly," I declare.

Damon gradually loosens his hold on me and relaxes.

"If he had hurt you, I would have killed him," he states as a simple fact. "Anyone who dares to lay a hand on you will have to answer to me."

"He didn't hurt me, and I would rather not talk about the last three days."

"Why?" he asks suspiciously. "Are you holding something back from me because you're scared of what I'll do?"

"No, it's not that. I could barely sleep and couldn't keep any food down while I was on Alek's ship. I learned very quickly that my body was not made to live on a boat. I'm a land lover, through and through."

Damon chuckles. The deep rumbling sound inside his chest makes me smile.

"Good. In all honesty, I don't particularly like being on boats either." He pulls the covers up over my shoulder. "Why don't you get some rest? My change is about to happen, and I think we could both use the sleep."

I lay my head against Damon's chest and close my eyes. Tiredness overcomes me. The next thing I know I'm waking up to a semi-dark room and have my head lying on something furry. When I pull away, I see that Damon has transformed into his wolf. The cool purple flames of his coat is the only light illuminating the room. I watch them dance along his body for a little while, marveling in the fact that he's just as beautiful in his wolf form as he is in his human one. I close my eyes and rest my head against his fur again, feeling protected by him no matter what shape he takes.

I'm startled awake by a loud, and rather obnoxious, knock on the door. When I open my eyes, I see that Damon is in his human form again and already dressed for the day.

"Please tell whoever that is to go away," I moan, grabbing his pillow from the other side of the bed and covering my ears with it like a makeshift hat with earmuffs.

Damon looks over at me and laughs as he walks to the door and opens it.

"What's so urgent, Oliver?" he asks, revealing the identity of our visitor.

"I think you need to come up on deck," I hear Damon's best friend say worriedly. "Alek is screaming at the top of his lungs that he wants to talk to you, and Captain Nahla is about ready to throw him overboard."

"What does he want?" Damon asks gruffly.

Even from my position on the bed, I can see that his expression has harden when Oliver mentioned Alek's demand.

"I have no idea." Oliver sounds as clueless as his words indicate. "All I know is that he said he won't shut up until he sees you."

"Fine." Damon's growl of the word tells me that I need to be there when the two men talk, or he's liable to shove Alek into the sea before the captain of this ship has a chance to. "Tell him I'll be there soon."

Damon shuts the door and stares at the doorknob for a few seconds as if contemplating his next move. When he looks over at me, the lines of anger on his face soften.

"Don't kill him," I request, knowing such an action would only burden Damon's soul with another death. He still hasn't forgiven himself for killing his father. I don't want him to kill Alek because he feels a need to avenge my kidnapping.

"He deserves to die for what he did to you," Damon replies angrily.

"No, he doesn't." I sit up, holding the covers to my breasts so we can clearly see each other. "He was only doing what he thought best for his people. If you'll let yourself remember, you kidnapped me first for the very same reason."

"That was different," he protests.

"Only by your standards," I say.

"Why are you trying to defend him?" His eyes narrow on me. "Did you develop some sort of feelings for Alek while the two of you were alone together?"

I feel offended by his questions.

"No," I state in no uncertain terms. "My only concern here is for you. Killing your father has left a scar on your soul that may never be healed. Killing Alek might not leave as deep of a wound, but it would be a decision you would second guess for the rest of your life. All I'm asking is that you don't let your anger at him make you do something foolhardy. I don't want our reunion to be marred by death." I throw the covers off and stand from the bed, completely naked but not uncomfortable with Damon watching my every move. "You and I have something building between us that's worth fighting for, and I will do whatever it takes to make sure we don't lose it."

Damon's gaze rakes my body from head to toe with undisguised desire. The need I see in his eyes mirrors my own and makes me lose my breath.

"If you're trying to distract me," he practically growls, "it's working."

When I smile at his words, the scales tip in my favor. With just a few long strides, Damon reaches me. His arms wrap around my shoulders in an embrace that's rough and possessive. When his lips touch mine, they're demanding. And when he plunges his tongue inside my mouth, I moan for more and meet his demands with a few of my own.

My fingers find their way to his curly mane of hair. When I grab it, he moans against my mouth and slides his hands down my back. His hands grab my bottom and squeeze, pressing me farther into him so I can feel the proof of his desire, as if I needed it. I tighten my hold on his hair and he tightens his hold on my bottom.

"Oy!" a female voice says before we hear a rather harsh banging against the door. "King Damon! I respectfully ask you to step your ass out here and handle your prisoner! I'm tired of hearing his blimey caterwauling!"

With a groan of aggravation, Damon reluctantly pulls his mouth away from mine.

Both of us are breathing hard and the ache between my legs instinctively knows it won't be satisfied anytime soon.

Damon briefly stares into my eyes before planting a gentle kiss on my swollen lips.

"I need to handle this," he says regretfully.

My throat is too tight to make a reply. I simply nod my head in response.

With a sigh, he steps away from me and turns to head for the door. When he reaches it, he yanks it open.

"Your timing is less than opportune, Nahla," he snarls.

"And your prisoner is driving me up the blooming wall," the woman counters. "Now get out here and handle Alek before I dump him over the side of my ship."

"I'll do that if you do something for me in return."

"And what is this something?" she asks with clear suspicion.

Damon glances my way before returning his attention to the captain. "Ivy needs some clothes. Do you have any to spare in here?"

"Ha! First you commandeer my cabin and now you want to take the clothes right off my back? It's gonna cost you another bag of gold when I return you to your home."

"Fine. Where are your spare clothes?"

"There are some drawers at the foot of my bed. She can find something to wear in those."

Damon looks over at me to make sure I heard the captain's words. I nod, letting him know that I did.

"Come up when you're ready," he says. "I'm going to go handle Alek and see what the bastard needs to tell me."

"Remember what I asked you *not* to do," I remind him.

He nods curtly before leaving the room and shutting the door behind him.

I quickly go to the foot of the bed and find two drawers built into the bottom of it. When I pull them open, I grab a white linen shirt, black drawstring pants with wide legs, and a pair of black slip-on shoes. Without wasting any more time, I leave the room in case I need to act as a mediator between Alek and Damon. I honestly don't care what happens to Alek, but I won't let Damon lose a part of himself by hurting the other man unnecessarily to avenge my honor.

CHAPTER 5

As soon as I reach the main deck, I have to use a hand to shade my eyes against the glaring sun. Shouts can be heard coming from the crew who have formed a circle around the main mast on this level. To my surprise, all of them seem to be women with just as many wolves roaming the deck. I can only assume Captain Nahla's crew is similar to Castor's and Alek's. Half of them are from Dawn and the other half from Midnight to make sure the ship always has a crew to man her sails.

"You should rip his blooming head off for what he did to your woman," one of the crew shouts angrily.

"Aye!" another one agrees. "If he had taken my woman, I would tear his balls off and shove them up his ass!"

This rather gruesome suggestion earns a few hearty laughs all around.

"Oy!" I hear the captain of this vessel shout out to her rowdy crew. "Let the men talk, you scallywags! Let's hear what Alek has to say for himself."

"You mean what excuse he's going to spew to save his own head," another of the crew jokes.

"I don't have to defend myself," Alek says rather defensively. I can't see him through the crowd, but I know he's somewhere in the center of it all. "I did what I did for my people. For you ungrateful heathens!"

"Excuse me," I say to the women directly in front of me, being careful to stand back a few feet in case they accidentally touch my skin.

They turn to peer at me and quickly part, granting me a wide berth to walk through their ranks until I'm standing in the inner circle. Alek is sitting on the deck with his arms pulled back around the main mast and his wrist tied together with a length of rope. I see a metal cage directly behind the mast. It must be where Alek spent his night while he was in his wolf form.

Damon towers over him looking angrier than I've ever seen him while the captain stands between them off to the side watching the proceedings with keen interest.

"That's not a good enough excuse for what you did to her and you know it," Damon roars. Even though I told him to keep his calm while he spoke with Alek, it's evident he has either forgotten my advice or is unable to keep his anger in check now that he's face to face with my kidnapper.

"I did nothing that you haven't done to her yourself," Alek tries to reason. "All I want to do is protect my people. The same as you. You know as well as I do that without her we're all doomed."

"Doomed to what?" the captain asks, clearly confused by Alek's words.

Now that I have a clear view, I can see that the captain of the ship is a tall dark-skinned beauty with dreadlocks that practically hang down to her waist. Her dark blue eyes stand out against her milk chocolate colored skin. She's wearing a leather tricorn on her head, a white voluminous shirt similar to mine, a vest to match her hat, and a pair of brown pants tucked into knee high black leather boots.

"Doomed to have the next generation be born as wolves and never have the ability to shift," Alek states.

"Pfft," the captain waves Alek's concerns away like you would an annoying fly. "That'll never happen." Her gaze slides over to Damon as a pinch of uncertainty enters her eyes. "Will it?"

Damon's shoulders stiffen. "It's already happening. I thought you would have been aware of the situation by now."

"Well, sure I've heard the rumors." The captain shrugs. "But I thought it was just town gossip. Are you saying babies are being born in their wolf forms and staying that way? Permanently?"

Damon doesn't answer right away but he eventually gives a reluctant nod.

"But all hope isn't lost," he assures her. "My mother may have found a way to reverse the condition. We simply need to obtain more of the serum she's used to heal some of our babies in Midnight."

The captain fixes me with a steely gaze. "Why are the two of you fighting over her? What makes you believe she can solve this problem?"

For some reason, I thought Damon would have told her about me already. How exactly did he convince this woman to help him rescue me? Gold, probably. I do remember her mentioning that he owed her another bag of the precious metal for the clothes I'm wearing.

"Ivy is human," Damon says. "The only pure-blooded human left in the world."

The women around me give me an even wider berth.

"Is she the one who can kill you with just a touch?" the captain asks, eyeing me with a great deal of apprehension. "Is that the reason you wouldn't let anyone help you with her last night when you dragged her onboard?"

"Yes," I answer, not needing Damon to do it for me.

All the women take another step away. Their precaution is warranted. Even if I told them I mean them no harm, there's no way to know what might happen out on the open sea. A rogue wave might tilt the ship and inadvertently cause one of them to bump into me, ending their life by accident.

"Then how is it that the two of you can touch her?" the captain asks, looking between Damon and Alek.

"My mother gave us something to protect us from her poison," Damon says. "If I had known what a total bastard you really are," Damon fixes Alek with hostile eyes, "I would have followed my mother's advice and just let you die that day."

"Are you saying you somehow saved Alek's life?" the captain asks.

Damon nods.

The captain rears back her right foot and proceeds to give Alek a good kick in his side.

"Ow! What was that for?" Alek complains.

"Pirates may not have a lot of moral codes to live by, but we never double cross someone who has saved our life. What's wrong with you, Alek? I thought Castor raised you better than that."

"Who do you think encouraged me to steal Ivy for our own people in the first place?" Alek counters. "My father was all for it. Don't look so surprised, Nahla. Your mentor isn't as worthy of hero worship as he seems."

Nahla narrows her eyes to slits as she peers at Alek, not liking his words one bit.

"I don't worship people," she states. "Just the gold in my coffers and the ale in my tankards."

"Whatever." Alek rolls his eyes in disbelief.

"What did you call me up here for?" Damon demands to know as he stares daggers at Alek.

"I want you to let me go to the Barrens with you," Alek says. "Ivy told me that you plan to go there to find more of the cure your mother used. I would like to represent my people on that expedition."

Well, shit. I totally forgot about telling Alek the details of our trip to the Barrens. On the second day at sea, I mentioned it in hopes that he would turn his boat around and take a chance on Margaret's idea. He seemed doubtful that I was telling him the truth at the time, but now it seems he's singing a different tune.

"If you hadn't kidnapped Ivy, I would have considered it," Damon says. "As things are, I don't see how I can trust you around her. If I had my way, I would throw you overboard and be done with your sorry ass."

Alek seems to sense Damon isn't going to change his mind so he looks at me with beseeching eyes.

"Ivy, you know me. Please, help me save my people. I promise you I'll never ask for anything ever again."

"Can a promise from a pirate be believed?" I ask.

Quite a few uneasy murmurs erupt from the crowd of pirates and none of them look too sure their own kind can be trusted.

"A promise from a friend can be," Alek states.

"We are not friends," I remind him. "If you had cared about me at all, you wouldn't have taken advantage of me during a time I wasn't thinking straight. Boris needed me! I'll never forgive you for taking me away from him when he was on the verge of death. Never."

"Fine." Alek's face contorts into one of anger. He looks up at Damon with a twinkle of mischief. "Have fun raising my baby, Damon. I'm sure after all the fun Ivy and I had during our time together, she's carrying my child by now."

I gasp in horror. "We never had sex and you know it!"

Alek grins. "Do I? What do you think the good people of Midnight are more likely to believe? That you and I spent three whole days together in separate beds, or that I took advantage of you while you were with me? I'm a pirate, you know. People don't tend to consider us gallant or trustworthy. You just said so yourself."

"You son of a bitch," Damon growls. His hands clench into fists by his sides as he attempts to rein in his anger. "I'll kill you myself if you try to spread lies about Ivy to my people."

"Huh," Alek tilts his head up in defiance, "are you sure I'm lying? You have to be wondering to yourself who is telling you the truth. Me or her."

"I trust Ivy a hell of a lot more than I trust you."

Alek chuckles as he looks at Damon who towers over him. "That isn't saying much since you don't trust me at all. How will you deal with all the whispers once she has my baby? Are you ready to raise a bastard as your own child?"

"Untie him, Nahla," Damon growls, never taking his eyes off Alek.

"Listen," Nahla takes a step forward. "I know I threatened to throw him overboard earlier, but I can't let you do that. Castor will burn my ship down if he finds out I left his son out in the middle of the ocean to die."

"I have no plans to throw him overboard." Damon starts to roll up his sleeves. "I plan to beat him to a pulp for his lies, but I can't do that unless you release him."

"Damon," I say, hoping I can convince him to stop this madness but realizing I may not be able to. His anger has been building for three days now, and I'm not sure I can reason with him to end this before it starts. Instead, I decide to remind him about what he said down in our cabin. "Remember what you promised me."

Damon cuts me a sharp glance, looking annoyed by the reminder.

"I know what I said," he says curtly. "I won't break my word."

Nahla walks over and squats down behind the mast to cut Alek's bindings. After she stands back up, she offers Alek a hand to help him to his feet. He accepts her generous offer and stands on wobbly legs.

While he stretches his arms and shakes out his legs, Damon watches him like a predator ready to pounce on his prey.

I look around the crowd for Oliver, but he doesn't seem to be present. If anyone can talk some sense into Damon, it's him.

"Gentleman," Nahla says, "this fight is to be a friendly one."

Friendly? How can a fight be friendly?

"No maiming," she continues, "and no killing. Everything else is fair game. Do you both agree to those terms?"

Damon nods.

"Yeah," Alek says as he stretches his arms over his head not looking the least bit worried. "I understand." He looks over at me and gives me a roguish wink. "Don't worry, Ivy. You won't have to raise our baby alone. I'll never let a child of mine be raised like a spoiled brat."

Without warning, Damon slams his right fist into Alek's smug face, causing the other man to stumble backward with blood dripping out of his nose.

"Uh, okay," Nahla says, quickly getting out of the way. "Good luck, gentleman."

Damon pounces on Alek with the ferocity of a caged animal let loose on its enemy. He pummels Alek in the face two more times before targeting the other man's gut. Alek nearly falls to the deck, but

Damon allows him to regain his footing as if he doesn't want him to go down and end the fight too soon.

Alek spits a mouthful of blood onto the deck before grinning at Damon as he catches his breath.

"Who would have guessed that the great King Damon has a soft spot for whores." He begins to laugh when Damon comes at him again, fists swinging.

This time Alek is a bit more prepared. He quickly raises his own fists and dodges Damon's first swing while managing to take advantage of his opponent's forward momentum and knocking Damon off balance with a kick to his right kneecap. Damon falls onto his side, hitting the deck hard, but he recovers instantly by rolling once before regaining his feet.

Alek laughs but it's short-lived. Damon unexpectedly rushes him. He wraps his arms around Alek's waist and uses all his weight to propel him backward. Alek lands with his back on the deck while Damon straddles his torso and begins to pummel Alek's face with both fists, not letting up. Not giving Alek a moment to recover.

"Oy!" Nahla says. "I said no killing, Damon!"

Damon's too far gone to hear her words, or maybe he does and he's choosing to ignore her.

Seemingly out of nowhere, I see Oliver walk through the crowd of women who are shouting for Damon to not let up on his punishing blows. Oliver rushes over to pull Damon's arms back from behind, preventing him from slamming his fists into Alek's face anymore.

"Stop, Damon!" Oliver orders. "You're going to kill him."

"It's no less than he deserves," Damon says viciously, wrenching his arms out of Oliver's hands.

When he lifts his right fist to strike Alek again, I rush over and kneel down before him so he can see me.

"Damon, no!"

I'm not sure if it's my voice or the look of horror on my face, but Damon finally snaps out of his bloodthirsty trance as he lifts his eyes to meet mine.

He lowers his fist and stares at my face.

"You've won." I drop my gaze to Alek who passed out three blows ago and is bleeding from several breaks in his skin. "He can't even fight back anymore."

Damon, breathing heavily with rage still blazing in his eyes, lets out a guttural growl and pushes himself off Alek. He turns his back to me, to all of us, and storms off, returning below deck, presumably to the cabin we were in earlier.

"Grab Alek and take him below deck to his men," Captain Nahla orders two of her mates. "I'll tend to his wounds myself."

As I stand, the captain of the ship swaggers over to me with a confident stride.

"Thank you for stopping Damon," she says, holding out her hand for me to take.

I stare at it and shake my head. "I would but shaking your hand would mean your ship would lose its captain and enough bad things have already happened on this trip."

"Ahh, right." She slowly withdraws her hands and snaps her fingers before stuffing it into a front pocket in her pants. "Thanks for the reminder. Blimey, it must suck not being able to touch people."

"Yes, it truly does suck." I'm not sure why, but I smile which earns me a small smile back from the captain.

"Well, anyway, I'm sure Damon has told you who I am."

"I know your name is Captain Nahla and that this is your ship, but other than that . . ." I shrug.

"This here," she says, lifting her hands and looking up at the main sailing mast, "is the *Bonny Belle*. Feel free to roam around all you want." She looks at me with a serious gaze. "Boris and I are friends, you know. He's the one who helped me get this ship."

I tilt my head. "He's never mentioned you to me before."

"Ahh, well, he wouldn't," she says with a nonchalant shrug. "He always liked to keep his dealings with us pirates on the down low. Don't tell Damon this, but even if he hadn't offered me two bags of gold, I would have still come after you for Boris's sake."

"Thank you."

Nahla nods in acknowledgment of my gratitude. "Well, I best be tending to Alek's wounds. He'll be upset if his pretty face ends up being marred by scars because of this fight."

As I watch Nahla walk away, I have to wonder who else Boris has kept me away from over the years. I knew he had business dealings with some unscrupulous people. We're thieves, after all, but I wasn't aware he had any pirates as friends.

I turn to face Oliver.

"What's the best way for me to handle Damon? I assume you've seen him in this state before."

"Only once." Oliver nervously scratches his cheek. He seems reluctant to say more. I'm not sure if he believes sharing his thoughts with me will be a betrayal of Damon's trust, or if he simply doesn't want to tell me what happened in the past. Either way, I need to know what he's referring to if I'm going to help Damon move past his anger.

"You need to tell me," I say. "Nothing you say will go any further. I know how to keep a secret."

"It's not really a secret." Oliver turns his head slightly to look out across the ocean. He bites his bottom lip for a second as he considers his next words. "I haven't seen him this upset since he killed his father."

I gasp in surprise. "Are you telling me Damon might have killed Alek if we hadn't stopped him?"

Oliver gives me a side-eyed glance and shrugs. "I don't know that for sure. All I know is that he had the same look on his face as he did the day he fought his father for the throne."

"I see." This is worse than I thought, but Oliver's insight into Damon's current mental state steers me in a direction to help him. "I'm going to go talk to him."

When I turn to leave, I know exactly how I'm going to approach Damon. Whether or not he's in any state to listen to what I have to say is yet to be seen.

Before I reach the stairs to go below deck, the hairs on the back of my neck stands on end. I quickly look up into the clear blue sky as if to catch the person peering at me, but all I see are puffy white clouds floating across the sky, propelled by a cool wind. With a shake of my head, I silently berate myself for my jitteriness.

Yet, I feel like I'm being watched and my actions judged.

But by whom?

And most importantly, why?

CHAPTER 6

Before I open the door to the cabin, I steel myself for which Damon might be waiting for me on the other side. The almost uncontrollable rage he displayed during the fight is a side of him that's new to me. With a deep breath to steady my nerves, I slowly open the door and step into the room. I half expect to find the interior of the cabin in shambles, realizing his pent-up anger has to be let out in some way.

To my surprise, the room is intact, and Damon is pacing back and forth in the small area like a caged animal ready to pounce on its next victim. I pray his anger doesn't find me a suitable target. He cuts a glance my way as I enter the room, but that's the only reaction I get from him.

Closing the door behind me, I'm careful to do it quietly, not wanting to draw more attention to myself. I decide to remain by the door, not daring to take another step forward until I'm certain Damon has calmed down enough to have a rational conversation. The only sound that can be heard is the lapping of water against the hull of the ship and Damon's booted heels clicking along the wood floor.

Suddenly, Damon stops walking and turns to face me.

"Do you have feelings for Alek?" he asks curtly. "Is that why you stopped me?"

I'm taken aback by his questions, not quite understanding where his suspicion is coming from.

"The only thing I feel for him is anger because he took me away from Boris when he needed me the most, and he took me away from you when we were just getting to know one another."

The lines of rage on Damon's face slowly fade, leaving him looking merely agitated. He rests his hands on his hips and hangs his head.

"Do you know why he said those things up there?" He looks up to meet my gaze.

"What things exactly?" I ask in confusion.

Damon's lips tighten. "That you might be carrying his child."

"You know he was lying." I feel my own temper start to flare. "I already told you he didn't lay a hand on me while I was with him."

"I know that. You know that, and he knows that, but every person in Nahla's crew probably believes he had his way with you." Damon takes a deep breath before continuing. "He said that to sew a seed of doubt in everyone's mind, and to make sure I don't touch you myself."

"I don't understand." I take a step forward.

The wrinkles between Damon's brows deepen. "If I made love to you right here and now and you became pregnant, people would always doubt whose child it was. Mine or Alek's. He did that to insure I keep my distance because he knows I never want people to whisper behind our backs that the next king or queen of Midnight is actually his bastard child."

"That's crazy." I scoff, but I see the seriousness in Damon's eyes. He's not joking.

I take another step forward now standing only three feet away from him.

"You're not going to let that affect what's growing between us, are you?" I search his eyes, desperately seeking my answer, but I end up seeing it so clearly. I don't even need him to say his next words.

"Physically, yes," he says with deep regret. "I have to. Waiting a month or two will be worth it to make sure your child never has to doubt who his father is. No one should have to live that way." Damon averts his gaze, not wanting to look me straight in the eyes as he finishes his thoughts. "I lived that way, and I won't put my own son or daughter through it."

My lips part in surprise. "What are you talking about?"

"My mother had an affair with the captain of the castle guards," he says, "and my father never let her or me forget about it. Even though he killed the guard, he always doubted that I was his son." Damon looks back up at me. "I never blamed my mother for the affair. I can only imagine she was simply looking for someone to love her because my father sure as hell didn't.

"For years I lived with people whispering behind my back that I was the bastard son of that captain, and that my father should have kicked me and my mother out of the castle when I was born. Can you believe there was a time when they actually called that son of a bitch a saint for allowing us to live there? My mother . . ." Damon's voice trails off and his eyes become unfocused as his mind takes him back to another time. "My mother was the one he punished the most. There's a reason she always wears long-sleeved dresses."

Although it's morbid, my curiosity is piqued.

"What's the reason?" I whisper.

"After I was born, he publicly humiliated her by stripping off all of her clothes in front of everyone in the castle and whipping her with a leather strap that had been soaked in vinegar. She'll die with the scars he left all over her body. The only parts of her he didn't touch was her face, neck, and hands. He thought if he scarred her enough no man would ever touch her again."

I cover my mouth with both hands. Tears spring to my eyes for Margaret.

I don't know what to say. How do you respond to something so inhumane and horrible? No wonder Damon killed his father as soon as he was old enough to take the throne. The Midnight pack should consider themselves lucky to have him as their king instead of King Reginald.

It takes me a moment to pull myself together and form a response.

I wipe the tears from my eyes. "How can you feel any guilt for killing him?"

"He was a bastard, but he was still my father." Damon runs the fingers of one hand through his hair. His stance remains stiff as his conflicting emotions continue to battle each other. "Now, anytime someone I care about is hurt by someone else, the monster I had to become the day I killed him rears its ugly head and takes control of me. It feels like someone flipping a switch between the man I want to be and the man I was back then. I don't feel like I have any control over that person until I calm down and realize what I've done and how close I am to becoming just like my father."

"You could never be as cruel as him." I grab hold of Damon's arm, realizing he just stated his true fear. "You will never become your father. It isn't possible."

His desire to believe my words shines plainly in his eyes, but a sliver of doubt prevents him from trusting himself.

"Half of him will always be a part of me," he states.

"And half of your mother will always be a part of you too," I remind him. "Your mother is strong. She would have to be to survive what your father did to her and still be sane. The monster, as you call it, only comes out when someone you care about is in trouble because—"

I stop myself short from saying my next words as I realize something that hasn't been said between us yet.

"Because what?" he whispers, urging me to finish my thought as he searches my expression for the truth.

I swallow hard. "Because your love for them is as strong as your hate for the person who hurt them."

"Hmm." He slowly nods as he considers my words. "How do you suggest I get rid of that part of myself?"

"I don't think you should."

Now he looks completely perplexed. "Why not?"

"As you said, it's a part of you. It's what makes you human."

"Half human," he corrects. "When I'm a wolf, all my actions are controlled by instinct. I don't really have to think. I just do, if that makes sense."

"I can understand that, even if I haven't experienced it myself. I think you need to embrace the side of you who loses control in order to learn restraint."

He shakes his head slightly. "What do you mean?"

"By nature, you're protective of those you care about most. You protected your mother and the people of Midnight from your father the only way you knew how. He never would have just stood by and let you take the throne away from him. You need to remember that he was trying to kill you too. It seems like you focus so much on ending his life when yours could have ended that day just as easily. Or was he so old that beating him was easy?"

Damon scoffs. "It wasn't easy. He definitely would have killed me if I had slipped up and made a mistake."

"Then all you did was defend yourself. There's no shame in that."

Damon reaches out and takes one of my hands with his. "And what about what just happened up on deck?"

"You let Alek goad you into that fight. He knew exactly what buttons to push to incite your anger. You can't let people do that, Damon. Not if you truly want to be a leader. Maybe if you embrace the part of yourself that loses control, you can learn how to make it act in your favor and not completely take you over next time. There are things in this world worth fighting to the death for, but you also need to walk into those situations with your eyes wide open."

"I know what you're saying is right, but I'm not sure if I'm strong enough to pull back when I need to. All I do in those situations is see red."

"Then think about something else. Think about something that makes you happy instead."

"Very few things make me happy. If you haven't noticed, I don't exactly break out into a fit of giggles very often."

I smile. "That's because you don't have enough good memories to fall back on. Come on."

I tug on Damon's hand and lead him toward the bed.

"Sit down," I instruct as I kneel on the floor in front of him.

"Am I about to get a very happy memory?" he asks, sitting on the edge of the bed with a twinkle of amusement in his eyes.

"I hope it will be a happy memory, but I believe you're going to be disappointed in what I have in mind versus what you're hoping will happen next."

Damon sighs as I pull his boots off and set them by the nightstand.

"Now lay back in bed." Gently, I push his shoulders until his head is lying on the pillow.

He doesn't fight me. He does look intrigued though. I slip off my shoes and crawl into bed until I'm snuggled next to him with my head resting on his shoulder.

"Now, tell me the happiest memory you have from your childhood."

Damon remains quiet for a long time. So long, in fact, that I lift my head to look at his face to make sure he hasn't fallen asleep. He's wide awake and staring at the ceiling, but his eyes move like he's searching his brain for at least one memory to tell me.

"There has to be something," I say.

"I suppose there's one," he finally says. "I thought about it the other day when I was with my mother."

"What was it?"

"I was thinking about her hair."

"Her hair?" I can't help but grin at how odd that sentence sounded coming out of his mouth.

"She used to wear it down when I was a child," he goes on to say, lost in the memory. "I remember it being so long it went well past her shoulders, and it always smelled like fresh cut roses. When my father wasn't around, she was such a different person. Carefree. Loving. Fun."

I prop my head up with a hand while the other one traces the outline of a button on Damon's shirt.

"That sounds like a good memory."

He looks away from the ceiling to meet my gaze. "What's your favorite childhood memory?"

I smile as a memory easily comes to mind.

"Boris would always tell me stories right before his change. Sometimes it would be a story he heard from traveling bards who would perform in the tavern he used to own, and sometimes it would be a story from his own past. Those were the ones I loved the most."

"Which story was your favorite?" Damon covers the hand I have laying on his chest with one of his own as he waits for my answer.

"I loved the story about how my grandmother almost took his life but then saved it."

Damon looks intrigued. "How in the world did that happen?"

"Boris tried to steal the Queen's Circlet once. At the time, my grandmother was one of the queen's maids and stopped him from getting away by hitting him over the head with a copper bed warmer. He lost his balance and fell down two flights of stairs. From his side of the story, the fall nearly cracked his head open. He said all he remembered was opening his eyes and seeing my grandmother leaning over to look at him. The next thing he knew, he was waking up in his own bed with her sitting beside him. She claimed to have used magic to heal his wounds and warned him to never try to steal from the castle again. That happened a few months before I was born, and it's the reason he felt obligated to take me in. He owed her a life debt and adopting me was how he repaid her."

"What happened to your grandmother?"

Damon begins to twirl a lock of my hair around his index finger.

"I think I killed her."

Damon's hand stops playing with my hair. "How could you possibly know that?"

I look into his eyes before I tell him something only Boris and I know.

"Boris said she was coughing when she left me with him, and that she was found dead the next day at the castle."

"Was she old?"

I nod.

"Maybe she simply died of old age. I assume no one suspected foul play."

"The story was that she died of natural causes. Possibly a heart attack."

He starts to twirl my hair again. "Then there you go. That seems more likely."

To change the subject from something so morbid, I come up with another way to get to know the man I'm sharing a bed with.

"Tell me something that no one else knows about you," I challenge.

Damon narrows his eyes. "Hmm. I feel like my life is an open book. There isn't a lot that doesn't go unnoticed by others at the castle."

"There has to be something that you do behind closed doors that no one else knows about."

After a few seconds, he grins. "There is one thing that I like to do in the bathtub when I'm all by myself."

"Oh?" I lift my head a little higher. "Well, I know what you do in the tub when you have someone sharing it with you. Does it happen to fall along those lines with a bar of soap, perhaps?"

Damon chuckles. "No. It does not. It has to do with acoustics."

Now I'm stumped. "Explain."

He shrugs. "I sing."

"You sing?" Surely, he's joking.

"Yes. I sing," he says, sounding slightly offended. "Why does that seem odd to you? The bathroom is the perfect place to sing, haven't you noticed?"

"Uh, no. I don't sing."

"What?" He looks downright appalled by my answer. "You've never sung a note in your entire life?"

"I don't know any songs."

With a shake of his head, Damon sits up, forcing me to sit up on the bed too.

"Then I need to teach you a song." He clears his throat. "I learned this one when I was a boy. My mother used to sing it to me."

Down by the sea
There's a girl in glass slippers who chases the moon
She searches the night sky for the star that will take her home
Loneliness runs away with her heart
Leaving her forever forlorn and cold

Never never gonna get back home
Never never gonna find what was lost
Never never gonna reach the stars
And the wind and the sea swallowed her whole.

"Are you telling me your mother sang that song to you when you were a child?" I ask in disbelief. "Is it supposed to be a lullaby?"

"I think so," he says uncertainly. "I really don't remember. I just remember her singing it to me. Why?"

"It's completely depressing." How does he not see that? "This girl was trying to find her way home and ended up drowning in the ocean."

"No," he protests. "That's not what happened."

"And I quote, *And the wind and sea swallowed her whole.*" I lift my eyebrows, challenging him to argue against my assumption. "What else could that possibly mean?"

Damon scratches the side of his head. "I don't know. Maybe she decided to give up trying to find a way home and decided to stay where she was instead."

"And here I thought you were a pessimist." I peer at Damon with a new sense of hope. "Sounds to me like you're an optimist instead."

"Optimist," he grumbles, but I see a seed of doubt in his eyes.

My lips spread into a smile of their own accord because I feel like I've cracked his armor just a little.

"Admit it," I say. "You're a glass half full kind of guy, aren't you?"

"And what if I am? Does it matter?"

"No, but it tells me there's hope for you. For us."

I quickly learn I've planted another seed when I see desire light up Damon's blue and brown eyes.

Before I can react, he has me pinned underneath him on the bed.

"Say that one more time," he murmurs, lowering his head to kiss the bridge of my nose.

"Which part?" I close my eyes as my breath becomes more labored.

Damon kisses my chin. "You know which part, Ivy. Don't play coy."

"The part about us?"

He hovers over me, looking into my eyes so deeply I feel like my very soul has been laid out naked for him to dissect.

When he lowers his head to place his lips so close to mine we're sharing the same breath, I swallow hard and feel every inch of my body yearn for him to touch me.

"Yes," he whispers into my mouth.

"I have hope for us." The words are softly spoken, but he hears them well enough.

With a fleeting touch, he brushes his lips against mine, stirring my body into a frenzy of need that I've only experienced twice before, and each of those times involved Damon.

"Do you want me, Ivy?" He kisses each corner of my mouth, waiting for me to answer his question.

"You already know the answer to that." Each breath I take is quick and unsteady. I can't seem to fill my lungs before Damon's touch steals it away again.

"I want to hear you say it." He glides a possessive hand over the side of my breast, dipping it into the curve of my waist until it lands firmly on my hip. When he slides his hand down between me and the bed, I moan from want as he grips me, pressing my hips against his to feel the proof of his own desire.

Nothing else matters to me in that moment. I would say anything, do anything to have him.

Sliding my fingers into his curly hair, I pull his face back down to mine.

"I want you to touch me." My words come out as a whimper of need. "I want you to take me and finally claim me as your lover. I freely give you my body, Damon. All you have to do is give me yours too."

"And what about your heart? Is that mine to claim as well?"

I never get to answer his question. A loud metallic sound fills the room, causing Damon to sit up straight. The alarm on his face instantly sends a wave of panic into my heart.

"What's wrong?" I ask, sitting up next to him.

"Nahla has dropped the anchor," he says, a cold hardness to his voice.

"Is that bad?"

He looks me straight in the eyes. "It could be *very* bad."

CHAPTER 7

Damon grabs his boots and pulls them on. I leave the bed to slip my feet back into my shoes.

"You should stay here," he says. "I don't know what's going on up there, but you'll be safer if you stay in the cabin."

"No."

Damon shakes his head, clearly irritated with my response. "This isn't the time to be stubborn, Ivy. I failed to protect you once, and I'll be damned if I do it again."

"If you want to make sure I'm safe, keep me by your side. That's the best place I can be."

"Then at least stand behind me," he says, with a look of resignation.

"Why? So you can take a bullet for me? Or worse? Not on your life." I take one of his hands with mine. "If you really want to claim my heart, treat me as your equal and not like something fragile little being that needs to be shielded every time we run into trouble. I'm not a child, so don't treat me like one."

"I know you're not a child, but I also don't want to place your life in danger unnecessarily."

Before he can stop me, I stride to the door. I'm halfway up the stairs before Damon even makes it to the threshold. When I reach the deck, I find Nahla leaned up against the main mast waiting for us.

Once we're standing within three feet of her, she pushes her shoulder off the mast and faces us straight on.

"Why have you stopped the boat, Nahla?" Damon asks. "What do you want?"

"I want to go with you on this mission to the Barrens," she says. "The people of Midnight and Dawn aren't the only ones who need this miracle cure and you know that."

"Fine."

Both Nahla and I stare at Damon in surprise.

"You're not even going to argue about it?" I ask. "Taking her with us complicates things."

"That may be so," Damon admits, "but agreeing to her terms gets us home a lot faster than standing here arguing about it. Whether or not I like it, she's our only way back to Midnight."

Nahla's generous lips spread into a smile. "You're smarter than you look."

"What exactly are you implying?" he asks, taken aback by her statement.

"Most pretty boys don't have two brain cells to rub together," she chortles. "I can see I'll need to keep my wits about me when I'm around you."

Damon does not appear amused by Nahla's summary of his intellect.

"How much longer until we're back in Midnight?" he asks.

"Fortunately for you, the wind is cooperating with us. We should be making port by morning."

"If I were you, I would keep an eye out for Castor," Damon advises. "He blew the last ship I was on out of the water and left us stranded on the side of the river."

"Oh, don't worry about that old coot." Nahla waves away Damon's concerns. "He has no idea what happened to his son's ship yet, and he and I don't have a beef with each other. As long as you keep your pretty head out of view, he'll be none the wiser that you're on my ship."

Nahla looks me up and down. "Can you cook?"

"I can but I don't particularly like to."

"Our cook is sick at the moment. Why don't you go to the galley and start some lunch for my crew. We've all got to pull our weight around this ship to make it work."

"I paid you plenty of gold for your services," Damon protests. "Now you expect Ivy to do menial labor?"

Nahla places her hands on her hips. "No. I expect you both to get your asses in the galley and cook us all a meal. We can't sail this ship on empty bellies."

Damon looks flabbergasted. "Do you honestly think I know anything about cooking?"

"Of course I don't." Nahla shakes her head like Damon didn't even need to ask the question. "But I'm sure Ivy can put you to work. All you have to do is make us some potato and fish head soup. Any fool can throw that together, even someone who has never cooked before."

Damon opens his mouth to protest again, but I know it will be a waste of his breath.

I slip my arm around one of his before he can say anything else. "If you lead us to the galley, we'll get started right away."

"Just make a large pot of soup. Enough to feed us for lunch and supper. When the Dawn crew changes, their cook will prepare their meal."

We follow Nahla to the bow of the ship and into the galley. It's cleaner than I thought it would be, but with a ship run entirely by women, I'm not entirely surprised.

Nahla walks over to the side wall where wooden bins are set up. She lifts one of the lids.

"Got plenty of potatoes and onions in here," she points out before stepping in front of a barrel set beside it. "And this has all the salted fish you could need. Anything else you see," she waves her hand in the air indicating the produce sitting in open crates all around, "you're welcome to put into the soup. We just want it to taste good. Can the two of you handle that?"

I push up the sleeves of my shirt and walk between the prep counter and the stove.

"We've got it from here." I pick up a small knife from the counter. "Damon, grab about ten potatoes and start peeling them with this."

Flipping the knife in the air, I offer it to him handle first.

"So I guess I'll get to do all the grunt work," he grumbles.

I raise a disapproving eyebrow in his direction. "Overprivileged much? Are you too good to do the peeling?"

"I'm a king," he states before setting the knife down on the counter and walking over to the bin of potatoes. "I was raised to rule people, not do manual labor."

"Wow," I say in disbelief. "I didn't realize you thought of yourself as better than everyone else."

"You're putting words in my mouth." He pulls out ten potatoes and cradles them in his arms. "I didn't say that."

"Maybe not outright, but that's exactly what you implied. Whether you like to admit it or not, you're not any better than anyone else. We're all born. We all live, and we all die. Nothing separates us except for the way we choose to live the years we're given."

"I never got a choice." He turns back to the counter and sits on a stool across from me. "I was born into the life I have now."

"And if you hadn't been born to rule, what would you have chosen to do with your life?"

Damon picks up the knife and starts to peel his first potato.

"I'm not sure. I've never given it much thought." He looks up from his task to meet my gaze. "Did you always want to be a thief, or did you fall into the job because of Boris?"

"I think I've always had a mischievous side to me," I confess. "And stealing from the rich in town made me feel like I was paying them back for being so cruel to me."

"I can understand that." Damon sets his first peeled potato aside before he reaches for the next one. "Do you think you'll change much after you become queen?"

"I probably won't be stealing from the people of Midnight if that's what you're really asking."

Damon chuckles. "The thought did cross my mind. My mother told me before I came to find you that I should place you in charge of redecorating the castle. She seems to think you can turn it into the home I always deserved."

"Margaret said that about me? I wasn't sure she even liked me."

"She does. She has difficulty showing people how she feels about them. I blame that on my father. He beat her every time she showed kindness to anyone."

I let that thought simmer for a moment while I fill the stock pot with water from a barrel beside the prep counter.

"I think Margaret might have a crush on Boris." I remember how flirtatious she was with him when they first met.

"Boris?" Damon sounds aghast at the thought. "Please tell me you're joking."

I set the pot on the iron stove and add another log into the fire before I turn to look back at him.

"Are you telling me you're a snob too? It sounds like you're implying Boris isn't good enough for your mother."

"He seems like a nice enough fellow, but to be honest, I'm not sure anyone is good enough for my mother. She needs someone with a kind heart who will be patient with her."

"Boris does have a kind heart and your mother would be lucky to have him!"

I didn't mean to shout, but Boris is my dad in every way that counts. Anyone who puts him down or dares to call him common has to answer to me.

"Look," Damon places his knife down to give me his undivided attention, "I didn't mean to upset you, but you caught me off guard. I had no idea the two of them might have a thing for one another. Maybe you read their reactions to one another wrong. Besides, they're both pretty old. Why would they be looking for love at this late stage in their life?"

I laugh. "And who are you to put an age limit on when someone can fall in love? I hope Boris finds someone to share his life with. He's already spent so much of it taking care of me that I would like to see someone take care of him for a change. Don't you want that for your mother?"

"Of course, but . . ." Damon picks up the knife and starts to work on another potato. This time his cuts are quick and I can clearly see how irritated he is. "Well, I just can't imagine she really needs the company that badly."

"Again, offensive," I point out but keep my temper in check. "What's wrong with Boris?"

"Well, he's old and out of shape. I don't imagine he has much stamina and the thought of him and my mother together turns my stomach."

"Oh, I see. You can't imagine the two of them having sex is what it boils down to, right?"

Damon visibly shivers. "Don't put it so bluntly. The images that just popped inside my mind were horrific."

"For your information, Boris isn't fat. He's fluffy like a teddy bear with a heart just as pure." I rest the palms of my hands on the counter and lean toward Damon. "You're not going to interfere with whatever happens between them, are you?"

"My mother is wise enough to make her own decisions about such things. Besides, I doubt she would listen to any advice I gave her."

"Good. At least you know when to stay out of other people's affairs, especially when they deal with the heart."

I grab a clay bowl from off the counter and walk over to the salted fish barrel. After I have four of the cod fish in the bowl, I dump them into the pot. Onions are next. I have those peeled and sliced before Damon is through with his sixth potato. Since Nahla said I could use whatever is available in her galley, I decide to add in some cloves of garlic, sliced carrots, chopped green onions, and a few sprigs of dill that's growing right outside the door in a small makeshift herb garden.

"How are those potatoes coming?" I ask as Damon peels his last one.

"Almost done. What do you want me to do with them next?"

"Dice them up and add them to the pot. That'll be the last ingredient."

I look through a small pantry by the stove and find a bag of flour and some lard. When I walk back, Damon looks at me funny.

"I thought you said the potatoes were the last ingredient."

"They are for the soup, but I bet these ladies wouldn't mind some freshly made biscuits to go with it. I might even make them a pie. I just saw a crate of apples in the pantry."

"I thought you said you didn't like to cook?"

I shrug. "I usually don't, but it's a nice day and being up here with the wind blowing is sort of calming. I don't hate cooking. It's just that Boris is a better cook than I am, so I never did much of it at home."

All this talk about Boris is making me miss him even more. Tears threaten to pool in my eyes, but I quickly blink them away. The last thing I want is for Damon to see me get all sappy.

After I mix the flour with some baking powder and salt, I cut the lard into the mix with a fork. I add in just enough water to make it wet and knead the dough before dumping everything out onto the counter and rolling it flat. With a nearby cup, I cut the biscuits out and lay them in a cast-iron skillet before shoving it into the belly of the oven.

Damon has the potatoes diced and boiling in the soup by this time.

"Is there anything I can do to help with the pie?" he offers.

"Yeah." I shove ten red delicious apples over to him. "Peel."

"Ugh." He flops down onto the stool again. "What am I? The great peeler? Can't I do something else?"

"Hey, you asked what you could do for me and that's it, buddy. Peel or don't peel. It's up to you."

Damon growls but he picks up his knife and starts to peel.

"I would much rather be peeling something else off," he says as he works.

"Oh?" I measure out the amount of flour I need to make the crust. "And what would that be?"

"I'll give you one guess."

A roguish grin appears on his face. It doesn't take a genius to decipher what Damon would rather be doing.

"Although I would love to have you peel my clothes off, I thought we can't have grown up playtime because of what Alek said."

"There are other ways we can satisfy one another without running the risk of you becoming pregnant," he states. "I believe I've already proven that to you a couple of times now."

"And so you have." My cheeks feel warm from the reminder of our intimate moments together.

"I like it when you blush," he says, a smile on his lips and in his voice. "Especially when we talk about sex."

I nervously clear my throat. "Do you always put things so bluntly? It makes me uncomfortable sometimes."

"Why?" He sounds genuinely intrigued, so I decide to answer his question.

"I suppose it's because all of this is new to me." I briefly glance up at him. He's stopped peeling his apple and is staring straight at me. "It's not like anyone else has touched me like you have. They couldn't even if they wanted to."

"Hmm." Damon continues with his task and falls silent.

A tension builds up between us and I can sense he wants to ask me a question.

"Spill it," I say. "What do you want to ask me?"

"I was wondering if you'll always regret never having another lover besides me."

I look up in surprise, but the expression on Damon's face is thoughtful.

"Why in the world would I want someone else?" I ask.

He shrugs. "Do you think you'll regret never having experiences with other men?"

"No," I say curtly. "I don't. Why? Do you want me to go jump Alek? He's the only other man I can have sex with besides you."

"I didn't say that." Damon's voice has dialed into anger. "If I have my way, you'll never know the touch of another man for as long as you live. Even thinking about you being with Alek turns my stomach.

If he had taken advantage of you, I would have killed him with my bare hands and not thought twice about it afterwards."

I smile. "Then you *do* like me."

Damon doesn't answer right away. He simply continues to peel the apple in his hands.

"I more than like you," he finally says. "In fact . . ."

I wait for him to finish his thought but he doesn't.

"Never mind," he says. "This isn't the time or place for such a conversation."

What was he going to say? How much does he like me? Is it a lot? I think so. In fact, I think he may even be falling for me just like I am him.

"Oy!" Nahla walks in and sniffs the air. "What smells so good in here? I smell the soup cookin' but there's something else."

"Biscuits," I tell her as I add in other ingredients for the pie crust. "And an apple pie will be going in as soon as the biscuits are done."

Nahla moves beside me, but not close enough to place her life in danger from my touch.

"Well, if you ever get tired of the grouch over there, you're always welcome to join my crew, Ivy. From what Boris told me, you're quite the thief. I could always use a good one on my ship as long as she isn't stealing from me."

Nahla laughs. It's a rich, easy sound that strangely puts me at ease with her.

"I'll keep that in mind if things don't work out with the grouch." I chance a glance in Damon's direction and notice a cocky grin on his face as if to say there's no chance in hell I'll ever leave him.

He's probably right, but I won't be giving him the satisfaction of boosting his ego any further.

"Well, all right then," Nahla says, pushing herself off the counter. "I'll leave the two of you to it. I'm looking forward to eating your meal, Ivy."

"You know I helped," Damon reminds her. "Where's my thanks?"

"Men." Nahla rolls her eyes in exasperation. "Always wanting a pat on the back for doing the little things. Thank you too, King

Damon. I'm sure the meal would have been a complete disaster without your expert peeling." Her tone drips with condescension causing Damon to narrow his eyes at her in displeasure.

Nahla laughs as she leaves the room having succeeded in provoking the exact responses she was hoping for from Damon.

"You shouldn't let her goad you." I dump out my pie dough and begin to roll it out. "Rising to her bait is exactly what she wants."

"I know, but sometimes I can't help the way I react to people. It's not like I have a switch to turn my emotions on and off." Damon slams a peeled apple on the counter before snatching another one off the pile.

"The first step in controlling your temper is doing just that. The next time someone provokes your anger, try to think about something that calms you. Go back to that memory from your childhood with your mother if that brings you happiness."

"I suppose it could work, but I don't think that's the memory I would choose."

"It doesn't matter which memory you pick as long as it's one that calms you."

"Then I have the perfect memory."

I expect Damon to share which memory he's chosen, but he doesn't. Should I pry into his thoughts? No. If he doesn't want to share it, he doesn't have to.

Still.

My curiosity is piqued. The more I think about it the more I want to know which one he chose, but his expression gives nothing away.

After a few minutes of silence, I decide to tuck my inquisitive side away for now. Maybe he'll be more comfortable sharing his thoughts with me later.

Maybe.

CHAPTER 8

My lunch ends up being a hit. So much so that I earn the nickname Chef from the crew. Even Damon is impressed with my culinary skills.

"These are delicious," he declares, dunking a second biscuit in practically as many minutes into his bowl of soup and taking a healthy bite out of it. "I know I watched you make them, but I had no idea I was watching a master in the kitchen at work."

I point my soup ladle at him. "Didn't Margaret teach you not to talk with your mouth full?"

He swallows what's in his mouth. "Sorry."

"Hey, Chef!" Nahla practically bounces back into the galley. "Give me another bowl of that soup."

"Aye, aye, Captain."

I give her a mock salute before scooping out another ladle full of soup and dumping it into her bowl. She grabs another biscuit and proceeds to do what Damon did, dunk and eat.

"If I had known you cooked this good," she says with her mouth full, "I would have stolen you away from Boris years ago with promises of adventure and bounty on the open water."

"And I would have promptly told you no. I never would have left Boris for life on a boat like this. Being on the water makes me sick to my stomach."

"Really?" Nahla looks at me queerly. "You seem fine to me."

She shrugs and grabs the apple pie from the counter.

"Hey!" I protest. "That needs to cool a little while longer."

"You snooze you lose on this ship, Chef. If I don't snatch it now, one of the others will. I don't need a fight to break out between my crew. It's best if I just take this for myself and let the others dream about how good it tastes."

"You haven't even tasted it yet," I point out. "It may be a total disaster."

Nahla lifts the pie to her nose and inhales deeply. "Oh no. This will taste just as delicious as it smells." She gives Damon a meaningful look. "You best marry Chef here and be quick about it, or I might just steal her for myself."

"If Alek hadn't kidnapped her, we would already be married," he declares.

With a laugh, the captain spins back toward the opening to join the rest of her crew who are all eating out on the deck.

When Damon looks back at me, I feel my cheeks practically burst into flames.

"Why are you blushing, biscuit?"

My embarrassment instantly gets pushed aside. "Biscuit?"

He nonchalantly shrugs. "Nahla calls you Chef. Why can't I call you biscuit, biscuit?"

"Biscuit," I mumble under my breath while I grab what's left of the pot of soup off the counter and return it to the stove. Secretly, I love Damon's cute term of endearment for me, but I'm not about to give him the satisfaction of knowing it pleases me.

I drop the ladle in the pot and turn back around to face him. I don't have to look far. While I was busy, he left his stool and is only standing a little over a foot away from me now.

My body tingles from his closeness, and I'm finding it incredibly difficult to breathe.

With a look of open desire in his eyes, he reaches out and . . . grabs another biscuit from the cast-iron skillet on the stove.

Wait . . . what? Does he actually desire my biscuits more than he does me now?

Damon smiles mischievously as he takes a bite out of his stolen treat.

"What?" he asks, after he swallows. "You look disappointed about something."

"I thought you walked over here to see me, not steal another biscuit from the pan."

He grins and I find it incredibly difficult to stay mad at him.

Without warning, he wraps his free arm around my waist and yanks me up against him.

"Is that better?" he murmurs.

"Only if it's what you really want and not something I goaded you into doing."

Damon sets his half-eaten biscuit back on the stove top. He places both of his hands on my waist and easily lifts me off the floor in one swift motion. Once he has me sitting on the prep counter, he leans into me, nuzzling the side of my neck with his lips before placing them close to my ear.

"I would much rather be eating you, biscuit."

His teeth gently tug on my earlobe, accentuating his words and sending delicious tendrils of delight down my body.

While his lips plant tiny kisses down my neck, I close my eyes, allowing myself the pleasure of enjoying our little interlude. His hands slide up inside my shirt from the back and leisurely make their way to the sides of my breasts.

"Oy! Don't be getting handsy where we make our food! I may be a pirate, but I run a clean ship, and I don't want all your sex germs on my counter."

With a growl of frustration, Damon turns to face Nahla. "I swear, woman, you choose the worst times to interrupt us."

"Pfft." Nahla walks over to the other side of the counter to set her empty bowl down while I promptly hop off it to readjust my shirt.

"If you ask me, I'm doing you a bloody favor, mate. Every person on this ship heard Alek's boast. Do you really want people to wonder if any child Ivy has is yours or his?" She pauses but it seems to be more for dramatic effect than waiting for an answer from Damon. "Of course, you don't. I grew up in Midnight, remember? I know how cruel the lords and ladies at court were to you because of Margaret's affair with her guard. There's no way you want that type of gossip plaguing your own child."

Nahla's keen perception of Damon is crazy good. I'm impressed with her ability to read him so well. In fact, I'm a little jealous of her skill. Life would be so much easier if I knew what he was thinking.

"I was going to be careful," Damon weakly protests.

Nahla laughs. "The day a man can keep the thing between his legs under control when there's a willing woman in his arms is the day I'll believe in miracles."

Nahla looks between us and seems to come to a decision about something.

"The two of you need to make more soup and biscuits," she orders. "You might as well throw in a couple of more pies to boot."

"I thought the Dawn crew had their own chef," I say.

"Oh, they do, but she's a horrible cook." Nahla shivers in revulsion. "The last thing I need is for half my crew to feel cheated out of a good meal. Besides, if your hands are busy with work, there won't be any time for fooling around. As long as you're on my boat, there won't be any baby making, understand?"

My cheeks instantly warm up. The scowl on Damon's face would wither lesser people, but Nahla simply laughs.

"Get to work, you two. I have a hungry crew who needs to be fed."

Nahla strolls out of the galley without a care in the world, completely ignoring Damon's displeasure with her.

"I'll get you some more potatoes to peel."

Before I can take a step away, Damon reaches out and grabs me by the wrist. He pulls me to him until our bodies practically meld into one. When his lips find mine, I feel more desired than I ever have in my whole entire life. His kiss leaves a brand on not only my lips but also my soul.

The intimate moment ends as quickly as it began, leaving us both breathless.

"Maybe Nahla's right," Damon murmurs, lifting his free hand to cup the side of my face. "Maybe we should keep busy . . . for now."

He releases his hold on me, and I take two steps back.

"I . . . I'll get the potatoes," I say again. When I turn around and face the bin where the potatoes are stored, the shuffle of Damon's feet tells me he's returning to his stool.

What would have happened if Nahla hadn't interrupted us? A few pleasurable scenarios run through my mind, making me ache for the day when we don't have to worry about such things. I sigh in anticipation of that time and pray that it happens soon.

I quickly discover that Nahla seems to believe it's her mission in life to keep both me and Damon busy on her ship. In fact, we don't get another moment alone.

Not long after she ordered us to make another meal, one of her crew skips into the galley and says she was sent by her captain to help us. I soon discover that the young blonde was sent as a distraction. She yammers on about her exploits with Nahla and neither Damon nor I get a chance to say a word much less a full sentence. Eventually, I tune the girl out and let my mind drift to other matters.

I suddenly realize that I haven't thought about Simon once since Alek kidnapped me. I wonder what the king of Dawn is thinking. Is he suspicious of how long it's taking Damon to return to Midnight with me?

Perhaps, but it certainly wasn't for lack of trying on Damon's part. He found me much sooner than I expected and just in the nick of time. If he hadn't been there during the octopus attack, the fish would be eating me instead of the other way around right now. It's the closest I've ever been to death, and I have no intentions of ever letting it get its hands on me again.

When the twilight hour rolls around, we end up feeding the whole crew this time. The Midnight crew decides they need a second full meal that day before taking on their wolf forms, and the Dawn crew jumps at the chance to eat after watching their counterparts enjoy their lunch with such gusto earlier.

After everyone has been fed and all the dishes have been washed, nighttime settles, and I lose my chance to be alone with Damon again before his wolf takes over. It's just as well though. After cooking all day, I'm so tired all I want to do is sleep.

I follow Damon down to the cabin. He jumps up on the bed and curls into a ball of fur that I promptly snuggle up against for added comfort. The warmth of his body and my own tiredness soon propels me into a restful slumber.

When I wake up the next morning, it's to the sound of angry voices. Damon is no longer in the cabin. I quickly run my fingers through my hair and hop out of bed. After I slip my shoes on, I open the door and hear both Damon and Simon yelling at one another.

It seems we've made it back to Midnight just in time for the morning twilight hour, and the king of Dawn isn't only angry, he's livid.

"You should have taken me with you," Simon's voice booms across the deck as I peek out from the stairwell before making my presence known to the others. "You had no right to leave me behind."

"Ha!" Damon scoffs, shaking his head at the other king. "I had every right. Bringing you along would have complicated things unnecessarily. Besides, what would have happened if that monster had taken this ship down too? Our people could have lost both their leaders."

Simon tightens his lips, glaring at Damon for being logical, but I don't have time to stand here and listen to the two of them bicker. There's no way to tell how much twilight is left, and I'll be damned if I let either of them keep me from seeing Boris before he changes into a wolf.

I stroll onto the deck and immediately draw Simon's attention since he's facing me. A gentle breeze off the water lifts his hair away from his face, and his blue eyes capture mine with a possessiveness that doesn't go unnoticed.

"If I were you," Damon says in a low voice, "I would prepare myself for disappointment. Ivy will never be yours, not as long as I have breath in my lungs."

Simon drags his eyes away from me to look at Damon. "I guess we'll have to fix that when we get back from the Barrens, or are you going to chicken out and cancel our duel to the death?"

"I've never backed down from a fight, and I'm certainly not afraid of losing to someone as pampered as you."

"I'm going to the castle," I tell them as I make my way past the crew toward the dock. "I want to see Boris before he changes."

"I'll walk you back to the castle," Simon offers first.

"You most certainly will not," Damon says. "It's my castle. Not yours. If anyone is going to walk her back to my home, it'll be me."

"You've had her to yourself for what? Almost two days? I would like to ask her a few questions about what happened while she was being held captive."

"And I—"

"Oy!" Nahla says from her perch near the wheel of the ship. She looks down at the two men on her boat like their squabbling children instead of kings. "Neither of you are going to walk her up to the castle. I'll do it myself."

"I don't need an escort," I argue.

Nahla probably hears me, but she doesn't give any indication that she does. Once she's on the main deck she walks straight over to my side.

"I need to go up to the castle anyway," she says. "Damon said I could refill my galley with whatever he has in his food cellar."

"Within reason," Damon says.

"Yeah, yeah. I won't steal you blind."

Before Nahla steps onto the ramp that leads down to the dock, she looks over and gives me a conspiratorial wink.

"I hear tales there's some pretty good wine in the Midnight cellar," she whispers to me. "Maybe if I get there first, Damon won't notice that some of it is missing."

"I tend to think he notices a lot of things."

Nahla looks back over her shoulder at the two kings. "You men stay at least twenty feet behind us. Ivy doesn't need you crowding her with your inflated male egos."

I'm starting to like Nahla more and more. All I want to do is see

Boris before I lose my chance. I love Damon, but he can be so over-protective at times.

Wait . . .

I stop midstride down the ramp.

What did I just say to myself?

Do I actually love Damon or was that just a turn of a phrase that didn't mean anything?

"Oy!" Nahla calls out to grab my attention. By this time she's halfway up the dock. "What's the hold up, Chef? Having second thoughts about joining my crew?"

She cackles in glee while I shake my head to clear it and continue to make my way down to her. When I reach her side, she falls in beside me, matching her stride with mine.

The people in town are milling about preparing for the day ahead. I close my eyes and raise my face up to the sun for a few seconds, soaking up its warm rays.

"Sun lover, eh?"

I reopen my eyes to look over at her. "It feels nice after being cooped up in a hot kitchen all day yesterday."

Nahla grins with zero guilt. "Listen, my crew hasn't had a decent meal like that in ages. I feel like they deserved it after all we went through chasing after you in Alek's ship, don't you?"

"I suppose," I begrudgingly admit. "But didn't Damon pay you handsomely for your services?"

"Of course, he did. What kind of pirate would I be if I didn't get paid up front?" she softly chuckles.

I realize why I like Nahla. She says exactly what she thinks. I can appreciate that kind of honesty. Even admire it.

"So what's this nonsense about a fight to the death between the two of them?" she asks, having heard the men mention the duel.

"They have this stupid idea that a fight will settle who gets me once and for all, but I'll never let it happen."

"You don't say?" She sounds intrigued by my boast but dubious. "How exactly do you plan to stop them?"

"I've already chosen who I'll marry."

"Ah, well, here's to hoping they let your choice stand, but from what I know about the two of them, they're as stubborn as it comes and neither of them will let you go so easily. Even if they find this miracle cure in the Barrens, there's no guarantee that it will work. Alek said you told him it only worked on a few of the cubs here in Midnight, not all of them."

I forgot about that fact.

"Well, even if they keep me barefoot and pregnant, I can only have so many children during my lifetime. It would take several generations to spread my humanity to everyone."

"True," she concedes, "but you're a sure thing. This magic cure isn't. No king is going to gamble the future of his people on a maybe. I think you need to prepare yourself for the fight and an outcome you may not expect."

Nahla is right. The cure is no guarantee, but I am.

A glance over my shoulder assures me that neither Damon or Simon can hear our conversation. Just as Nahla requested, they're walking exactly twenty feet behind us. Returning my attention to the road ahead as we leave town, I focus on the castle and everything it represents here in Midnight, both past and present.

"Did you know Damon's father?" I ask her. "He sounds like a real son of a bitch."

"I didn't know old King Reggie personally, but my mother did. They were lovers for a time, but Damon's father changed out his bed mates about as often as he changed his underwear. In fact, Damon and I might even be half brother and sister for all I know."

I peer at her in shock. "Really? Does Damon know that?"

She shrugs. "I have no idea. I'm sure ole Reggie has a few bastard children running around this town. It doesn't mean Damon is going to befriend each and every one of us. Besides, I don't want my reputations sullied by his memory."

"I've heard about some of the things he did here." I try to block out the imagery of Margaret being whipped in public for her infidelity but my imagination is a little too vivid. "I'm a little surprised someone didn't kill him before Damon did."

"Reggie had anyone who was a threat killed before they could get him first. From what my mother said, there were a lot of people in town who wanted him dead, but none of them made it very far. Reggie may have been a bastard, but he wasn't stupid."

"Was your mother like you? A pirate?"

Nahla laughs like I've said the funniest thing she's heard in quite some time.

"Hell no. She was a laundress in the castle." She wipes away tears of laughter from her amber eyes. "When she got knocked up with me, Reggie threw her out into the streets. If it wasn't for a few kind souls here who took her in, I would have grown up homeless."

"What made you want to become a pirate then?"

"I wanted the freedom to choose the rules to my own life." She raises her chin up a notch higher. "I swore to myself that I would never become a sad sack like my mother. For whatever reason, she truly loved King Reginald, despite his cruelty to her and everyone around him. I never wanted a man to rule my life like he did hers. It almost killed her when Damon executed his father."

"Wait, is your mother still alive?" I ask in surprise.

"Yea. She still lives here. I come to visit her every once in a while, but not as often as I should. Sometimes I can't stand looking at her sad face," she says in disgust. "It's like she's still in mourning over his death and it turns my stomach."

"She'll definitely know you're in town since your boat is anchored at the docks."

"True," she says with a heavy sigh. "I guess I'll need to go see her, but I would like to grab of bottle of wine first before I visit her."

"I'm sure Damon wouldn't mind you taking her a basket of food too."

"Even if he did, do you honestly think I would care?"

This time it's my turn to softly chuckle. "No. I don't think you would. You know, I wish Boris had introduced us. I think we could have been friends."

"It's never too late to become friends," she says with a wink. "I think he kept me away so you wouldn't be tempted to join my crew. Losing you would have torn his heart in two."

"I never would have done that because leaving him would have hurt me just as much. He should have known that."

"Maybe he wasn't confident enough to test it out."

"Maybe."

The rest of our walk to the castle is made in silence as we each become lost in our own thoughts.

The fight between Damon and Simon is foremost in my mind. One way or another, I'll find a way to stop it, whether they like my interference in their affairs or not.

CHAPTER 9

The closer we get to the castle, the faster my legs start to move.

By the time the front entrance comes into view, I'm at a flat out run. Nahla attempts to keep up with me but fails. Maybe she doesn't have her land legs yet, but she ends up having to stop.

"You go on," she says with a wave of her hand, bent over and attempting to catch her breath. "I'll catch up."

I hear her but slowing down for her was never an option for me. I'm too close to Boris to care if she finds me later in the castle or not. The twilight hour is quickly ticking away, and I have to see him before he changes into his wolf form. If he had been the one kidnapped, I would be beside myself with worry and any rest I got would not be peaceful.

The castle doors are wide open, allowing the morning coolness to naturally permeate the interior. When I run through the doors, the entryway is practically empty of people except for a few servants preparing to attend to the needs of those staying in Damon's home. I hear one of the maids gasp in surprise when I rush by her on the grand staircase, but I don't give her a second thought. By some miracle, I remember how to navigate through the castle's maze of corridors and locate the hallway where not only Boris's room is located but also mine.

His door is open, and I slow my pace to a walk just outside his room in case he's already fallen asleep. When I peek inside, Margaret is removing some gauze away from the wound on his throat. With her back to me, she's mostly blocking Boris's view of the doorway and obscuring my presence.

"Ahh," she says with immense satisfaction. "That looks much better. See! I told you the stitches would hold even through your transformations."

Margaret stands away from her patient to deposit the gauze in a waste basket by the nightstand. When she does that, Boris's gaze is drawn to me.

His eyes fill with tears and a tremulous smile spreads his lips. The joy on his face makes me realize just how much I've missed seeing him.

"There's my poppet," he says in a choked voice. "I knew you would come back to me."

I rush into the room and have my arms around him before he can wipe the tears away from his face. He rests his cheek against the top of my head and holds me close like he may never let me go again.

His body tenses. "Are you hurt?"

"No," I reassure him. "No one hurt me."

I leave out the part where Alek knocked me out when he first kidnapped me. Boris doesn't need to know about that. If he did, Alek would surely be a man marked for death. If Boris didn't kill him with his bare hands, he knows plenty of unscrupulous people who would do the deed for a price.

Boris relaxes and kisses the top of my head.

"Let me look at you then," he says.

I sit up on the side of the bed so he can see for himself that I'm perfectly fine.

"I assume my son has returned with you?" Margaret asks.

When I look at her face, I can see she's holding herself with her usual aloof demeanor, but there's a shallowness in her breathing that tells me she's awaiting my answer with bated breath.

"He should be in here soon. I ran part of the way while he and Simon walked behind me."

"Behind you?" Margaret looks perplexed. "Why would he walk behind you? That doesn't sound like him at all."

"Nahla made them walk behind us because they wouldn't stop arguing."

Boris chuckles. "That sounds about like her. She can be quite the spitfire when provoked."

"I like her." I take hold of one of Boris's hands, not wanting to lose physical contact with him. By his grip, I can tell he doesn't want to let me go either.

"I was afraid you might," he sighs. "Has she convinced you to go gallivanting off with her to live a pirate's life yet?"

"No," I laugh. "There's no way I would leave you. You should know that."

Boris grins, pleased with my answer. "I had no intention of ever letting the two of you meet, but desperate times called for desperate measures, and I knew her ship was the only way Damon was ever going to catch up to Alek's vessel."

"And I made it just in time," Nahla says as she walks into the room with Damon and Simon on either side of her. Is she between them on purpose to keep the two kings from squabbling again? I have a feeling that's exactly why she's so strategically positioned.

Damon greets Boris with a single nod of his head. Boris returns the nod with an expression of thanks.

"I'm glad to see you made it home in one piece, Damon," Margaret says. "After all the stories Boris told me about that one," she gives Nahla a scathing look of disapproval, "I was having my doubts you would return to me in one piece."

"Oy!" Nahla looks rightly offended. "What's that supposed to mean?"

Margaret lifts her head a notch higher. "Oh, I think you know exactly what that means, young lady."

"Mother," Damon says reproachfully, "Nahla helped us rescue Ivy. You should show her a bit more gratitude."

"Hmph." Margaret obviously disagrees. "Anyway, we should leave these two alone so they can catch up with one another. Besides, you have someone else you need to go talk to, Damon. That fae man keeps lying naked out in the backyard. It's quite appalling and causing a bit of a scandal. He hasn't listened to me or Edmond, but maybe you can talk him into keeping his clothes on for a change."

Damon appears amused. "I'll try, but I can't make any promises."

"I suppose that will have to do." Margaret makes shooing motions with her hands as she ushers the others out the door. "Let's go everyone. I'm sure Ivy would appreciate some privacy to regale Boris with her little adventures at sea."

"Little adventures," I scoff. "I wouldn't call coming face to face with a giant octopus little."

Boris looks confused. "A what?"

"But I haven't had a chance to speak with her at all," Simon protests like a petulant child.

"You need to get ready for the change anyway." Margaret points him toward the door.

With a look of irritation, Simon leaves the room.

After everyone else has left, Margaret slowly closes the door.

"Have fun you two," she says to us.

"Thanks, Maggie." Boris gives her a wink and a smile.

I don't get to see Margaret's expression, but I do hear her giggle as she pulls the door closed.

Margaret giggling? I believe someone has some explaining to do.

"Maggie?" I ask, crossing my arms. "What happened while I was away? Did you and Margaret profess your undying love for one another or something? And what's up with her giggling? I didn't even know she was capable of that sound."

Boris chuckles softly. "You know I've always had a way with the ladies. Maggie is no exception. She was helpless against my charms."

"Well, you're a fast worker. You were able to charm her with only two hours of actual speaking time a day. It sounds more like you're a miracle worker to thaw her icy heart."

"You and I talk, in our way, when I'm in wolf form. It was the same with me and Maggie. I would tell her about my life while she was a wolf, and vice versa. That woman has experienced more hardships than you might realize. If I can give her even a moment of happiness, our time together has been well spent." Boris narrows his eyes at me. "You're not jealous that I'm giving her attention, are you? That would be absurd. You will always be my main priority no matter who else I might like to spend time with."

"No. I'm not jealous. Well, maybe just a little," I amend, "but that's only because I've never had to share you with anyone else before. Honestly, I hope you can give her some joy. From the things Damon has told me about the way his father treated her, she deserves to have someone as kind as you in her life. Did, uh . . . did she tell you why she always wears clothing that covers her body?"

Boris looks surprised. "Damon told you about the whipping?"

I nod. "He also told me about the affair she had with her guard, and that he may not be the son of King Reginald. I think he secretly hopes that he isn't, and I can't say I blame him for that."

Boris sighs. "I guess we'll never know for sure, but he doesn't seem to be anything like the old king. Has he treated you well, or do I need to have a talk with him?"

"He treats me just fine." I can't help but smile as I think about Damon.

"Oh dear."

I look Boris in the eyes and see worry. "What?"

"You're in love with the dolt. I can see it all over your face." He shakes his head at me. "The two of us are in trouble now, aren't we?"

"Why trouble?" This time it's my turn to look confused.

"You've fallen in love with Damon while I've fallen for his mother. It seems like we're both in well over our heads. Neither of us have ever felt this way which means we can't give each other advice."

"I see what you mean." I slip off my shoes and prop up some pillows beside Boris. After I sit down closer to him, I decide to switch the subject and tell him all about my time on both Alek and Nahla's ships.

"Sounds like quite the adventure," he says. "Oh! Before I change, I have something for you. It's behind my pillow."

Boris leans up, and I pull his pillow away from the headboard to discover the Queen's Circlet .

"Maggie found it when she was cleaning up that mess in your room." Boris leans back once I let go of his pillow. "It must have been knocked off your head when that fae attacked you. She found it underneath your bed."

"Damon told me what Vamir claims about our past," I say. "Do you think he's telling the truth about the war between his people and ours?"

"I'm not sure, but I believe you may hold the key to that question."

I rotate the Queen's Circlet in my hands until I find the off-color diamond.

"What if I discover that he's lying?" I look to Boris for advice.

"Then you have to tell the others. We need to know if we can trust him before we go traipsing off into the Barrens with him leading the way."

"You're not going. You're staying here."

"The hell you say! I could be missing a leg, and I would still hop after you."

The imagery of Boris hopping after me on one leg tickles my funny bone.

"I hate to do this, poppet, but the change is about to happen. Why don't you go lock the door and use that thing to look at another memory about that couple you mentioned? What were their names again?"

"Emily and Mark."

I hop off the bed and walk over to the door to lock it. After I'm settled back into my spot beside Boris, I hold the circlet firmly in my hands.

"Go on," he says. "I'll keep watch over you."

"Okay." I close my eyes and take a deep breath before touching the slightly pink diamond.

Just like the times before, I'm sucked back into the past where Emily and Mark lived.

I instantly see Mark standing on what looks like the roof of a tall building. His eyes are filled with not only panic but also mortal fear.

"Are you recording this?" Mark asks anxiously.

"Yes," I hear Emily say in a much calmer voice. "It's recording."

"Against all odds," he says into the diamond necklace Emily is wearing, "the Earth has finally made first contact with an alien species. Or should I say they made contact with us."

He moves out of the frame revealing a silver pyramid shaped object hovering in the sky a good distance away from where they are standing.

"I can't believe this is happening, can you?" he asks Emily.

"It's pretty incredible," she agrees. Still, she sounds detached, distant even.

"What do you think they want?"

Emily doesn't make a reply.

"No guesses?" he prods after her silence.

"No," she replies, not sounding at all worried or interested in what had to be a profound experience for all of humanity.

Since the circlet not only allows me to peer into the past but also feel what Emily feels, I know she's worried about the unearthly visitors, but she's also mad for some reason. She clearly doesn't want them there.

"Don't worry, Em." Mark places his hand on Emily's protruding belly. "Junior here doesn't have anything to worry about. I'm sure they come in peace. They wouldn't travel all this way in their spaceship for nothing, and if they wanted to attack us, they probably could have done that from outer space."

Still, Emily says nothing, but I can feel her panic so clearly. Why isn't she sharing her thoughts with Mark? From the few memories I've watched, she's never been this closed off from him.

While Emily is still facing the spaceship, I see it start to spin in the sky as it makes its way toward their building.

"We should probably go back down to our apartment." Mark attempts to pull Emily along, but she resists him.

"I want to watch it," she says. "I need to see what happens next."

Mark sighs. "Where you go, I follow."

With their hands firmly clasped together, they watch as the spaceship floats even closer. When it hovers over their building, it comes to a stop.

Emily no longer feels worry or panic. She simply feels resigned to her fate, without any hope for a reprieve.

She lets go of Mark's hand and turns to face him.

"Remember that I love you." She doesn't know if this will be the last time she ever sees him or not, but she's trying to prepare for the worst. "Our marriage and this baby means everything to me, and I will fight to my last dying breath to protect both you and our child."

"You're scaring me, Em." Mark places his hand on her arm. "Let's go home."

"I love you."

There's a flash of blue light that nearly blinds me.

When the light fades, Emily finds herself standing in a field of tall grass with even taller pink flowers.

A man with long blond hair, porcelain white skin, and pointy ears stands before her. He's wearing a sky-blue silk ceremonial robe with a white collar and cuffs.

His expression is haughty and the look of disdain on his face as he looks at Emily is nothing short of the scariest thing I've ever seen in my life. He has to be a fae.

The man's eyes travel the length of her and stop at her baby bump.

"They told me you were pregnant, but I had to see it for myself," he says in disgust. "How could you, Emily? How could you let yourself become impregnated with one of their filthy progeny?"

Emily holds her head up a little higher. Her defiance is strong, and I silently cheer her on.

"They're not as horrible as you made them out to be, Father. In fact, I've come to care about many of them as much as I do you."

"Nonsense! They're all a bunch of uneducated primates who made it up the food chain because they learned how to speak and use their thumbs." The man turns his back to Emily as if he can't bear to look at her anymore in her current state. "You are a great disappointment to me, Daughter. If it wasn't for your mother . . ." his voice trails off as if he doesn't want to finish saying what's on his mind.

"What? You would kill me for falling in love and wanting to have my husband's child?" she mocks. "This is how we save our people. We can share this world with the humans and integrate ourselves into their lives. I've proven we can mate with them too and have viable offspring."

Emily's father whirls around in a fit of rage.

"That wasn't your mission. All you had to do was live among them and gather data."

"I've done that! I've spent the last two years doing exactly what you wanted me to do. Maybe it wasn't the way you envisioned me doing it, but nothing can be done about that now."

"Two years and you couldn't keep your legs closed because of that human?" Her father takes a menacing step closer to her. "I hope disgracing our family because of your wanton ways was worth it, Emily. You've brought shame to the House of Sangard and I will never forgive you for that."

"I will not apologize to you for what I've done."

"Then go back to your precious humans, daughter," he sneers. "We'll gain control over this world soon enough, and you can join them in death for all I care. You're already dead to me, so why not make it for real?"

The blinding flash of blue light appears again.

Emily finds herself standing on the sidewalk beside her building.

She collapses to the ground in a fit of tears. Her heartache is so strong my own chest hurts like someone just struck me with a red-hot poker. Her sorrow is all too real, and I breathe a sigh of relief when I'm woken up by a warm tongue on my face.

Boris, now in his wolf form, has his head over mine. He whines softly before pulling away. After I sit up on the bed, I wipe away the tears I shed over Emily's sadness. I drop the circlet on my lap before wrapping my arms around Boris's neck. Even in his wolf form, he's able to bring me comfort.

I continue to cry for Emily, but I also shed tears for everything humanity lost.

CHAPTER 10

After Boris falls asleep, I decide to stay in his room for a little while longer. Emily's memory was haunting, and after recounting the story to Boris, the last thing I want to do is run into Damon and have to relive it all over again. He needs to know the information I was able to gather, but I need some time to recover.

If I had just watched it as a bystander, I don't think it would have affected me so deeply, but I felt her heartache like it was happening to me. I'm not sure what I think about the fae now after seeing how atrociously Emily's father treated her. How could he cut her out of his life so easily? I can't imagine Boris ever doing that to me. He would die for me just like I would for him.

I lay back against the pillows with the circlet in my hands. I'm not sure if there are more memories stored in the diamond or not, but I need to know how Emily's story ends before I mention any of this to Damon. It would also help to know how the diamond became part of the circlet in the first place.

With a deep breath, I locate the diamond again and touch it to learn what other secrets it has to share.

Mark is in the bedroom franticly pulling out clothes from a chest of drawers before tossing them into an open suitcase on the bed.

"Mark, there's nowhere we can go to hide," Emily tells him. "The fae will eventually win, and when they do, our only chance will be that my father changes his mind about our marriage."

Mark scoffs as he closes the suitcase and zips it up.

"From what you told me, it doesn't sound like there's much hope in that happening." He looks up at her. "We have to get out of the city. It's bad enough your people have forced almost all of us to change into wolves at some point during the day, but now they expect us to let them rule us. It's not going to happen, Em! Not when the governments of the world have one more card to play."

"But nuking the whole planet doesn't make any sense." Emily is clearly frustrated. "Why destroy your own home like that?"

"You've spent two years among us, but you still haven't learned what it means to be human," Mark says harshly. It's the first time I've ever heard him talk down to her.

"Don't be cruel," she begs. "I thought you said it doesn't matter what I am and that you would always love me no matter what."

"I'm sorry." He hangs his head in both frustration and shame. "I do love you, Em. I love our son, and I also love my world. The one thing you haven't learned about my species is that we don't play well with each other or apparently aliens who give us ultimatums. We would rather destroy our planet than let it be taken over by a race of creatures who want to take half of it away from us."

"To them, it was a generous offer. They could have asked for all of it."

"Generous." Mark shakes his head. "And which nations were supposed to give up their lands? They didn't *ask* either, Em. They *demanded*. That didn't go over well with anyone."

Mark pulls the suitcase off the bed and starts to walk out of the bedroom.

"Do you really believe running away to the mountains will protect us?" Emily chases after her husband just as a baby starts to cry in a different room.

"If you have a better idea, I'm all ears." Mark sets the suitcase by the front door before turning to Emily. "My family has lived in those mountains for hundreds of years. Maybe we'll get lucky and be able to live out our lives there in peace. All I know is that we need to leave this city because it's bound to be one of the first ones hit if they decide to go nuclear."

"But I still don't understand why the leaders of Earth would choose to do that. No one wins in that scenario."

Mark throws his arms in the air. "No one is winning now! Most humans would rather destroy everything than hand it over to a bunch of aliens. Besides, your people are the ones who struck first. This spell, or whatever, that transforms us into wolves started all of this. It would have been better for the fae if they had killed us instead."

"My people aren't normally violent. Desperation for a new home is the only reason they reverted to using that kind of magic."

The baby cries louder. Both Mark and Emily turn toward the sound.

"He probably needs to be changed and fed," she says. "Why don't you pack up his stuff while I take care of that."

Emily walks down a hallway and enters a nursery with Mark following behind her. She heads directly toward the white crib and picks up the baby swaddled in a yellow blanket.

"I've got you, Jack. Mommy has you," she says while patting the baby on the back to soothe him.

For the next few minutes, Emily takes care of the baby's needs as she changes his diaper and sits down in a rocking chair to breastfeed him. The boy has the distinctive pointy ears of the fae, and I wonder how they explained that to their friends and family after he was born.

I suddenly realize, I've never seen Emily. I have no idea what she looks like or if she has the same distinctive ears. Since she was sent to Earth on a two-year scouting mission, I can only assume her ears were altered in some way to conceal her true identity from the humans she was supposed to interact with.

Still, I wish I knew what she looked like, but I'm not sure how many more memories are stored in the diamond. In fact, I'm not sure why this memory was recorded. The past ones were of important events in Mark and Emily's life together, but this one is so normal. Why would she record it?

When I hear Emily start to cry, I feel her sense of loss, and instantly understand why she decided to record this moment. It was her last day in the home she and Mark had built together. Everything was about to change, and there was no way of knowing what would happen next. Mark's plan to live in the mountains was a last-ditch effort to find somewhere safe for his family, but in Emily's heart she knows it will fail. Yet, she went along with it because Mark needed to do something to protect his wife and child.

After Emily burps the baby, Mark finishes packing up Jack's belongings and looks anxious to leave. He escorts Emily and the baby to the door, but before she follows him out, she turns and looks back at her home one last time.

"Em, we need to go." Mark's words are gentle. He seems to sense how hard it is for her to say goodbye to their home, but there's also an urgency in his voice that tells her their time is running out.

Emily turns away from the apartment and follows him.

They don't bother to close the door. What's the point? They're never going to return and anything left inside their apartment will probably be destroyed in the war to come.

When they make it outside their building, they're met with pure chaos. Hundreds of people are packing up their belongings into metal contraptions with four black wheels. It appears to be a carriage of some sort because I see some people traveling down the road in them.

"Looks like everyone is trying to leave," Mark says worriedly as he tosses their suitcases into their own metal carriage on the street. "I knew we should have left last night."

Emily opens the carriage door and sits down on a black leather seat inside, holding Jack close to her chest.

An ominous sound fills the air.

Its metallic wail is like nothing I've ever heard before. It instantly fills Emily with dread and fear.

"Oh no," Mark says as he pulls away from the carriage and looks up into the clear blue sky.

Emily hops out of the car to stand beside her husband. I don't see anything overhead at first, but then I see something shoot across, leaving a wake of white smoke behind it.

Mark looks down at Emily. His eyes are filled with tears.

"We're too late," he says. His voice is filled with regret and missed opportunities.

He pulls her in close as if to shield her from what's coming next. His body is shaking uncontrollably, and Emily begins to cry.

"I'm so sorry," Mark says, tightening his hold on his family. "I should have done more sooner."

"It's not your fault. It's not your fault." Emily keeps repeating this over and over again, but I'm not sure if she's saying it to Mark, herself, or both. She feels a great deal of guilt over what's happening, which I can understand. If it wasn't for her people, the world wouldn't be on the brink of total annihilation.

Emily pulls away so she can look into Mark's eyes one last time. It's a final lasting memory she can take with her to the grave. The baby cries, not completely understanding what's going on but feeling the fear that surrounds him.

Mark cups her face with his hands lovingly as tears for a lost future together stream from his eyes.

"I love you," he declares leaning in to plant small kisses on her lips and cheeks. "You're the best thing that has ever happened to me, and I don't regret one second of our life together."

There's a bright flash of light that draws both of their attention. As Emily looks to her right, she sees a huge cloud of smoke that looks a lot like a mushroom for some reason.

"Don't look at it," Marks says, drawing her back into his arms, holding her so tightly they practically meld into one.

"Em, I love—"

Mark's declaration of love is cut off, and Emily finds herself standing in the field of grass and pink flowers again. Jack wiggles in her arms, reminding her that he's there.

Emily whirls around.

"Mark?" she cries, already knowing that he won't be answering her back but holding out hope that he will. "Mark!"

"He's not here."

Emily turns to find her father standing beside her. His eyes are focused on the baby in her arms.

"I suppose that's my half-breed grandson," he says haughtily.

"Where is my husband?" Emily demands to know. "Why isn't he here with us?"

"You ungrateful girl," her father says. "The only reason *you're* here is because your mother begged me to save you and that *thing*."

"Where is Mark?" Emily screams.

"I assume he's dead just like all the other people in the city you lived in."

"You could have saved him!" She falls to her knees in the grass. Her pain is debilitating. I've never felt agony so all-consuming in my own life.

"Be thankful you're still alive, daughter, and pull yourself together before you shame us even more than you already have. We didn't destroy the planet. Humanity did. Feel lucky you've been given the chance to raise your child. Otherwise, you would be a smudge of soot like your husband marking the sidewalk you just stood on."

"You should have left us," she cries. "We should have all died together."

"Perhaps," her father cold-heartedly concedes. "But only time will be able to tell us whether or not you deserve this second chance at life. Now pull yourself together. I'm supposed to take you to see your mother."

The memory ends, but the lingering effects of Emily's sorrow doesn't.

When I open my eyes, I still feel her heartache in every bone in my body. The loss of Mark was like losing half of herself. After I slide the circlet underneath my pillow, I curl up into a ball and cry myself to sleep.

When I wake up, Boris's room is darker, and I see he's transformed back into his human form.

"Are you okay?" He stops slipping on his boots as he looks over at me. "Did you sleep in here all day?"

Still groggy from sleep, I nod. "I guess I did. I must have been more tired than I realized."

"It's no wonder considering the week you've had."

What happened in Emily's last memory comes rushing back to me, and I know there's only one person who can help erase it from my mind.

"I need to find Damon." I get out of bed and slip my shoes back on. "I assume you're getting ready to spend some time with Margaret."

Boris stands from his chair and pulls the ends of his vest down.

"You assume correctly. We normally share supper during this twilight hour."

"I'll find you later then, if I get the chance."

I make my way out of the room and through the castle. I have no idea where Damon will be during this time of day, but I plan to ask the first servant I run across where he is right now.

Unfortunately, my plan gets derailed by the one person I was hoping to avoid.

"There you are," Simon calls out to me.

I had just turned the corner to a new corridor when I hear his voice. I know I'm only two hallways from the grand entryway, but he's directly in my path.

"I don't want to talk to you, Simon. Get out of my way."

I walk straight ahead, not caring if he touches me or not. If he's foolish enough to reach out to stop me, that's his own fault.

To my disappointment, he simply matches my stride as I reach him.

"I get the feeling you and I have gotten off on the wrong foot," he says amiably enough. Though, I hear a hint of disingenuousness in his voice.

"Whatever could have given you that idea?"

Simon smiles, having picked up on the sarcasm that was practically dripping from my words.

"I know my initial kidnapping of you was foolhardy, but it wasn't anything worse than what Damon has done. Surely, even you can see that."

I stop. I turn. I look Simon straight in the eyes.

"What is that supposed to mean? If I didn't know any better, I would say you were calling my intelligence into question. Even you wouldn't be that stupid."

"Oh, good grief." He throws his hands in the air. "Is there anything I can say to you that won't be taken the wrong way? It seems like you have it set in your mind that I'm a monster. For the record, I'm not. I simply know what I want. Is that so wrong?"

I cross my arms. "And tell me what it is that you want so we don't misunderstand each other."

"I want you to become the next queen of Dawn," he states. "I want you to become my wife and bear me children who will save my people. I want exactly what Damon wants yet you don't seem to be running away from him every chance you get. In fact, where are you headed in such a hurry?"

My arms slowly fall back to my sides. "I'm trying to find Damon."

Simon points an accusing finger at me. "See! What is it about him that's more pleasing to you than me?"

Ahh, I see. The king of Dawn wants his ego stroked. Maybe if I'm up-front and honest with him, he'll leave me alone.

"Look, Simon, I'm sure there are literally thousands of women in Dawn who would love to become your next queen or even your mistress, but I'm not one of them. Yes, you're handsome, and I'm sure, in your way, you can be charming when the need arises, but for whatever reason, I don't find you the least bit attractive. In fact, the thought of sharing a bed with you makes my stomach feel like I've swallowed a whole pitcher full of spoiled milk."

"Well, don't hold back, Ivy, tell me how you really feel," he says with his own brand of sarcasm.

"None of what I said was meant to bruise your ego. I'm simply telling you the truth as I see it. I can also promise you that if you go through with the duel with Damon and somehow win, you will, in fact, lose because I would rather die than live the rest of my life with you."

My words act like a slap in the face. Simon not only appears shocked, but he also looks worried.

"You don't mean that." His words don't match his tone. Since he's looking me straight in the eyes, he should be able to tell just how much I mean it.

"You can test your theory, but you will lose. The people of both Dawn and Midnight would also lose because their last hope for a better future would no longer exist. I won't live as a prisoner in my own skin, Simon. I just won't."

I turn and continue to make my way through the castle. Simon doesn't follow me. If the look on his face is any indication, he took my words to heart. Maybe they were enough to stop the fight from happening, but I doubt it. His ego won't let him walk away from the fight with Damon, even though I just told him he won't actually be winning anything. He would rather see me die than concede to his rival.

When I reach the grand staircase of the entryway, there are quite a few people walking around. It doesn't take me long to find Damon. He's tucked away in a corner speaking with Anya. If the tears in her eyes are any indication of what they're talking about, I would have to say she's putting on a good show of denying her involvement in the destruction of my clothing. Perhaps she's trying to convince him that my fae assassin is the real culprit, but I hope he doesn't fall for that ploy. Ripping my new clothes to shreds was an act of pure hate and the only person who truly hates me here is Anya. Even though she doesn't know me, the fact that Damon cares for me more than her must be eating her alive.

I can't say I blame her for the way she feels. Damon never should have used her as a friend with sexual benefits and no strings attached. That rarely works with women when affairs of the heart are in play. I thought he would be smart enough to realize that, but maybe he was letting his little head think for his big one in the past.

Anya catches me looking at her and the expression on her face completely changes. She wipes away her tears and nods at something Damon says. She makes a clipped reply before pushing past him and disappearing down one of the main corridors of the castle.

When Damon turns, he notices me on the staircase and smiles. The sight warms my chilled bones. I race down the stairs and run straight for him. I don't stop until I'm in his arms with my head against his chest, listening to the beats of his heart.

"Not that I mind you running into my arms but is everything all right?" he asks worriedly.

"I just need to feel you against me," I whisper, remembering the soul rending pain Emily felt after losing Mark. What would she have given to hold the man she loved one last time?

"What's happened? I was a little worried something was wrong since you spent most of the day in Boris's room. I just assumed you needed rest after everything you've been through the past few days." He tightens his hold as if his arms can protect me from all harm.

I don't answer right away. A few seconds later I feel Damon's body stiffen like he's suddenly raised his guard.

"Was it Simon?" His voice is as hard as steel. "Did he do something to you?"

I look over my shoulder and see the king of Dawn descend the staircase. His full attention is on me and Damon.

"No." I pull back slightly to look up at Damon's face. His jaw is firm and his gaze steady on the other king. "Simon didn't do anything, but I need to tell you something in private."

"Follow me," he says, taking one of my hands with his. "Let's go for a walk outside. The palace tends to have too many ears sometimes."

We head straight out the front door and into the waning sunlight of the day. As we stroll across the lawn, I begin to tell Damon about the power of the circlet and all of the memories it's shown me so far. Damon listens intently, soaking in all the information I've gained from Emily's life.

"So what Vamir told us is true," he says after I tell him the details of the last memory.

"As far as I know, yes. He's told you the truth."

"I suppose that's a relief to some extent but having his words confirmed from a reliable source is troubling. If we can learn more about the fae before we head into the Barrens, that would be helpful."

"There may be more memories stored in the diamond. If there is, I might be able to learn more about them."

"Are you sure you want to do that? I would rather not know anything else than see you upset again."

"Does that mean you care about me just a little, King Damon?" I tease.

He smiles. "Only just a little."

"I only care about you a little bit too." I demonstrate this by lifting my hand and measuring out how much I care with my thumb and index finger spread less than an inch from each other.

Damon laughs softly. He begins to close the distance between us, but a new voice barges into our conversation.

"King Damon!"

I look toward the castle and see a man I've never met before. He's tall and lean with short blond hair and green eyes. It doesn't take a genius to figure out he's Anya's father. The resemblance is too uncanny.

"Can I have a word with you?" the man asks. He eyes me with barely contained contempt as he approaches us.

"If you're here to ask me to reconsider my decision, don't waste your words, Klaus. Anya has broken the rules of my home and has been ordered to leave in the morning. There's nothing else to be said about the matter."

Klaus's face turns beet red. "You can't just throw her out. She has served you well over the years and doesn't deserve to be treated this way. Just because she lost her temper, doesn't mean she should be thrown out of court. Let me pay for the clothing that she ruined. Surely, we can come to an understanding about this."

"Anya leaves in the morning. That is the only thing you need to understand." Damon's voice is hard and unyielding. The crestfallen look on Klaus's face indicates that he knows there is nothing he can do to change Damon's mind on the matter.

"Fine." Klaus straightens his shoulders. "We'll all be leaving first thing tomorrow and returning home."

"Then I wish you a swift journey."

Klaus turns his back to us but not before giving me a scathing look of reproach. It seems uncalled for since I'm the victim here, but I suppose I can understand his position. He loves his daughter. He may have even thought she would become queen of Midnight one day, but then I came along and ruined all of his plans for her. I can't say I'm sorry about that because Damon deserves a hell of a lot better than Anya. She showed her true colors, proving to Damon she can't be trusted.

"Have you made an enemy for life?" I ask, turning to Damon as he watches Klaus walk away.

"Maybe," he admits, "but Anya has to go. I won't allow anyone who is a danger to you stay in the castle."

When his eyes meet mine, my heart misses a beat. Is it love I see in his expression? I'm not sure, but there is a softness in his gaze that gives me the courage to tell him how I feel.

"Damon, I think I'm falling in—"

"Damon!"

My declaration of love is rudely interrupted by Margaret, of all people.

I turn my head to see her waving to us from the entrance of the castle. Damon's hand cups my face and turns it back to him.

"What were you about to say?" he murmurs, choosing to ignore his mother and keep his focus on me. He searches my face for an answer, but his expression is guarded for some reason.

"Damon! I need to see you and Ivy," Margaret yells across the lawn.

"It can wait," I say. "We better go see what your mother wants before she loses her voice from yelling at us."

Reluctantly, Damon drops his hand away from my face and sighs in disappointment.

"Why do you think people keep interrupting us at the worst possible times?" he asks before taking my hand as we walk back up to the castle.

"I don't know, but it's becoming rather irritating."

Damon laughs. "Yes. So irritating I may just have to kidnap you again and take you somewhere no one can find us."

"Promises, promises," I tease, earning a pleased grin from Damon.

"Finally!" Margaret says in exasperation. "You have got to do something about that fae. I can see why the king of Dawn kept that man in the dungeon for so many years."

Damon sighs. "What's he done now? When I spoke to him earlier, he promised to keep his clothes on."

"Oh, he's fully clothed all right, but Nahla showed him where we keep the good wine and now he's drunk off his ass and swinging from one of the chandeliers in the ballroom."

"How—"

Margaret holds up her hand to stop Damon's question.

"Don't ask me how he got up there. I have absolutely no idea, but he's refusing to come down. Both Edmond and Boris are in there now trying to coax him off the blasted thing."

Damon lets go of my hand as he quickly strides in the direction of the ballroom. It's the same room where I was first introduced to the challengers for the contest.

Margaret and I follow in his stormy wake.

"Before I forget," she says as we walk together, "I had some clothing made for you while you were gone to replace what Anya ruined. They're hanging in your closet."

"Thank you. I appreciate that."

"I also took it upon myself to have an outfit made of leather for our trip to the Barrens. It's no place for a dress, and you'll need the added warmth the material will give you."

I smile at her thoughtfulness as we enter the ballroom and find a half-naked man singing something unintelligible as he sits on one of the chandeliers, swaying it back and forth like it's a child's swing.

"Vamir!" Damon shouts as he stands between Boris and Edmond. "Get down here this instant!"

"Not unless you have another bottle of this wine in your hands," Vamir says, chugging down what's left in his bottle before throwing the empty vessel against the far wall. It shatters, creating a mess on the floor and a red wine stain on the wall.

Vamir starts to sing again, but when his gaze falls on me, his body tenses and blood drains from his face as he becomes as white as a sheet. In one fluid motion, he leaps from the chandelier and somehow lands on his feet only three feet in front of me.

He's so intoxicated that he begins to sway from left to right, as if the world as he knows it is swaying too.

"You," Vamir slurs. "It's really you."

Vamir's eyes roll back in his head as he collapses to the floor like a limp noodle, leaving us all wondering how he could possibly know me.

CHAPTER 11

"I guess this shows us one thing about the fae," Edmond says as he and Boris pick Vamir up off the floor. "They can't hold their liquor worth a damn. One bottle and this bastard is swinging from a chandelier."

While Damon leads the men to the connected sitting room, I can feel a pair of inquisitive eyes peering straight into my soul, or at least that's what it feels like. I attempt to ignore Margaret's hard stare, but she refuses to let me go that easily.

"How do you know Vamir?" she asks.

I look her straight in the eyes. "I don't know him. He must have me confused with someone else."

"Hmm." Margaret doesn't sound convinced as she turns her head to watch the men wrangle Vamir through the doorway to the other room.

"He's been in the Dawn dungeon practically all my life," I remind her. "There's no way we could have ever met, because the first time I ever stepped foot inside the castle was the night I went there to steal the Queen's Circlet. The simplest explanation for his reaction is that he's drunk and mistook me for someone else he knows."

"I suppose," she concedes, literally shaking off her own question with a shrug. "No matter. We'll simply ask him to explain himself once he's sober."

Boris walks back into the ballroom. "Ivy, are you up for a little fae babysitting duty? I volunteered us since we both slept all day. Besides, the others will be changing soon."

"I don't think we have much of a choice." My lack of enthusiasm translates a little harsher than I intended, but it can't be helped. Truth be told, I was hoping to have a moment alone with Damon before he went through the change tonight, but maybe this is for the best.

"What's going on here?" Simon strolls into the ballroom like he's the king of Midnight instead of Damon. His arrogance seems to know no bounds.

"Your fae drunk himself into a stupor," I inform him.

"I don't claim that creature as mine," he says with mild disgust. "He's simply a leftover responsibility from my father's reign."

Margaret lifts a hand in the air to gain Simon's attention. "Do you know of any reason why he would think he knows Ivy?"

Inwardly, I cringe. I wish she had kept quiet about that.

Simon peers at me with confused intrigue. "No. He's never met her before, as far as I know."

"Considering how drunk he is, who knows what he was seeing? For all we know, he could have thought I was a pink elephant."

Simon grins. "Well, will wonders never cease. You actually do have a sense of humor. Where have you been hiding that all this time?"

"You haven't exactly given me any reason to share that side of myself with you. The first time we met in person you had just locked me in your tower to offer me the glamorous position of your royal concubine, remember? It wasn't exactly a fun filled night for me."

"Yet, nothing worse than anything Damon has done to you," he politely reminds me.

"Did I hear my name mentioned?" Damon walks in from the connecting room and gives Simon a cursory glance before he focuses his attention on me.

"Only in passing," Simon notes, visibly irritated by his rival's interruption. "I hear Vamir has been a bad boy. Where is he?"

"In the other room." Damon tosses his head back slightly to indicate the room he just came from. "Boris and Ivy will be looking after him this evening."

"I can help with that," Simon eagerly volunteers.

"We don't need your help," Boris curtly informs him. "He's one man. He can't be that hard to look after, especially in the state he's in."

"He's still my captive," Simon states, "and my responsibility. I'm afraid I have to insist upon it."

"That might not be a bad idea." Damon gives me a meaningful glance, but it's all I need to know what he's thinking.

If Simon is with us, he won't have time to go snooping around Damon's castle and sticking his nose into places where it doesn't belong.

"Sure." My smile feels forced only because it is. "The more the merrier."

From the grin on Simon's face, he seems to take my acceptance of his presence as a sign that my feelings are softening toward him. The complete opposite is true, but he doesn't need to know that. I'll let his arrogance rule his thoughts for now. If need be, I can always snap him back into place later.

"Come along, Damon." Margaret goes to her son. "We should prepare for the change."

Damon fixes me with his eyes. "I'll be back afterwards."

"Are you worried I'll sweep Ivy off her feet with my charm?" Simon jokes. "I promise to behave myself. Besides, Boris will be with us. Isn't he enough of a chaperon?"

"No," Damon says bluntly. "I trust you about as much as I trust a snake not to bite me."

"On that note," Margaret says, "why don't we leave and both come back to spend time with everyone. Just because we're wolves doesn't mean we can't communicate with each other."

Margaret tugs on Damon's arm. With a warning glance in Simon's direction, Damon follows her out of the ballroom. The rest of us make our way into the sitting room where Vamir is snoring so loud the sound reverberates off the walls.

"The two of you should turn him onto his side," I say to Boris and Simon. "Otherwise, his snoring is bound to give us all headaches by morning."

While the men tend to Vamir, I open the doors in the room that lead out onto the back veranda and gardens. With a deep breath, I detect the scent of jasmine in the air.

"Ivy," Simon calls out behind me, "do you know how to play poker?"

I turn to find Simon rummaging through a drawer in the side table by the couch. He pulls out a stack of playing cards.

"You do know who raised me right?" I ask.

Boris laughs heartily. "Ivy could play poker when she was four years old and beat the best of them at it. If you're planning to play her, you might want to make sure it isn't for anything you really want."

Simon looks around the room, searching for something. Out of curiosity, I watch him walk over to the fireplace mantle and grab a vase filled with colorful marbles.

"We can use these," he says, holding up the vase.

"You might as well deal me in too," Boris says. "It's been a while since I played."

We set up three chairs around the coffee table so we can all keep a watchful eye on Vamir. Considering how drunk he is, I doubt he'll be waking up anytime soon.

Simon shuffles the deck while I divide the marbles out between the three of us. In no time at all, we're playing our first hand of the game.

"I haven't seen Tripp since I returned," I say. "Where is he?"

Simon's brow furrows. "Since Oliver returned with you, Tripp hasn't left his side. He seems to prefer his company to mine."

"Shocker," I say under my breath. If I were Simon's son, I wouldn't want to spend time with him either. "Don't you feel even an ounce of shame that you're trying to replace his mother with me?"

"Not even the slightest." Simon rearranges some of the cards in his hand.

"It isn't her fault Tripp was born the way he is," Boris says gruffly. "I don't see why you're punishing Sophia for it."

"That isn't the only reason I divorced her." Simon shifts uncomfortably in his seat, but he doesn't clarify his statement.

"Then what was the other reason?" I'm not about to sit here and let something like that go unexplained.

"Does it matter?" His voice is strained, and I can tell I've hit a sore spot.

"I would like to know," I say. "Everyone thinks you kicked her out of your bed because she gave birth to Tripp. Are you telling us that isn't the real reason?"

"She cuckolded me," Simon blurts out in a rush of heated words. "Does it make you happy to know that her infidelity caused me so much pain that all I want to do is cut her out of my life?"

His question and outburst catch me off guard.

"No. It doesn't make me happy. I'm sorry she cheated on you, but why haven't I heard that story before now?"

Simon scoffs. "I sure as hell wasn't going to tell anyone my wife whored herself because she thought *I* was the reason why our son is cursed. It's not exactly something I want known, but if we marry, I don't want to go into our union with any secrets between us."

I have no intention of ever marrying Simon, but saying that aloud would just lead to an argument. Instead, I study my cards and let our discussion naturally fade as we continue to play our game.

A few minutes later, Damon and Margaret reenter the room in their wolf forms with a little surprise following behind them, Tripp. Simon's son runs in and launches himself onto his father's lap, adoringly looking up at him with his beautiful blue eyes. Eyes he inherited from Simon.

The look on Simon's face is comical. It's obvious he didn't expect his son to be joining him this evening. He looks surprised, dismayed, and a little uncomfortable all at the same time.

"Hello, Tripp." Simon awkwardly pets his son on the head. "I thought you would be asleep by now."

Tripp yaps at his father before curling himself up on Simon's lap and closing his eyes.

Simon's face relaxes as he gently runs his hand along Tripp's fur. From what I'm seeing, there is love between them, but it feels like Simon is holding himself back from fully giving his son his heart. Simon catches me watching him. He clears his throat and pulls his hand away from Tripp while returning his attention to his cards.

Damon pads over and sits down beside my chair, all the while keeping a wary eye on Simon. Margaret goes to Boris and lays next to his chair. I suddenly realize this is the first time I've seen anyone else from Midnight in wolf form. I'm not surprised that Margaret's coat is a mixture of black and gray fur. It seems befitting of her personality, beautiful yet wise.

After a few hands, things become more relaxed in the room. So relaxed that Boris feels comfortable enough to strike up a conversation about my grandmother with Simon.

"You knew Mabel quite well, didn't you, Simon?" Boris shuffles the deck of cards before dealing out another hand.

"I did." Simon nods. "She was the only one of my mother's servants who remembered that the queen had a child. Mabel always made sure we spent some part of the day together."

"Does that mean you knew my parents?" I ask, hoping Simon might be able to provide some answers about my past.

Hope fades from my heart when Simon shakes his head.

"To tell you the truth, I didn't even know she had a family. I was only ten when your grandmother died, and at the time, I was going through my own grief over losing my mother."

My heart stops. "Are you saying they both died around the same time?"

"That's what I was told," Simon says. "My mother had been sick for quite some time before she died. I was only allowed to see her a few minutes each day until her death. During her last few months, I wasn't allowed to see her at all."

"I never did hear what she died of," Boris says. "Do you know?"

"I don't have a clue." Simon shrugs. "All I know is that my father was madder than I had ever seen him before. I know he loved her, but after she became bedridden, he never visited her again. I'm not sure why, and I was too afraid of him to ask. I assumed if he wanted me to know he would have told me."

I breathe a small sigh of relief. For a moment there, I thought I might have inadvertently killed Simon's mother with my curse, but since she was sick for months beforehand, blame for her death doesn't fall on my shoulders. I guess it's just an odd coincidence that they both ended up dying around the same time.

Out of the corner of my eye, I notice Vamir's fingers twitch. When I look at his face, a single tear escapes the corner of his eye. Is he dreaming about something sad, or is he listening to our conversation? A few seconds later his snores fill the room again, leaving me with more questions about him than answers.

Around two o'clock in the morning, I start to yawn and can't seem to stop.

"You should go to bed," Boris encourages me. "Simon and I can look after Vamir. We have a big day tomorrow, and you need all your wits about you in the Barrens."

"I want to argue that I should stay, but I just don't have the strength," I admit with embarrassment. "Come and get me if he wakes up before I do."

"Would you like me to come up and tuck you into bed?" Simon asks with a straight face.

Damon growls in response from his spot by my chair as he stands to all fours.

"That won't be necessary. I have an escort."

Simon grins. "Just an offer."

Damon's growl becomes louder as he bares his teeth, glowering in Simon's direction.

I stand from my chair and rest my hand on top of Damon's neck. "Let's go."

As one, Damon and I leave the room and make our way up to my bedroom. I decide to make a small detour and fetch the Queen's Circlet from Boris's room. I'm desperate to find out if Emily recorded any more memories on the diamond. After losing Mark in such a horrific way, was she ever able to find peace living among her people? Especially her father. He could have saved Mark's life yet he chose not to. How do you forgive someone for killing the love of your life? And her poor son. Was he treated like an outcast by the fae because he was half human?

I hope Emily found happiness again, but I don't see how she could. Mark was her world. I felt her love for him as if I were standing in her shoes and experiencing it in my own heart. There's no way she ever fully recovered from his death. Happiness would have eluded her for the rest of her life.

When we enter my bedroom, I close and lock the door. The last thing I want is an ill-timed interruption while I delve back into Emily's memories.

Damon hops up on the bed and curls up on one side of it while I lie down on the opposite side.

"I'm going to see if Emily recorded anything else with the diamond," I tell him.

He growls softly in response and repositions himself to keep a watchful eye on me.

Even in the dim moonlight streaming through the windows of my room, I easily find Emily's diamond in the crown and touch it.

"The humans can't be trusted!" Emily's father says to a large gathering of fae.

He stands in the center of a small, crowded amphitheater. Most of the fae are cheering him on, obviously agreeing with his rhetoric while the others remain silent and thoughtful.

"We should finish them off now and spare this world from any more harm," he bellows.

Emily stands from her seat. "Have you forgotten the reason why the humans almost destroyed their world in the first place? We're the reason why. They felt threatened by us, and we gave them no reason not to. You mutated their DNA, Father. You turned them into animals just to make them fear you."

"They were animals long before we ever arrived," her father

argues, staring Emily down with no love in his gaze. "I simply helped them realize it by turning them into real ones."

Emily turns her gaze away from her father and looks at the other fae.

"Please, I beg you to find it in your hearts to let what remains of humanity live. I realize some of you may believe they're savages, but that couldn't be further from the truth. They are capable of so much more than you realize. Since I'm one of the few of you who was able to live among them, I can tell you that they are capable of great beauty and innovations we could only dream about making. Let what remains of them live alongside us. I promise you won't regret it."

Emily's father scoffs harshly. "I regret not taking them out before they poisoned this world. That's the only regret I have."

Several fae grumble in agreement with his statement.

"That can't be changed now," Emily reminds them all, "but we can show them compassion and help them acclimate to their new world. In a few hundred years, this planet will be livable again. It's only a blink of an eye to us, but for them, several generations will come and go. Surely, given all that time, the human race can prove their worth to you."

A woman slightly older than Emily stands on the other side of the small arena. She has long white hair and wears a green robe like dress.

"I agree with Emily," the woman says, daring those gathered to argue against her. "We are not barbarians who selfishly throw life away. I say we follow Emily's suggestion and let the humans prove they can change."

"And how exactly do you propose we do that?" Emily's father asks the woman.

"Divide what's left of humanity and see if Emily's prophecy comes true."

Emily's father laughs harshly. "They'll kill each other within a few years or at the very least devolve into their wolf forms and lose what makes them human forever."

"Perhaps." The woman nods. "You keep telling us we're the superior race, yet you're acting just like them if you don't agree to this."

His eyes narrow on the woman. "How so?"

"You keep telling us how greedy they are, but aren't we the ones who demanded they share their world with us? I don't think anyone here can argue that humanity would have gone on living their lives if we had never come here. We are as much to blame for their demise as they are, and if you can't see that, then you're a fool."

The gathered fae grumble and shift in their seats. It's obvious the woman has touched on a sore point for many of them.

"I suggest we give them time to become used to their new way of life," the white haired woman states.

Emily's father shakes his head. "That won't change who they are."

"I have an idea," Emily says. "If we take all of their memories away, maybe we can view them as they really are. Without a shared history, they'll be forced to make the best of what we give them."

A burly man dressed in white robes stands. "I say we let Emily and her mother perform their experiment. It's the least we can do."

Ahh. The white haired woman is Emily's mother. Interesting.

"It will take quite some time for Earth to become inhabitable again," Emily's mother points out. "By that time, we should have our answer about the humans. If they prove themselves unable to change, then we can end their existence easily. But, if they prove to be worthy of a second chance, we will have saved a race who can contribute to our lives as much as we can theirs."

Silence enters the amphitheater as Emily's father considers his wife's suggestion.

"Run your experiment then," he begrudgingly agrees. "But let it be known that I predict it will fail. Humans can't even live in harmony with themselves much less those who are the slightest bit different from them."

"We shall see." Emily's mother tilts her head in her husband's direction, but her eyes are fixed on her daughter.

The memory ends, and I'm brought back to my world.

As I place the circlet underneath my pillow and curl up onto my side, a chill of uncertainty for humanities fate makes me shiver.

Damon uses his teeth to pull the blanket on the end of the bed over me for warmth.

"Thank you." I reach out to pet the spot between his ears. The purple flames along his fur dance in response. "I'll tell you what I saw in the morning."

Damon grunts and lays his head on the pillow beside me. As we both drift off to sleep, all I can think about is the last scene I watched.

What will it take for humanity to prove its worth to the fae? Have we done enough or are we running out of time?

CHAPTER 12

I wake up to a room with only me as its occupant. Damon is nowhere to be seen, making me wonder if something happened while I slept, forcing him to leave my side.

From the dim morning light filtering in from the balcony's double doors, it's easy to tell that another twilight hour is upon us. Today we travel into the Barrens to find more of the magic elixir Margaret used to cure the wolf pups in Midnight and help them regain their ability to transform between their wolf and human forms. Finding it could be the key to my freedom by diminishing Simon's desire to make me his queen.

With this in mind, I hop out of bed and open my wardrobe to search for the outfit Margaret had made for me while I was away. Not only do I find the leather jacket and pants, I also discover five new dresses that are even prettier than the ones Anya destroyed.

Before I put the outfit on, I decide to take a quick bath since I haven't bathed in a few days.

After I'm clean and dressed, I walk out of my room to discover the one person I didn't expect to see: Anya.

She's pacing up and down the hallway with her hands clasped tightly together. The look on her face is one of more than worry. She looks deathly frightened.

When she sees me, a quick, judgmental glance takes in my outfit before she meets my gaze with her own.

"Good morning," she says with a small bow of her head.

I almost look behind me to see if Damon is standing there. Anya has never shown me any reverence and this new attitude is surprising.

"I realize I'm probably the last person you want to see, but I came here to ask you for a favor."

This should be good.

I step into the hallway and close my bedroom door behind me.

"What kind of favor?" I ask, crossing my arms in front of me as I wait for the answer.

"I . . . I," she stammers before clearing her throat nervously, "I came to ask you for your forgiveness."

"Forgiveness for what exactly?" Of course I know what she's referring to, but I want to hear her admit her crime.

Anya closes her eyes and takes in a deep breath as if she has to draw on all her strength to admit the truth to me.

"Out of my jealousy, I destroyed your dresses and left the remnants scattered across your bedroom. I can only beg for your forgiveness."

"And?"

Anya looks perplexed. "And what?"

"You seem to have forgotten about putting poison ivy in my dress."

Her cheeks turn red from either shame or embarrassment at being caught in yet another childish act.

"I'm sorry for that also," she whispers, dropping her gaze from mine in shame. Whether or not she truly feels apologetic for her act, I'm not sure, but at least she has enough sense to appear remorseful.

"I can forgive you for what you did, but I'll never forget it, Anya."

Hesitantly, she returns her gaze to me. "Does your forgiveness mean my family and I can stay at court?"

"That isn't my decision. I'm not queen yet. Damon is the only one who can decide your punishment."

"He's ordered us to leave this morning, but I was hoping you could talk to him and—"

I raise my hand to stop her next words. "I'm not going to ask Damon to change his mind, if that's what you're hoping. What you did should have consequences. If you ask me, you're getting off easy. I'll feel a lot safer without you here."

Anya's expression completely changes. Hate blazes in her eyes as they narrow on me. Her lips tense to the point of becoming white lines across her face.

There she is. The *real* Anya. I wonder how hard it was for her to come to me and beg for my help. From the look of hatred on her face, she must have traded in every ounce of pride she had to do it.

"You will never be my queen," she snarls. "You're nothing but a freak of nature who can't be trusted with the future of Midnight!"

I smile. "Do you honestly think I haven't had people call me worse? That's the difference between us. You've been protected by your parents and Damon all your life, but I've had to face the worst humanity has to offer. I've lived with my curse since the day I was born, and I've had to deal with bigoted people like you in every stage of it. Even though I have every right to turn my back on all of you, I won't. I care what happens to the people in Midnight and even Dawn, and I have no desire to see the next generation suffer ridicule just because they're different. You can curse me. You can tear up my clothing, but the one thing you will never do is shame me. I know who I am and *what* I am. Can you say the same and come out stronger?"

Anya purses her lips even tighter. I can physically feel her anger like a hot cloud that's filled the space between us as she huffs loudly and stomps down the hallway, retreating from me as fast as she can.

As I watch her walk away, a slow clapping of hands draws my attention to the entrance of Boris's room. My father stands there with a proud smile on his face. He stops clapping and walks over to me.

"Good for you, poppet. I couldn't be prouder of the woman you've become. There was a day not so long ago that you would have wanted to punch someone in the mouth for talking to you like that."

With a nervous laugh, I straighten out my leather jacket. "I guess we all have to grow up sometime, and I've learned words can sting even deeper than an upper cut to the jaw."

"Quite right," I hear Margaret say as she walks out of Boris's room twirling her long white hair into a bun at the nape of her neck. She's also wearing a leather outfit but instead of a short jacket like mine, hers is longer and flares out at her waist almost reaching her thighs.

I look between the two of them. A slight blush colors both of their cheeks. It doesn't take a genius to decipher the reason why Margaret just walked out of my father's room. Uncomfortable isn't strong enough of a word to describe how I feel. Mortified fits it perfectly though.

I can't even force myself to look Boris's way. Being faced so blatantly with the fact that he's still a sexual creature may have traumatized me for life.

As I often do when I feel out of my element, I decide to move on to another subject.

"Do either of you know where Damon is?"

"Of course, dear." Margaret waves her hand in the air in no particular direction. "He went to find Alek and his men."

My heart drops with dread. "What do you mean he went to go find him? I assumed he put Alek and his crew in a jail cell in town since this castle doesn't have a dungeon in it."

"Oh, he did," Margaret says. "But the town constable snoozed while the pirates escaped sometime during the night. I don't know why Damon felt the need to go chasing after them. I'm sure they're long gone by now. Alek's father probably has them on his ship and halfway across the ocean."

"I hope so." I don't even try to keep the worry out of my voice. There's no need for me to put up a front around these two.

"That pirate won't steal you from us a second time," Boris says, scratching at the bandage on his neck.

Margaret tugs on the sleeve of his white shirt. "Come along, you. The twilight hour is almost over. I'll need to redress your wound after you change so it doesn't get any dirt in it while we're traveling today. Although, I do wish you would reconsider going with us. A few more days of rest would do you more good than traipsing around the wilds of the Barrens."

"We've already had this argument, Maggie. I'll not have it with you again." Boris wraps his arm around her waist. "Now come on. Let's go change it before you get your panties in a wad."

Margaret snaps her fingers in the air as she remembers something. "That's what I forgot to put back on. My underwear!"

Boris turns even redder. I look down at the wood floor between my feet and study the wood knot I find there. Margaret simply laughs as Boris ushers her back into his room.

Once they're behind closed doors, I breathe a sigh of relief.

Talk about awkward.

"I'm telling you, we need to go after them." Simon's voice carries down the hallway as both he and Damon round the corner.

"And I'm telling you that's a waste of time." Damon scowls at his unwanted companion. "They're trail led straight into the Barrens. More than likely, Alek thinks he can find the cure before we can. Let's not make his assumption a reality."

When Damon turns his head away from Simon and looks down the hallway at me, his expression softens. His eyes travel the length of me in a second and an instant grin transforms his face from angry to pleased. The new warmth in my cheeks does nothing to hide how the sight of him affects me too. All he's wearing is a black velvet robe loosely closed at the waist by a sash. Someone must have given it to him when he returned to the castle. It makes sense. He would have been completely naked after his transformation back into his human form.

"I see the woman of the hour is finally awake," Simon says. Surprisingly, he isn't leering at me. Maybe he's simply too tired or maybe he finally realizes I'll never be attracted to him. Whatever the case, I'm thankful. The last thing I need is for him to think I'm even remotely interested in him. There's only one king in this hallway who has a claim to my heart and his name isn't Simon.

"So Alek is on the hunt for the cure?" I ask as the pair come to a stop in front of me.

Damon sighs. "Looks that way. We need to get a move on as soon as the Dawn pack change."

"Did Nahla go with Alek and the others?" For some reason, I desperately hope she didn't betray us. I kind of like her.

"No," Damon assures me. "She's preparing to travel with us."

"Do you think she helped Alek and the others escape?"

"It's a possibility I considered, but it's not a question I asked her. I assume she helped in some way. It could be that she's going with us to maximize their chances of finding the cure for their people, but I'm not going to ask her point blank. We'll see how loyal she is to Boris, and who's side she's really on."

Damon takes my hand, leading me to my bedroom.

"If you'll excuse us, Simon," Damon says, not even bothering to look the other king's way. "I need a few minutes alone with my future queen."

When I glance over my shoulder, Simon's lips are pressed so tightly together they practically disappear. He may not be pleased by Damon's actions, but I'm certainly curious to know what the king of Midnight has instore for our stolen moments behind closed doors.

As soon as we walk into the bedroom, Damon shuts and locks the door before pulling me over to the bed. My body aches to reach out and bring him into my arms, but I don't get the chance to follow through with my desires. Instead, Damon sits me on the edge of the bed but remains standing in front of me.

"Tell me what the diamond showed you last night." His eyes narrow on me, taking on a seriousness that is all Damon. "We don't have much time, so just give me the gist of what it showed you."

I comply with his request and tell him quickly what I saw in Emily's memory.

"How exactly are we supposed to prove ourselves to them?" he asks once I get to the end of my retelling.

"I have no idea." For some reason I feel like I'm failing him by not having the answers he needs, but there is a solution. "I can try again. Maybe there are other memories stored on the diamond that will tell me more."

Damon nods. "Do it. We need to be armed with as much information as possible before we meet any more fae out in the Barrens. The last thing we can do is fail whatever test they might have in store for us there."

I reach across the bed and pull the circlet out from underneath my pillow. With it in my hands, I rollover onto my back and take a deep breath before touching the pink hued diamond.

All I end up seeing is the very first memory I viewed of Emily and Mark when he gifted her with the memory device. Squeezing the diamond tighter doesn't help matters. It only makes my hand sore against the sharp point and doesn't change what I'm seeing. Once the memory ends, I sigh in disappointment and sit up, still holding the circlet in my hands.

"The first memory I saw played again. The memory I saw last night must have been the last one. I'm sorry."

Even though it's not my fault that I'm unable to view more memories, I feel like a failure and hang my head.

Damon drops to one knee before me and tilts my head back up with a gentle hand.

"That isn't your fault."

When I look into his eyes, I feel a sense of relief. His gaze is gentle and understanding.

"You did the best you could. Besides, there might be another way to get the information we need."

It only takes me a second to realize what he's talking about.

"Vamir," I say.

Damon nods. "He has to know about this test. In fact, I'm wondering if he and the fae who attacked you were sent here to watch us. Maybe their mission was to judge whether or not we deserve to go on living."

"I hope he hasn't judged us all by the way Simon and his father treated him."

Damon stands. "Me and you both."

With a tug on my hand, Damon helps me to my feet.

"I passed Anya on my way here. Did she come to speak with you or my mother?"

"Me. She wanted me to ask you not to make her and her family leave court."

Damon lets out a harsh laugh. "Indeed. Well, how did that go?"

"About as well as you might expect."

He laughs again but this time there's true humor in the sound.

"From the look of hatred on her face when she passed me, I can only assume you were firm in your no to her."

"Yes. I was rather blunt about it too."

Damon brings me into his arms. "Were you now? I would have liked to have been a fly on the wall and overheard that conversation. Your feistiness is one of the things I admire the most about you."

"Really?" I tilt my head as I look at him. "I seem to remember you getting rather irritated with me whenever I argued with you."

He pulls me even closer against him. So close in fact, I can feel a particular part of him stir underneath his robe. An invitation to explore? Or simply a natural reaction to the mutual attraction we feel for one another.

"That doesn't mean I don't find you irresistibly sexy when you argue with me," he murmurs.

His eyes immediately notice my quickly warming cheeks. He smiles.

"I like it when I can make you blush too."

I bury my forehead against his shoulder so he can't see my cheeks grow even warmer. His chuckle at my embarrassment manifests as a slow, deep rumble inside his chest. The sound makes me happy for some reason, and I wrap my arms all the way around his waist. He reciprocates and we silently stand there simply holding one another.

"While we're in the Barrens, please be careful," he says. "If I lose you, the world might as well end because my life would never be the same again."

I pull back to look him in the eyes. No words come to mind. Only action.

I grab the front of his robe with both hands and yank him as close as two people can get. I capture his lips with mine as if I never intend to let him go. I want him. I want all of him, inside and out. My heart races within the walls of my chest so hard I can feel each beat like the strike of a drum. My blood rushes with a need to make our union official, final.

When I tear his robe open, he does the one thing I didn't count on.

He pulls away. Two steps backward and the spell between us is broken.

Damon stands unashamedly with his robe open. My gaze drops to the evidence of his arousal making me question why he pulled back.

"You want me," I say, breathless from our all too short kiss. "Why did you pull away?"

"When I have you, there won't be any question about whose baby you carry," he says in a strained voice. "I will never put our child through the torture of having people call him or her a bastard behind their back. I care enough about you to pull away because I never want you to have to suffer other people's ridicule either. My mother may never admit it, not even to herself, but having people doubt her honor did its damage. I swear to you that our life together will be better than what my parents went through. If you believe nothing else, believe that."

He pulls his robe together and reties the sash around his waist. Without saying another word, Damon walks out of my room, leaving me yearning for a physical release I obviously won't be able to get for a very long time.

CHAPTER 13

F rustrated. Yeah. That's what I feel. Frustrated and in need of a cold bath.

With a growl, I pick up the closest thing to me and hurl it against the door of my room. The second the circlet passes over the tips of my fingers, I gasp in horror at my foolishness, but it's too late. Helplessly, I watch it slam against the back of the door so hard it makes a loud thud. One of the diamonds flies out of the setting as the rest falls to the floor.

I scramble over to the circlet and drop to my knees to pick it up and discover the pink diamond is the gem that fell out. Frantically, I search for it, all the while cursing myself for being so stupid and careless. A few minutes later, I breathe a sigh of relief when I find the diamond propped up against the leg of a chair in the nearest corner. With quick strides, I go to my wardrobe and find a small white handkerchief to pick the diamond up with, not wanting it to automatically show me one of Emily's memories.

Three knocks resound on the other side of the door.

"Ivy?" Boris says. "Can I come in?"

I get to my feet and tuck the now wrapped diamond in the front pocket of my pants before opening my bedroom door.

"Is everything all right?" he asks worriedly, glancing into my room. "I thought I heard a commotion."

"All you heard was me losing my temper," I confess. "Sometimes it seems like Damon is bound and determined to test the limits of my patience. Anyway, shouldn't you be getting ready for the change instead of worrying about me?"

"I still have a few minutes of humanity left." Boris cocks his head at me looking ready to defend my honor. "How exactly is the boy testing a virtue we both know you lack? Do I need to have a talk with him? I will, you know. I don't like seeing you so upset, and he seems to always be upsetting you."

"Look, I can handle my own problems, thank you very much. He's simply being bull- headed, that's all."

Boris chuckles and a twinkle of amusement enters his eyes. "Doesn't he realize by now that you can be just as stubborn as him? I would bet all my earthly possessions that you'll wear him down and make him give in to whatever it is you want from him."

"From your lips to his ears," I sigh. "I'm not so sure he will though. He seems set in his ways. I may have to bide my time and learn how to be patient for his sake."

Boris looks surprised. "Well, this is a miracle I'll have to witness for myself."

Boris laughs off the scathing look of irritation I shoot his way.

I decide to change the subject.

"While you're still human, I should tell you about the last memory that was stored in the diamond."

As quickly as possible, I tell Boris everything I learned from Emily's last memory. After hearing it, he looks troubled but not hopeless.

"You need to speak with Vamir and question him about what you saw," he says. "He's the only one we know who can tell us more."

"But what if he was sent here to judge us? What if I make matters worse by telling him what we know about his people?"

"I don't see how we could make matters worse. They seem rather dire as is. Don't you agree?"

I nod. "I suppose there's no harm in asking him.

"Good. Now, I need to go. I can feel the change about to happen." Boris leans in and kisses me on the forehead. "Keep your eyes and ears open while we travel through the Barrens today. There's no telling what might be out there waiting for us."

"I will." Even as I make my promise, I silently hope I'll be able to keep my word.

Lately, my mind has begun to wander, especially when Damon is around. The man is starting to consume my thoughts more and more and my heart yearns for him to say what I mean to him. After our time together, surely he views me as more than simply a way to save his people, but I want to hear him say it. He doesn't have to tell me he loves me. Even though I can't honestly say I wouldn't like to hear those words. I would also take any verbal note of affection he might like to cast my way.

"Maggie is downstairs watching Vamir until we're all ready to leave," Boris says. "Why don't you take this time to get to know him better?"

"Should I ask him about the fae testing us or wait until he gets to know me a little better?"

Boris spreads his hands palm up in the universal sign of uncertainty. "Honestly, I think you need to play it by ear. I don't know him very well either, but he seems like a reasonable fellow when he's sober. I suggest seeing what kind of connection you can make with him first. Then, maybe he'll open up to you on his own. If you remind him enough of this person he mistook you for last night, it might give you an advantage. He may tell you things he wouldn't feel comfortable telling the rest of us."

"Should I remind him about what he said last night?"

Boris shrugs. "Again, I would wait to see how he reacts to you. He might bring it up himself. You never know."

"Okay. I'll see how his mood is when I go downstairs and take it from there. Who knows? He might spill his guts out to me without me even having to say a single word."

Boris laughs. "Ever the optimist."

His sarcasm isn't lost on me. An optimist is something I've never been. I always approach situations with a healthy dose of skepticism. It's not something I can stop myself from doing. It's simply my nature.

As I approach the grand staircase at the front of the castle, I hear a lot of yelling. Most of it is high pitched and coming from a familiar voice.

Anya is berating a poor servant for dropping one of her bags and spilling clothing all over the entryway. I feel sorry for the servant, but I also feel a modicum of relief that her attention has been diverted for the moment, allowing me to slip past undetected as I enter the sitting room where Margaret and Vamir are having breakfast.

"These are simply delectable," Vamir tells Margaret before stuffing half of a flaky croissant in his mouth.

Margaret lifts a dainty teacup from its saucer on the table, slowly bringing it to her lips.

"They are rather buttery," she says. "My late husband could eat a plate full of those things in one sitting."

Vamir nods his bald head. "I can well imagine that. But alas, I am not such a glutton. I suppose living in that dungeon and subsisting on the gruel they fed me for all these years shrunk my stomach to the size of a pea."

Margaret laughs. "Well, eat up! Perhaps we can enlarge your appetite by filling your stomach with croissants."

I close the door behind me a little harder than I need to. It has the desired effect of drawing their attention to my presence. In the room stands four of Damon's guards, keeping a wary eye on our guest.

"Ivy!" Margaret smiles with true joy. It's not a look I'm accustomed to receiving from her, but I suppose she has every right to feel happy. After all, I did catch her walking out of Boris's room still putting her clothes on. "Come join us, my dear. We were simply enjoying a small breakfast while everyone else gets ready for our trip into the Barrens."

As I walk over to the table, I can't help but notice how openly Vamir is staring at me. I can't tell anything from his expression, but I've certainly captured his attention. When I meet his gaze, it's unwavering, but for some reason, his stare doesn't bother me. Normally, someone staring at me would make me self-conscious, yet the easy way he holds himself and the soft twinkle in his eyes shows affection, not disdain.

"Good morning." Vamir stands from his seat at the table. "I've been told you and I got off on the wrong foot last night during my drunken antics in the ballroom. Please accept my humblest apologies, Ms. Ivy. I meant you no disrespect. I hope you can forgive an old fool for his momentary lapse of judgment."

"There's nothing to forgive." I stop just short of the table while one of Damon's men brings me a chair. As I sit down, so does Vamir. "As you said, you were drunk. I assume you mistook me for someone you know."

Vamir clears his throat, appearing either nervous or embarrassed by his behavior the night before. I don't know him, so I can't quite tell which emotion he's feeling. Either way, it's nice to know he realizes what an ass he made of himself in front of me and everyone else who was present. At least he has the decency to act ashamed.

"You do resemble someone from my past," he admits. "In the state I was in last night, I must have assumed you were her."

I pick up a blueberry muffin from a basket of baked goods. "Who do I look like?"

Vamir smiles. "My mother. You resemble her in many ways. I haven't seen her in years, but I hope to be reunited with her one day soon."

"Does she live in the Barrens?" I ask. "Isn't that where the fae live now?"

Vamir cuts his eyes away from me. It instantly makes me suspicious.

"I don't believe so," he says, stuffing the other half of the croissant in his mouth. I suspect he did that to keep me from asking him more questions. He obviously doesn't know me very well.

"Then where is she?" I watch him eat what's in his mouth, letting him know I expect an answer.

After he swallows and takes a sip from his teacup, he clears his throat and looks my way.

"Some fae are in the Barrens and some are not in this world. Knowing my mother, I assume she's . . . *off* world at the moment."

"I see." Slowly, I peel off the paper wrapper on my muffin as I consider his words.

Why did he hesitate before saying where his mother is? And why place an emphasis on the word off?

"Is she circling around us in one of the fae spaceships?" I take a bite of my muffin and watch his reaction.

I don't have to wait long for one. His eyes immediately grow larger in surprise.

"How do you know about those?"

"I've seen them." Both Margaret and Vamir give me their full attention.

"Did you see it in the diamond you told me about when we first met, dear? The one in the Queen's Circlet?" Margaret asks.

"Yes." I take another bite of my muffin and turn my attention to Vamir in anticipation of a question from him.

"What diamond?" Vamir asks out of general curiosity.

I pull the pink diamond out of my pants pocket and hold it up for him to see.

"This one. Have you ever seen it before?" I ask.

Vamir shakes his head. "I'm afraid not. Should I have?"

I sigh in disappointment. A part of me was hoping he had some knowledge about the diamond and could tell me more about Emily.

"How long do the fae normally live?" I ask, wondering if Emily could still be alive.

"Oh, that's hard to say." Vamir sits back in his seat. "Some have lived for thousands of years. I would say the average life span for my people is three thousand years. It's one of the reasons we had to leave our home world. It was becoming overcrowded, and the resources on our planet were running out. We hoped to make Earth our new home and live with your kind in peace, but that isn't what happened. Humanity saw us as a threat and decided they would rather destroy their own home than share it with us."

Good. He's opened up a dialogue about what happened in the

past without much prodding by me. Maybe I can get him to tell me more about the test I learned about in Emily's last memory.

Since learning Emily's true heritage and her championship for humanity, it seems logical that she is the one who placed the diamond in the circlet. She may even be the person who made the prophecy that a queen of Dawn would one day be able to see the past with aid from the crown. What I don't know is why I'm the one who brought her prophecy to life.

I lean forward in my chair toward Vamir, maintaining eye contact with him. "Why can I see the memories stored in it? Do you know?"

Without missing a beat, he answers my questions.

"I don't have a clue. You would have to ask the owner of the diamond that question."

I slip the precious gem back into my pocket and continue to eat my muffin. Dead silence enters the room as I seem to have reached an impasse with Vamir. Although, he may be able to answer one more question for me. Let's see how far he's willing to go to help us.

"I learned that the fae are putting humanity on trial. They're testing us to see if we're worthy enough to live. Do you know anything about that?"

"Are you serious?" Margaret asks aghast. She looks from me to Vamir. "Are the fae watching us? Is that why the one who attacked Ivy was invisible?"

Vamir nods slowly. "He was a scout. One is assigned to each city to watch and report back what he or she learns from watching all of you. I was a scout once." Vamir raises a hand to rub the side of his bald head. "That's why I have no hair. It's permanently removed so the suit can make direct contact with our skin. Our body heat keeps the suit's power supply charged to maintain our invisibility."

Vamir didn't even try to hide the fact that the fae are watching us so closely. I'm not sure if that's good or bad. It seems like a good thing, but appearances can be deceiving.

"But you've been in a dungeon for the last twenty or so years," I remind him. "If you were the scout sent to watch Dawn, there's no way you could have reported back to your superiors after you were caught."

"Once I missed my check-in time, they would have sent out another scout to take my place," he explains. "There has been one watching your city since then. In fact, I would wager there have been several. Most scouts don't do it for more than a year at a time. We have family and friends who we love and want to spend time with too."

"How *did* you get caught?" Margaret questions. "You seem like a smart man, when you're sober at least. What mistake did you make that led to your arrest?"

"I fell in love with a human." His words sound like a confession but not one he's ashamed of making. "She was the love of my life." He looks between me and Margaret. "And there is nothing I would change about our time together. We both felt like our love was always meant to be."

"Who was she?" I ask.

"Someone long gone," he says sadly. "I'm sure you would have loved her if you had been given the chance to meet her. She had a way of putting people at ease and making them feel like they were important. At least, that's the way she always made me feel."

"Did she ever visit you after you were locked up in the dungeon?" Margaret asks.

Vamir shakes his head. "She wasn't allowed to come anywhere near me. It was just as well. I didn't want her to see me living that way. She was far too beautiful and lively to squander herself on someone who was doomed to live behind bars for the rest of his life."

"If she loved you as much as you seem to think," I say, "she should have found a way to get you out of that dungeon. I would never let someone I loved stay locked up like an animal for over twenty years."

"Not everyone is as strong as you," he says wanly. "And those who are weaker, shouldn't be judged for what they do or don't do."

I feel somewhat ashamed for what I said, but not so much so that I would apologize for it. All I said was the truth about myself. I wouldn't let someone I loved waste away in a tiny prison cell for twenty minutes much less twenty years. Whoever his lover was, she obviously didn't care about him as much as he thinks she did, but I won't say that to Vamir. I'm not that cruel.

"Is there any breakfast left?" Damon strides into the room fully clothed for our trip into the Barrens.

It appears Margaret had a black leather pair of pants and matching jacket made for him too. Unfortunately, it doesn't fit his body as tightly as my own, but it does accentuate enough of his assets to make him look devilishly handsome. As he strolls confidently over to the other side of the table, I find it impossible to take my eyes off him. He notices my attentive stare and smiles. He's in a rare, good mood, and I'm happy to see it.

"I've been meaning to ask." Vamir narrows his eyes at Damon. "How did you get that nasty scar on your face?"

Damon's smile slips and I silently curse Vamir for asking such an impertinent question.

"My father gave it to me," Damon answers, as one of his men brings him a chair to sit in at the table. "He clawed me right before I tore out his throat and ended his life."

It's the first time I've heard Damon describe the battle in such gory detail. The mental image of him ripping his father's throat out isn't a pleasant one, but it does make it easier to understand how such an act would mark a person's soul for life.

"You don't sound the least bit remorseful for such a barbaric act against your own flesh and blood." Vamir sits back in his seat, keeping a rather judgmental eye on Damon. "Why is that?"

"How dare you sit there and act all high and mighty while questioning my son," Margaret says in a raised voice. Her back has become as stiff as a viper about to strike its prey. "Damon killed his father to save me from an abusive man and our people from a king who only thought of himself. Don't throw stones at people when you are clueless about the turmoil in their own lives."

Vamir drops his gaze to the tabletop after being properly taken down a notch. "I humbly apologize if my questions came off sounding like accusations. That wasn't my intent. I was simply wondering why a son would have cause to kill his own father. In all of fae history, we've never had a similar incident mar our story."

"Then count yourselves lucky." Damon's terseness makes it evident that he hasn't forgiven the guest at his table for his insolence. When he turns his gaze to me, I see an unasked question in his eyes.

"Vamir has been frank about what I saw in Emily's memory. He was sent here to judge us as was the fae who tried to kill me."

"If you don't mind me saying so," Damon says to Vamir, "it seems like we should be the ones judging *you*, not the other way around."

"I apologize for my fae brother's lack of judgment." Vamir bows his head in my direction. "The fae who are sent here to watch you usually aren't part of the anti-human faction."

He has to be referring to Emily's father and those who think like him. I wonder if he knows Emily. Could they be friends? It's possible since the fae live so long, but I don't feel like asking him yet. I would like to get to know Vamir better before divulging everything I saw in Emily's memories. Even though I don't know her, I feel a strange sense of loyalty to her and everything she went through before and after Mark's death.

Edmond and Oliver enter the room. Walking side by side, it's easy to tell they're father and son. Their gates are similar as are the pleasant grins on their faces.

"Food!" Oliver jogs up to my side of the table and grabs a croissant from the basket of pastries. "I swear I could eat a horse I'm so hungry."

"Speaking of horses," Damon peers at his best friend, "are ours prepared for the trip?"

"Saddled and ready to go." Edmond lightly slaps Oliver on the back of his head. "I thought I taught you better manners, boy, especially when ladies are present."

"Sorry," Oliver says with his mouth full as he looks at me and then Margaret. "My stomach won over my manners."

"That's quite all right." Margaret stands from the table. "I need to grab a few things from my cottage before we enter the Barrens, so I'll be heading out now."

"I'll send some guards to accompany you," Damon says.

"That won't be necessary." Margaret waves her hand in the air as if the action will wipe away Damon's worry over her welfare. "Boris will be escorting me. I'm sure if I get into any trouble, he can help me handle it."

Margaret leans down and kisses Damon on the cheek. "I'll see you soon."

Since there's now an empty seat at the table, Oliver sits down and begins eating in earnest.

"Are you fattening yourself up for the journey?" I ask, feeling slightly amused by his ravenous appetite.

"We're bringing food with us," he says with a shrug, "but you never know what'll happen in the Barrens. Or so I hear. I've never personally been there, but there's a reason no one goes into that wasteland. Not unless they have a death wish."

"Do the fae have a city in the Barrens?" Damon asks Vamir.

"Of a sorts," he says. "It's always on the move though, so we'll need to start looking where your mother found the fae who was carrying his magic elixir."

"On the move?" I find it strange that he put it in those terms. "How is a city constantly on the move?"

"I said it was a city of sorts." Vamir grins at me. "It's actually a ship that comes and goes whenever those like me finish their tour of duty here."

"So the man my mother saw was he like you? Someone sent here to judge us?" Damon leans forward, fully intrigued by this new bit of information.

Vamir shrugs. "I have no idea. Do you happen to know what the man looked like?"

"I don't think he was someone sent to watch us," I say. "He wasn't bald like you. Margaret said he had the pretties long blond hair that she had ever seen."

Vamir looks confused. "Interesting. I have no idea who it was then. Several fae have long blond hair. It could have been anyone."

"I'm confused," Damon says. "What does hair got to do with anything?"

I quickly explain what Vamir told us about having to permanently lose his hair to maintain contact with his suit to stay invisible.

"Seems a bit drastic," Damon quips, touching the ends of his own shoulder length hair. "Why would you willingly do that to yourself?"

"In order to give you and the rest of the people here a fighting chance to survive," Vamir answers. "My people are split down the middle on whether humanity should be allowed to live with us. I wanted to give you all the best opportunity possible to pass our test."

"What test?" Edmond asks, looking completely confused about what we're talking about.

"I'll explain it to you and Oliver later." Damon grabs a biscuit stuffed with sausage and egg and takes a healthy bite.

I decide I should probably eat to. As Oliver pointed out, who knows what will happen in the Barrens? For all we know, this may end up being our last meal, and I, for one, don't want to die with an empty stomach.

A few minutes later, we all go out to the front of the castle where the horses are waiting for us. I look for a carriage for me to ride in but don't see one.

"Am I walking to the Barrens?" I ask Damon as I follow him to his mount.

He laughs. "No. You'll be riding with me. I assumed you have never ridden a horse before considering your curse. Am I wrong?"

"No. You aren't wrong."

"We outfitted one of my horses with a leather blanket. Between me, the saddle, and the blanket, the horse should be shielded from your poison. You don't mind riding with me, do you?"

I can't stop myself from smiling. "Nope. Not at all."

Damon returns my smile with a genuine one of his own. He looks at me with the gaze of a man who cares deeply about the person he's with, and it does strange but wonderful things to my insides. I feel like I could float all the way to the Barrens on joy alone.

"Good," he says before stopping in front of one of the largest black horses I've ever seen. It's at least a hand or two taller than the other horses and looks built for war. Damon turns to me and takes both of my hands with his. "Since we'll be riding together, I get to hold you during the whole trip," he murmurs. "Sounds like a win-win situation, if you ask me."

My own smile falters. "But what happens after the change tonight? Will I have to ride with Simon?"

"Uh, no." Damon drops my hands and grabs the reins of his horse before hoisting himself into the saddle. "You'll ride with Boris if we're forced to move during the night. There's no way in hell I would let Simon get anywhere near you. I don't trust him. For all I know, he would try to kidnap you just like Alek did."

Damon holds out his hand for me to take. With a little coaching on what to do, I find my way up into the saddle with Damon supporting my back and holding me between his arms.

I peer at him over my shoulder. "And if I was Simon's, would you steal me away from him?"

"In a heartbeat," he says without hesitation. "But you're not his. You're mine, and you will never be anyone else's."

With those words, Damon commands his men to head out, leaving me wondering how far Damon would go to ensure my safety.

I like the thought of him feeling so possessive of me because that's exactly how I feel about him. If anyone ever tries to separate us again, I don't have one doubt that we would both fight to the death to stop them.

CHAPTER 14

When we reach Margaret's cottage, she's sitting with Boris on the front porch, stroking the fur on his back.

"Well, it took you long enough," she says, standing from her seat on the steps. "I thought the lot of you might have forgotten where I live."

"Are you that anxious to return to the Barrens?" Damon asks.

"Not in the slightest." Margaret grabs a medium black bag from behind her before she and Boris walk up the stone path to meet us. Her own horse is tied to the white picket fence in front of her house.

After Margaret is comfortably in her saddle, Boris joins Simon's pack, and we set off to the Barrens where literally anything is likely to happen. I have very few expectations but several reservations about this trip. For all I know, Vamir could be plotting his revenge. What if he's leading us into a trap? I wouldn't blame him. After being held captive for so many years in the Dawn dungeon, he has every right to seek vengeance against us, especially Simon. Yet, I haven't seen anything to indicate that he wishes to do us any harm. In fact, he truly seems to want to help us, but he has no reason to. None that I can see, at least.

Within an hour of leaving Margaret's quaint cottage, the forest begins to change, and I sense we're getting closer to the Barrens. The change is subtle at first with the disappearance of birds chirping happily in the trees and squirrels rushing around in the brush to forage for nuts.

"Do you hear that?" I ask Damon.

"Hear what?"

"Exactly." I glance at him over my shoulder. "Where are the birds? I haven't even seen a squirrel or a rabbit since we entered this part of the woods."

Something straight ahead of us grabs Damon's attention.

"I would wager that," he says with a nod of his head, "has something to do with the disappearance of wildlife around here."

I turn back around and see what can only be described as total desolation.

As we reach the edge of the forest, the ground loses its grass, and the trees completely disappear. Now I know how the Barrens got its name. For what looks like miles, there is nothing except the remnants of charred earth.

"I always heard this is what the Barrens looked like," Nahla says, staring in horror at the devastation around us, "but I never could have imagined something so void of life. Give me the sea any day of the week."

"Did our ancestor's do this to the land?" I ask Vamir, as the ashen remnants of humanities history begins to fill my lungs.

"The bombs did indeed make a wasteland of much of the earth," he confirms, guiding his horse away from a gaping hole in the ground that leads to total darkness. "It saddened all the fae to see such a vibrant planet turn into a no man's land."

"Bombs?" Nahla asks. "What bombs?"

As we make our way across scorched earth, I tell the others all about Emily and Mark, and what I've seen in the memories stored in the diamond. Everyone seems captivated by the story, and I wish I could tell them more, but for some reason, Emily chose not to record her life after the gathering of the fae where they set an unknown challenge to determine humanity's survival.

For the rest of the day, we trek through the Barrens. The horses kick up so much of the ground with their hooves, that we leave behind a cloud of ash in our wake. By the time the twilight hour nears, we can see the peaks of distant mountains.

"Are those mountains where you saw your fae?" Damon asks his mother.

Margaret nods. "That's where he was all right. We would have to keep traveling through the night in order to reach the spot though."

Damon looks behind us to address Vamir.

"Do you sense your people nearby?" he asks. "Is this where their ship should be?"

Vamir shifts nervously in his saddle as he looks at Damon. "If your mother saw one of my brothers in those mountains, then yes, they should be close by, as long as they haven't moved on during the interim."

Simon emits a deep low growl as he stares up at Vamir. His flaming orange coat does nothing but make him look more menacing. Even in his wolf form, he has a way with intimidation.

Yet, does he sense something about Vamir that we don't? Simon hasn't kept it hidden that he has misgivings about the fae in our midst. I can't say I blame him. For all we know, Vamir could be leading us into a trap. After being Dawn's prisoner for over twenty years, who would blame Vamir for wanting revenge on the humans who kept him there?

"We should make camp for the night," Damon suggests. "Do you remember a place with water around here, Mother? The horses could use some."

"Yes. Follow me." Margaret softly kicks her horse in the sides to guide it forward.

Thirty minutes later, we enter the first signs of vegetation we've seen since entering the Barrens. The trees here are noticeably stunted in their growth, but some of them reach as high as seven feet tall. We're on the edge of the mountain range, but I still don't see the water source Margaret is leading us to.

"Are you sure this is the way?" Damon questions, not sounding so sure his mother's memory can be relied upon.

"I may be old, Damon," Margaret says crossly, "but I'm not senile.

There is a cavern just ahead with a natural spring. We'll need to boil the water we drink, but it should be fine enough for the horses. When I was in wolf form, I didn't feel any adverse effects from drinking straight from the pool."

It takes us fifteen minutes more to reach the cavern. It's entrance is slightly over grown with vines. Margaret turns in her saddle and gives Damon a satisfied smirk as we approach it.

"I'll never hear the end of this one," Damon whispers into my ear, sending shivers of pleasure along my skin with the warmth of his breath.

"I agree."

Damon chuckles and holds me tighter against him. "If the pool is deep enough, would you like to take a dip in the water with me?"

"I think I've done enough swimming to last me a lifetime." The memory of almost drowning in the ocean makes my stomach churn. "Besides, I don't have anything to wear in the water."

"Exactly." He leans in and whispers in my ear again. "It's been far too long since you've blessed my eyes with the loveliness of your body."

"Does that line work with most women?" I turn my head to look at him over my shoulder and am rewarded with a roguish, playful grin.

"You're the only woman I've ever said it to." His smile fades and our gazes lock. The warmth that enters Damon's eyes has the power to make my blood flow faster, hotter. My breathing becomes shallow as he leans in closer. Breathlessly, I wait to hear his next words. "I will never want anyone but you in my bed, in my arms and in my life. Destiny brought us together, and I won't let anyone tear us apart."

"Do you mean that?" With a gentle hand I reach up and cradle the side of his face with the scar. He turns his head and kisses the palm of my hand, answering my question. "Damon—"

"Oy! Love birds! Get off your high horse already. Some of us would like to get some fresh water."

With a growl of frustration, Damon spins in his saddle to pin Nahla with an icy glare.

"I swear, woman," he snarls, "do you have some sort of sixth sense? Every time Ivy and I start to have a serious conversation, you always manage to interrupt us."

Nahla throws her head back and laughs before dismounting her horse and gathering its reins.

"Look here, lover boy," she says, "Ivy isn't yours just yet. Alek is still roaming around here somewhere, and Simon," Nahla nods her head to the king of Dawn as he watches our conversation with immense curiosity, "well, let's just say I've heard about that death match the two of you are supposed to have. Winner gets to marry Ivy, right? That's a fight I'm excited to see, and I bet I'm not the only one."

With the reminder of the fight that's supposed to take place when we return to Midnight, reality splashes me in the face like a bucket of cold water.

I face forward again, as does Damon, neither of us commenting on Nahla's assumption.

She's right though. I'm sure a lot of people want to see Damon and Simon fight to the death when we return to Midnight. It's a winner takes all event. Two kingdoms separated for years by day and night will be ruled by the victor and me. No matter who wins, we all lose something of ourselves.

If Damon kills Simon, he'll never be the same again, and I'll have to find a way to help him put his soul back together after murdering yet another man who wants to rule his people. If Simon wins, I'll lose the only man I'll ever love and become a prisoner inside a gilded cage. My only hope for a life worth living is to locate more of the fae's magic elixir. If we can take some of it back home with us, maybe, just *maybe*, I can have the life I've always wanted. The real challenge will be to convince the fae to give it to us. I just hope the faction that wants to see humanity survive is more caring and in control of the elixir.

Damon helps me dismount from his formidable steed, and we all follow Margaret into the cave to find the pool of water she remembers so well.

As soon as we reach the entrance, I hear the splash of water falling and see the rather large pool she spoke of on the way here. For some reason, I imagined it would be smaller, not the size of a small pond.

"Well, that's interesting," Margaret says as she stares at the pool. "I don't remember it being this big the last time I was here."

"Really?" Damon peers around the dark space. The only light comes from the entrance of the cave. "How large was it last time?"

"No larger than a bathtub." Margaret shakes her head as if to jog her memory. "I must have misjudged it while I was in wolf form. Anyway, we need to build a fire by the entrance so we can boil some of this water for us to drink. Oliver, dear, would you mind gathering some wood for us? Take a few of the guards with you too. Ivy, why don't you help me set up our tent?"

"Our tent?" I ask.

Margaret places a fisted hand on her hip. "Of course, dear. You and I will be sharing a tent while the others sleep together out here."

Instantly, I look at Damon for confirmation.

"My mother believes your virtue would be safer in her presence," he tells me with a wry grin.

"Well it's certainly not safe with you around," Margaret says without a shred of doubt. "Besides, this way, Simon can't complain as much or corner Ivy unawares. Don't worry, son, I'll keep an eye on your lady love. Nothing will happen to her while I'm around."

I feel like Margaret has doomed me with her words. You should never boast something so confidently while fate is listening in on your conversation.

My gaze is drawn to a shadow beyond the pond, but as soon as I noticed it, it vanishes, making me wonder if it was ever there at all.

"What is it?" Damon asks, having noticed my divided attention. "Did you see something?"

"I thought I did, but it's not there anymore."

"There are shadows everywhere in here," he says, not sounding pleased about our accommodations. "It could have been a bat or even a shadow cast by one of us since the sunlight is at our backs."

"Yeah. You're probably right." Still, I could have sworn the shadow was in the shape of a small person. I shake my head to clear it and do what needs to be done next.

By the time we have our camp set up, the twilight hour is upon us and so is Simon and his men.

"Why didn't we just keep going?" Simon demands to know while he slips a white linen shirt over his head. "If we keep riding, we might reach the spot your mother is leading us to by morning. Isn't that right, Margaret?"

Damon's mother keeps a watchful eye on her pot of water over the fire.

"The horses need rest," she says without even looking Simon's way. "You can't exactly expect them to keep going without having water and food. We'll reach the spot by midday tomorrow and that's soon enough, if you ask me."

Simon gives a grunt of dissatisfaction. "Well I didn't ask you and I say we should keep going."

"Why don't you relax and take that stick out of your ass, Simon?" Boris says gruffly as he approaches the campfire we built near the entrance of the cave. "We could all use some rest after traipsing over that rough terrain today. Let's just enjoy the coolness of the night. Tomorrow will take care of itself."

"Well said, Boris." Margaret gives my father a welcoming smile as she takes in the clothing he's wearing. It's an outfit I've never seen him in before. He's wearing brown leather pants, a matching vest, and a white shirt. His black boots look newly buffed. In fact, they're so shiny I can see his reflection in them.

"I must say you look rather dashing in that outfit I had made for you."

Boris laughs but the hint of red on his cheeks tells me that her words have pleased him.

"Oh, Maggie, you are a sweet one. I'm just an old man trying to keep up with a couple of whipper snappers," he says, pointing a thumb in the direction of Simon and Damon. "We're we ever that arrogant at their age?"

"I dare say we were more so," Margaret says, casting a come-hither glance in Boris's direction. "Why don't you and I go explore the cave? Who knows what we might find?"

Boris puffs out his chest and offers Margaret his crooked arm. "I'm up for a little adventure if you are, Maggie."

"It seems like every minute with you is an adventure," she replies with a contented sigh. "Let's not waste a moment of our hour together."

While the two of them grab a torch from one of Damon's guards, I feel a sense of loss as I watch Boris walk away. I know I shouldn't feel jealous, but I also recognize how human my emotion is. For years, Boris and I only had each other. Now, we've found people we want to spend our lives with. That realization makes me both happy and sad. I don't want to let go of the past, but I also want to see what the future holds for us both.

"Are you hungry?" Damon asks, taking one of my hands with his. "We have plenty of provisions to choose from. Some cheese and grapes, perhaps? Or a sandwich?"

"All of the above?" I smile sheepishly. "I'm starving. Aren't you? We didn't even stop to have lunch."

"There wasn't a good place until we arrived here," he points out. "At least we have a roof over our heads, so to speak."

"Well, I'm starving," Simon states. "Where's the food?"

Damon has some of his guards bring in the bags of food from the horses. During that time, a windstorm kicks up, driving us farther back into the cave and closer to the water. It's the first time I've stood so close to the water's edge and being nearer makes me notice something.

"Are those bubbles?" I ask as I study the large pool.

Everyone turns to look. Damon drops to one knee to get closer.

"Seems that way," he says, dipping his hand past the surface. "I can feel them pop against my skin. The water is still cool, though, so it can't be a heat vent."

"Probably some sort of gas seeping in from an underground tunnel," Simon guesses.

"But what kind?" Damon stands back up.

"I don't think it's anything to worry about." Simon returns his attention to the entrance of the cave. "That windstorm outside is liable to do us more harm than anything in that water. We should probably bring the horses inside, don't you think?"

"That's the first smart thing I've heard you say all day."

Simon gives Damon a scathing look that would wither lesser men before he orders his men to start gathering the horses and bringing them into the cave. Damon follows suit with his own guards.

I hear a popping noise behind me and notice that the bubbles are larger now. So large, in fact that they are rising to the surface and popping. Laughter draws my attention away from the pond as Margaret and Boris come back from their little adventure.

"The two of you didn't go very far," I note while joining them back at the fire.

"There must have been an earthquake or something since the last time I was here," Margaret says. "That tunnel was completely blocked by a cave in." She looks around us. "Where is Damon at and when did that windstorm start?"

I answer her questions and also point out the bubbles in the pond.

"Do you think it's anything to worry about?"

"I don't think so, dear," she says with a dismissive wave of her hand. "Probably just a gas pocket causing that to happen. More than likely, whatever caused the cave in opened a vent somewhere."

It was basically what Simon said too, but still . . .

It gives me an uneasy feeling.

Out of the corner of my eye, I see Vamir sitting against the rock wall to my left. He's watching me. When I turn my gaze his way, he suddenly averts his attention to a pebble on the ground. He picks it up and studies it like he's never seen a rock before. Suspicious? Absolutely, but I purposely act like I don't notice. To me, it's obvious Vamir has secrets. Whether or not he ever plans to tell us any of them is yet to be seen.

Once all the horses have been brought in, Damon finally makes me the meal he promised. A hefty sandwich piled high with thinly sliced ham, cheese, lettuce, and tomatoes with a side of grapes already plucked from their stems. I finish my supper before he even takes the first bite from his own sandwich.

One of the guards begins to laugh, causing those around him to laugh also.

"I wonder what's so funny over there," I say, watching the usually silent and rather formidable guards smile and laugh like children.

"Not sure." Damon chuckles as he takes a bite of his sandwich.

Out of nowhere, I start to feel a little woozy. "Are you sure that ham wasn't spoiled? I'm starting to feel a little funny."

Damon laughs harder than he should. "It was fine, Ivy. Sometimes, you worry too much about things. Can't we just enjoy what's left of our twilight hour together?"

Damon shakes his head at me while he continues to eat his sandwich.

I hear more laughter but this time it's from Boris and Margaret.

"I need some fresh air," I tell Damon. "Would you like to join me outside?"

"In that wind?" he looks at the cave opening with disinterest. "Nah, I'm staying here to finish my sandwich. It's super delicious."

He takes a huge bite out of his sandwich and smiles up at me like a kid who just raided his parents' liquor cabinet. His eyes are unfocused, and I know there is definitely something weird going on in this cave.

"Come on," I say, grabbing one of his arms and attempting to drag him to his feet. "Something in here is messing with people. We need to get outside."

Damon yanks his arm out of my hold. "I said I wanted to eat my sandwich! Leave me alone!"

I look around for someone who can help me with Damon, but everyone, including Simon is laughing their asses off. I look over at the pond and notice that the bubbles I saw earlier are so large and plentiful now that the pond looks like it's boiling. Whatever gas is being expelled into the air is causing them all to go nuts.

When I look around the cave once more, I notice something else out of place.

Vamir is gone.

"Damon, Vamir left." I look down at Damon and see that his eyes are closed and he's snoring softly. I kneel and try to shake him awake. "Damon, wake up!"

He doesn't. In fact, he falls back and smacks his head against the rock wall. Thankfully, he has a hard head because I don't find any traces of blood when I touch the back of his head with my fingers. The others in the cave start to fall over and before I know it, they're all asleep except for me.

With a soft curse under my breath, I search Damon and find a dagger's hilt poking out the top of his right boot. I slip the weapon out and hold it firmly in my hand. Without wasting time, I run out of the cave to search for our wandering fae.

Through the short swaying trees, I catch a glimpse of Vamir's black cloak to the west and run after him. The wind is howling and blowing dust into my eyes. With the trees swaying, their limbs feel like small switches whipping my body this way and that. I do my best to keep my arms up in front of me to protect my face, but I still feel a sting against my right cheek as a rather determined branch lashes out at me.

The wind suddenly ceases to blow. It's almost like someone turned a switch, forcing Mother Nature to calm down. I catch my first glimpse of Vamir and discover he isn't alone.

Before he senses my presence, I crouch down and hide next to a tree trunk that's barely wide enough to conceal my body.

"What was that back there?" Vamir asks the cloaked figure. "I know you wouldn't hurt them, but what made them start laughing like that?"

"It was only a bit of nitrous oxide," the woman says in a voice I instantly recognize. "Don't worry about them. They'll be fine when they wake up. You know I want the humans to succeed. They're our future, if only your grandfather would listen to me."

"Mom, you know how stubborn he is. Even if he's changed his mind about them after all these years, he'll never back down."

Mom? But . . . I know that *voice.* I know who Vamir's mother is, but if she's his mom, then that means . . .

I stand and stare at the pair in front of me no longer caring if they see me or not.

"Emily?" I say, drawing their attention to my presence.

Vamir turns to face me, giving me a glimpse of the woman whose life I've been a part of since I touched the Queen's Circlet. After all this time I finally get to see her face. She's beautiful. Emily was probably in her twenties during her life with Mark and now, five hundred years later, she doesn't look a day past thirty. Most of her is covered up by the white cloak she's wearing, but her face practically glows as she looks at me. There's something otherworldly about her features yet somewhat familiar at the same time.

I drag my eyes away from her to look at Vamir.

"Jack?"

CHAPTER 15

Vamir stares at me in stunned silence.

I swallow hard. "You're Emily's son, aren't you?"

"He is," Emily answers, her eyes glisten with tears as she looks at me but her expression implies they're happy ones. "It's nice to finally meet you, Ivy. Although, I always dreamed we would meet under better circumstances."

"I don't understand." With only a few steps forward, I'm standing by both of them. "How did you get here? Where did you come from? Is the fae ship we're looking for close by? Did you bring us the elixir we need to cure the pups?"

"No, I'm sorry to say I didn't. In fact," Emily looks between me and Vamir, "there is no more elixir. One of the main ingredients needed to make it is exceedingly hard to come by now, and we quickly discovered that it doesn't work as well as we hoped it would. We had to abandon that project and start work on a new one. Hopefully, this new method will be more effective."

My heart sank when she said there was no more elixir but did a quick rebound with the promise of a new cure.

"So you're not sure this new cure will be able to help the pups?" I'm simultaneously fearful and hopeful to hear her answer.

"In theory, it should work, but we haven't been able to test it yet." Her words were said hesitantly, making me wonder what information she's withholding.

"What is this new method you developed?" Vamir asks. "I thought you would have perfected the elixir by now, not abandoned it."

"We did what we could to make the serum more effective," Emily turns her gaze to me, "but as Margaret discovered, it only works fifty percent of the time. Besides, it didn't work the miracle it was designed for."

"What do you mean?" I ask. "What were you hoping it would do?"

"Completely reverse what was done to humanity," she reveals. "Not all fae hate humans, Ivy. In fact, a number of fae have changed their minds and now wish to live in harmony with what's left of humanity. Before we integrate our people together, we want to offer you a sign of friendship by lifting the curse your people have had to live with all these years."

"That sounds grand and all, but it doesn't sound like you even know if your new cure will work. What is it? A new elixir?"

"No . . ." Emily leaves the word hanging in the air between us. I can literally feel her tension before she finishes her answer. "We've built a machine that may be able to extract the wolf DNA."

"DNA?" I ask in confusion. I heard it referenced in one of her memories, but I didn't know what it meant then. "What is that? Some fae term?"

Emily smiles at me with a great deal of understanding, but it doesn't prevent me from feeling like an idiot for not knowing what she's talking about.

"It's actually a human acronym. Think of DNA as a code that all living things have inside them. This code determines the color of your hair, how tall you'll be, and even what kind of personality you'll be predisposed to have as you grow."

"So is my DNA screwed up somehow? Is that why my skin secretes a poison?"

Emily glances at her son with a worried frown. I instantly get the feeling she would like him to answer my question rather than explain it to me herself.

"Jack," she says hesitantly, "I think it's time you had your talk with Ivy, don't you?"

Now I'm even more confused. "A talk about what?"

Emily calmly looks me straight in the eyes. "About who you really are and what your true purpose is in all of this."

My body suddenly feels flush with both excitement and worry. What is Emily talking about, and why does Vamir appear on the verge of having an anxiety attack?

"I don't understand," I admit looking from one to the other. "What do you want him to tell me? Why can't you do it? I know you, Emily. Between the two of you, you're the one I feel like I can trust."

Emily smiles, pleased that I have so much faith in her. "I know you've seen the memories I stored in the diamond, and I'm so grateful you were able to share my experiences that way. Although, I do wish I had been able to erase one of them, but if I had, all of them would have been corrupted. It was more important for you to understand my life with Mark than spare me a little embarrassment."

"What scene, and why didn't you ever show your memories to me? It would have been nice to see my father." Vamir appears hurt that she never shared the memories stored in the diamond with him, but maybe she can't. As far as I know, no one else has ever been able to access them except me.

"I'm sorry, Jack. I wish I could have, but I placed the diamond in the circlet right before the humans awakened here. Besides, the memory I'm referring to is one I never would have shared with you. There are some things a son shouldn't see his mother and father do."

"Oh." From the embarrassed look on his face, it seems Vamir knows exactly what his mother is referring to without any further explanation.

"So which name do you go by?" I ask him. "Jack or Vamir? Was Vamir your cover name while you were in Dawn?"

"No." His answer is brusque, verging on rude.

I've obviously hit on a sore subject. He clears his throat as if embarrassed that he let my question bother him. "Vamir is my fae name. My grandfather gave it to me so he wouldn't be reminded of my humanity."

"His true name will always be Jack," Emily says proudly, "but I'm the only one who ever calls him that." She looks at me. "Since you *do* feel like you know me, I would like to ask a favor from you."

Instantly, my guard goes up. People don't usually ask for a favor unless it's important.

"What kind of favor?"

"I want you to listen to what my son has to tell you and not judge him too harshly once his story is finished. You should also know that he had many chances to escape the dungeon in Dawn, but he chose not to."

"Why would you willingly stay there?" I ask him.

Vamir hangs his head, but I can't tell if it's in shame, sadness, or both. He looks lost or is this simply the look of a man who has lost so much in his life that thinking about it brings him unimaginable grief? Only his story will reveal the truth, and I have to admit that my curiosity is piqued.

"Once you hear what I have to tell you," he says, forcing himself to meet my gaze, "I hope you won't think any worse of me than you already do."

"To be honest, I don't know you well enough to feel anything for you."

Vamir flinches. It's a small movement, but one I notice.

"I think it's time for me to leave now, and Jack," Emily says, "you can tell Ivy about this world but only if she promises not to tell the others. If either of you disrupt the test, none of you will be allowed to ever leave."

"Leave?" I ask since she made the word sound so ominous. "What is that supposed to mean? Will the fae make us stay in the Barrens? Is that why people who come here never return home?"

"Jack will explain." Emily looks to her right as if someone is drawing her attention.

I look over to the same spot but see nothing but the stunted trees and brush surrounding us.

"Good luck," she says, returning her attention back to us. "I hope to see you both again soon."

Emily disappears right before my eyes.

"What the—" I can't even finish my sentence. Seeing someone disappear into thin air isn't something that happens every day.

"It was a hologram of my mother," Vamir tells me. "She wasn't physically here. It was just her image."

"Was that magic?" I wave a hand through the space where Emily stood but I don't feel anything different.

"No. It's technology my people possess, but it can't be used very often. If my grandfather found out it was being used to visit people here, he would punish that person, even if it was his own daughter."

"Your grandfather is a real piece of work. Is the only reason he hates humanity because the fae didn't receive a warm welcome when they came here?"

"I'm not sure. You would have to ask him that question." Vamir turns to fully face me. "Would you like to find a place to sit before I start?"

I shake my head. "I would rather stay on my feet."

He nods and starts to rub his hands together nervously.

"Well, I . . ." He clears his throat. "I, uh, well, I guess I should start by telling you about my first mission in Dawn."

"What made you want to be a scout? Was it Emily's idea?"

He tilts his head and looks at me like my questions are strange ones to ask. They seemed pretty reasonable to me considering everything I saw in Emily's memories.

"No. I came here all on my own. It was my decision, but I guess you could say my mother influenced my life choices. She kept me connected with the human world by letting me watch things that went on here."

"Watch?" I lift my gaze to the sky. "Are we being watched by your people right now?"

"Only the ones who want to help us." Vamir lifts a fist to his chest and places it over his heart. "I firmly promise that the only ones who are watching us are the ones my mother handpicked to help us succeed in this test."

"I see." Still, I feel as though a million eyes are watching us, and I'm not sure I'll ever feel comfortable again. "What happened on your first mission here and why did you stay in the dungeon all those years when you could have simply left?"

"I'll get to that second question," he promises. "As far as the first one, I met the love of my life the moment I stepped into this world."

"The one who let you rot in the dungeon?" I scoff.

Vamir's body bristles at my words. "As I said before, that wasn't by choice. I'm sure she would have come to me if she had been able to."

"So, who was this woman?"

Small beads of sweat pop out across his forehead. "She was Simon's mother, Queen Eleanor."

"Really?" I say in disbelief. "You fell in love with Simon's mother? Wait, you're not about to tell me you're Simon's father, are you?"

Vamir laughs. "No. Simon is the old king's son, not mine. When I met Eleanor, Simon was already nine years old."

The story Simon told me and Boris about his mother's death comes to mind and begs that I ask Vamir an important question.

"Did you inadvertently do something to the queen to cause her death?" It seems like too much of a coincidence, if you ask me. Vamir starts his new mission, falls in love with the queen, and she ends up dying not long after.

Vamir averts his gaze, unable to meet mine anymore.

"I guess I have my answer," I say, but not unkindly. It's obvious from his expression that the death of the queen caused him great sadness. "Is that why you chose to stay in the dungeon all those years? Was that your penance for her death?"

Vamir quickly wipes the corners of his eyes with his fingers and clears his throat before looking up at me. The pain of his loss still swims in the pools of his eyes.

"I thought it was the only thing I could do to honor her memory and our love for one another. At the time, I didn't realize there was another way for me to do that. In fact, I could have had a much different life. One that Eleanor wanted me to have but one her husband made sure I never would."

"What kind of life?" Vamir's tragic love story with the queen of Dawn has me caught in its web.

"One I could have had with my child with Eleanor."

"Child?" I ask in surprise. "But Simon doesn't have any siblings. Oh no." I cover my mouth with a hand, fearing I know what happened to Vamir's child. "Did the king kill the queen when he found out she was pregnant with your baby?"

"I wish it was his fault, but her death was because of me and my people."

"Wait," I take a small step forward and whisper, "did the fae kill her because you got her pregnant?"

"I inadvertently killed her because of what I am," he states. "I guess you don't know that part of the story from my mother's memories. If you did, I think you would have already guessed who our child is."

"Your kid is still alive?" I ask in surprise.

"Yes. She still lives, and if I have anything to say about it, she'll live a happy life for a very long time. I hope she'll even let me be a part of her life, but if she doesn't, I'll understand. I haven't been a very good father, but in my defense, I didn't know she was alive until the king told me right before his death. When Eleanor died, he came to me with a lie, telling me that she and the baby died during labor. As his last gift to me, he told me the truth. That my daughter was still alive and thriving without me in her life."

"Why didn't you leave the dungeon when you found out she was still alive?"

"I didn't want to disrupt her life. She had her own family and didn't need me."

"That was awfully selfish of you. I grew up without my parents, but I always wondered who they were and why they didn't want to be a part of my life."

"But you had Boris," he points out. "Wasn't he a good father to you?"

"The best. I wouldn't have wanted anyone but him to raise me, but it would have been nice to know who my real parents were."

"I always thought my daughter would be better off not knowing me, but you're saying the opposite. Do you think she would still like to know who I am even after all these years?"

"You should do it as soon as you can because she'll always wonder why you never came to see her. She needs to know her mother was Queen Eleanor too. She should have a claim to the throne if anything happens to Simon."

"Yes, I thought about that too. I'm sorry to say that Simon is a lot like his father. Self-absorbed and arrogant."

"You're a good judge of character." I can't help but chuckle at his astute observation. "I've already told Simon that I'll never marry him, even if he wins the fight."

Vamir looks alarmed. "Fight? What fight?"

"It's a long story, but basically, it's a fight between Damon and Simon for both kingdoms and me."

"You can't marry Simon."

"Didn't I just say that?"

"Yes, but . . ." Vamir's words trail off and he looks uncertain how to finish his thought. Finally, he looks me straight in the eyes. "You can't marry Simon because he's your brother."

Everything I thought I knew about my life suddenly comes crashing down all around me. Simon's story about his mother's death and how she was bed ridden for months finally makes sense.

She was pregnant with Vamir's child.

She was pregnant with *me*.

"Ivy." I hear Vamir's voice, but it sounds like it's a long way off. "Ivy, are you all right?"

I take in deep breaths to fill my lungs, but it still doesn't feel like it's enough. As the air enters my throat, I hear myself make a wheezing noise.

All my life I wanted to know who my parents are. Now that I do, the information is too much to take in. My body trembles. My mind whirls. I feel lightheaded like I'll pass out at any moment.

"Ivy!"

Vamir's shout finally breaks through my stupor, and I look at him crouched down in front of me. It's only then that I realize I've fallen to my knees like a broken doll that's been ripped in half.

"Do you see me?" he asks frantically.

Slowly, I nod. I can't seem to find my voice, but it doesn't matter. I'm not sure I could speak coherently even if it was available.

"I'm sorry," he says. "I didn't know how to tell you. I'm just thankful I didn't blurt it out last night while I was drunk."

"I saw you cry last night," I say, now understanding why tears spilled from his eyes when Simon told me the story about his mother's death.

Vamir smiles wanly. "I hoped no one saw that, but I guess I should have known there isn't much you don't notice. You inherited that from your mother. Eleanor was always able to notice the smallest detail about things."

"How exactly did my mother die?" I ask as tears blur my vision. "Did I kill her when I was born? Did my poison kill her?"

"Listen to me." He grabs me gently by the upper arms and looks me straight in the eyes. "You did not kill your mother. The fae did. We were simply pawns in their game. Do you understand me?"

"Then how did she die?" I have to know. I *must* know.

Vamir sighs heavily as he lets me go and sits on the ground.

"When the fae realized the humans were going to fight back, they manipulated their DNA so their skin would produce a poison if a human touched them."

"I don't understand. You were born before the war broke out. You couldn't have passed that along to me, right?"

"My DNA was manipulated along with everyone else's on the fae ships, but when I decided to become a scout, that part of me was reversed. Or so I thought." Vamir begins to pick at a strand of grass before he continues his explanation. "As a scout, you sometimes have to interact with people. There were times when I wouldn't be in my suit, so I could walk around and talk to people in person. You can't do that effectively if one touch can kill someone you're standing beside, as you well know. So, before a scout is allowed to come here, they have to have that part of their DNA excised. That way, they're no longer a threat to humans."

"If the ability was taken out of you before you came here, then how did I inherit it?"

Vamir grins grimly. "That's a very good question, and one I don't completely know the answer to, but it seems as though my sperm maintained the coding for the poison and passed it along to you."

"So when you said you inadvertently killed my mother, did you really mean that having me growing inside her is what actually killed her?"

"I can't say for sure. I wish I could give you the answers you're looking for, but I don't know enough about that sort of technology to tell you exactly what happened or whose fault it was. All I can tell you for certain is that it was the fae and their desperation to find a new home that caused her death. That's the way I look at it, and so should you. None of this was your fault, Ivy. You need to keep that in mind."

I sit on the ground, trying to grapple with everything I've learned in a very short amount of time.

"Emily said that you have something important to tell me about this world. What did she mean by that and why can't I tell the others this big secret?"

Vamir gives me a sideways glance. "Are you sure you're ready to know the truth about your world? I feel like you might need some time to accept what I just told you."

"If Emily believes I need to know what's really going on, then I trust her judgment. What's really happening here, Vamir? And how does it affect the test?"

Vamir turns to face me with his legs crossed.

"If there is one thing you must understand about the fae, it's that their science and magic go hand in hand. When they want something done, they find a way no matter what it takes. What I'm about to tell you will sound incredible. You may not even believe it at first, but you have to trust me. I promise to only tell you the truth from now until the moment I die. No matter how hard it might be for me to tell you certain things, I will never lie to you. Do you believe me?"

"I will until I catch you in a lie."

Vamir nods. "Good. Then that means we're starting to build trust between us. Now, all I ask is that you keep an open mind because what I'm about to say will be impossible for you to believe at first, but it's the truth. Are you ready to hear it?"

I take a deep breath. "Yes. Tell me what I need to know so I can save the people I love."

As Vamir begins to weave his tale of magic and how it applies to us, I begin to wonder if he's completely lost his mind. Yet, his words seem so sincere, but how can I believe what he's telling me? How can the world around me be real but also a lie?

CHAPTER 16

(Emily's Point of View)

Watching my son explain everything to Ivy breaks my heart in a million different ways. He's lost so much in his life. Will he lose her too? I'm not sure she can ever forgive him for not being there for her during her childhood, but what kind of life would they have lived if he had escaped that horrible dungeon in Dawn? They wouldn't have been allowed to come here to live with my people. At least, not yet.

Humanity is still on trial for the atrocities they committed. Making their planet uninhabitable was a spiteful act of destruction. The fae saw it as nothing less than an unforgivable sin. When I first returned, I wasn't sure I would be able to convince them otherwise, and it's taken me hundreds of years to persuade those around me that humans aren't the villains of the story. I'm constantly reminding them that if a similar situation had happened on our planet, we never would have given up half of our world to demanding invaders.

Humanity saw us as the aggressors. How else were they supposed to perceive us? To them, we were aliens hoping to reap their planet for our own survival. Who exactly was the one in the wrong? Them? Us? It all depends on who you talk to, but I, for one, always viewed us as the intruders. We demanded something of humanity they weren't able to give. Their race was young when we arrived. We were their first contact with what awaited them in the greater expanse of the universe. For all our knowledge, we were unwise in our dealings with the humans. We were demanding and cruel. We are the villains of this story, and humanity never had a chance against us.

My front doorbell rings, jarring me out of my reverie. I quickly switch off the hologram of my son and Ivy before leaving my opulently decorated living room to see who could be visiting me so late in the afternoon. The sound of my heels clicking against the polished wood floor breaks the silence in my lonely home. Before I open the door, I hang my cloak in the coat closet and smooth out my red hair. Luckily for me and my son, I had my hood up while I was talking with Jack. If Ivy had seen that we shared the same hair color, it would have been a dead giveaway to the familial connection between us.

I take a few seconds to look at myself in the mirror hanging on the wall above the entryway table. With the tips of my fingers, I pinch my cheeks to return some color to my face. I close my eyes and take in a deep breath before greeting my unexpected visitor.

Pulling the front door open brings me face to face with the disapproving glare of my father. The expression isn't a new one for him, especially when he takes time out of his busy schedule to visit me.

"Emily," he says tartly, "I've been told you visited Vamir. How many times have I told you that interference in the Choosing is not allowed?"

"I only went to check on him. I didn't interfere with anything."

He sighs in his own special condescending way. "I allowed you to visit him while he was a prisoner because it didn't affect the process, but now that he's out and with his daughter, you are no longer allowed to speak with him. Is that understood? By all rights," his tone turns menacing, "Earth 104 should be taken out of the running and immediately disposed of with your son still trapped there. Do you understand what's at stake?"

"Of course, I understand," I say snidely. "You remind me every chance you get."

The anger in my father's eyes is piercing, and I fear I may have gone too far this time.

He wags his index finger in my face. "Remember your place here, Emily. It's only by your mother's grace that we didn't let you and your son die during the war."

"And to her I will be forever grateful." I intentionally leave out his involvement in our rescue from the bomb that destroyed my home and killed the only man I'll ever love. He could have saved Mark so easily, but he chose not to. For that act of spitefulness, I will never be able to forgive him.

My father lifts a dubious eyebrow. He recognizes the fact that I didn't include him in my statement, and I'm sure he understands why.

"Watch yourself, Daughter. There are those within my faction who argue against giving the humans this chance at survival. We've played along with this game for what? Five hundred years now? And none of the worlds have been able to prove their worth yet."

"Earth 104 is different," I say stubbornly. "I know it."

My father snorts. "Why is that? Because Vamir and his unholy offspring are there?" He leans in closer to whisper. "That girl will never be a part of our family. I don't care if she *is* your granddaughter. Just because she's related to you doesn't mean her world will get any special privileges. Is that understood?"

I stare my father straight in the eyes. "Yes. I completely understand."

When he leans back, I see a self-satisfied grin spread his lips. "Good." He turns to walk away but stops on the porch just short of the steps to face me again. "Oh, by the way, your mother wants you to come to the party this evening."

"I already told her I don't plan to attend."

"Nevertheless, I think you should come for her sake. She wants to see you. For that fact alone, I think you should reconsider."

With a heavy sigh, I simply nod. "Tell her I'll be there, but only for a little while."

"Good. I'll let her know."

Watching my father walk away is both a relief and cause for alarm.

He may have used my mother to blackmail me into attending the party tonight, but I have a feeling his real agenda has nothing to do with her.

I close the door and press my back against it.

"What are you up to?" I whisper, knowing my father doesn't do anything without ulterior motives being attached. He holds the key to Jack and Ivy's survival, and with that power, he has me trapped under his thumb. It's a strange feeling to love and hate someone so fiercely, but my hate is quickly erasing my childhood memories of the loving man he once was.

For now, my fate has been decided and apparently, there's a party in my future. If I'm going to make it to my parents' event on time, I have to start getting ready. With feet that feel like they've been dipped in cement, I make my way up the staircase to the second floor.

An hour later, I leave my house and make my way through the city to my parents' home.

"Emily!"

I stop and turn to see my best friend, Aubri. She hops over a small crack in the street between us and hurries to my side.

"Fancy meeting you here," she says, taking my arm as we continue to make our way down the sidewalk. "I thought you were ducking out of the party this evening."

"I was until my father made it clear that I would be disappointing my mother if I didn't come."

"Hmm." Aubri is as shrewd as she is beautiful. Her long black hair is styled into an intricate updo this evening, accentuating her sharp cheek bones and bright emerald eyes. She's wearing a pale pink chiffon gown with a lace bodice that makes other parts of her body stand out. Her attire is a stark contrast to my unadorned black dress. "And do we believe that's the only reason he wants you to be there?"

"No. I'm sure he has an agenda. I just don't know what it is yet."

"Seriously, why does Eldon have to make everything so mysterious?"

We walk along in mutual silence for a few minutes before Aubri gasps.

"I think I know why he wants you there," she says excitedly. "A woman at work said Oberon will be attending. It wouldn't surprise me at all if your father is trying to hook you up with the dark fae king."

"Oberon is here?" Surprised doesn't even begin to describe how I feel. Worried, frightened, and mad are also the emotions Aubri's revelation is causing me. "I thought he and the others were still out searching for a new home."

Aubri shrugs. "I guess he finally gave up." She looks at me queerly. "I thought at least your mother would have mentioned his arrival to you. His ships made it here two days ago."

"I've been busy." Even though she's my best friend, Aubri doesn't know everything I do. If she did, her life would be in danger, and I refuse to lose another person I love because of my actions.

"So mysterious," she jokes. "Will you ever tell me all your secrets?"

"No." I look into her eyes. "I love you too much to ever put you in that much danger."

Aubri's smile falters before fading away as the reality of my life hits home.

"You know," she tightens her hold on my arm, "I would never tell a soul anything you tell me."

"I know that. Trust me, if I thought you would remain safe, I would tell you more, but my father has spies everywhere. I can't risk losing you. If I did, I would lose what sanity I have left."

Aubri sighs. "Well, I can understand that. I *am* pretty special."

"Special in the head maybe."

Aubri pinches my arm, but I laugh the pain of her retribution away.

Music drifts on the cool breeze coming from the direction of my parents' castle. It's an exact replica of the one they used to have on our home world of Aos. As a child, I remember thinking that there was no one as beautiful as my mother or as handsome as my father. Back then, I thought I had the perfect life, and that I was destined for a perfect future. When the resources on our planet began to run out, that future was forever altered. After all these years, I'm still not certain where fate is leading me.

As Aubri and I join the crowd filing into the castle, my father's personal butler sees me and waves me over to walk directly to the front entrance instead of waiting in line with everyone else.

"Come on." I gently tug Aubri's arm. "If I have to be seen as over-privileged, so do you."

"I don't mind," she giggles. "It's better than standing in line with all the other peasants."

I roll my eyes. "I can't believe you just said that."

"Well, it's true," she whispers after earning a few hard looks from the crowd who overhear our conversation. "At least that's how your father sees everyone else around him."

She's right, of course. My father looks down on most people, even me and my mother. Although, I have seen my mother put him in his place more than a few times. He may not realize it, but she's always been cleverer than him. The smartest thing she does is allow him to think he's in charge. A soft word spoken in his ear by her can change his mind more than a harsh word spoken in anger. He's a pushover where she's concerned, but he would never openly admit it.

"Princess Emily." Foster bows his head to me as we approach. He's been my father's butler for as long as I can remember. With his short black hair starting to gray and fine lines appearing at the corners of his eyes, age is finally catching up with him. His dark skin has turned ashen, making me wonder if he's caught some sort of illness since the last time I saw him.

"Hello, Foster. Do you know where my mother is right now?"

"No." His expression turns suspiciously blank, as if he's purposely trying to hide his true feelings to such a simple question. "But your father is waiting for you inside the ballroom. I believe he wanted you by his side before he announced his special guest for the evening."

"King Oberon?"

This time Foster can't hide his feelings as his eyes widen in shock.

"How do you know he's here?" he whispers.

Aubri leans closer to Foster. "I told her. Half the city knows his ship arrived here two days ago."

"Oh," he says in surprise. "Well, the king won't be happy with that news."

"Then let's not tell him," I suggest. "After he announces Oberon's arrival, it won't matter anyway. What he doesn't know now won't hurt him later."

Foster nods. "Quite right, Princess. You and your mother have always been quite intuitive where your father is concerned."

I'm not so sure about that, but maybe Foster is right. Maybe I do possess some of my mother's talent of persuasion where my father is concerned. Afterall, I did convince him to allow Jack the opportunity to become a scout when the time was right for him to go there and fulfill his destiny. His fate is one I've known the secrets to for quite some time. Sending Jack to live with the humans was the hardest thing I've ever done, but I did it. You can't run away from your future. All you can do is run toward it and hope for the best.

"I suggest you find your father as quickly as possible." Foster turns to the side, giving us a clear path into the castle. "The last time I saw him, he seemed rather anxious to introduce you to King Oberon."

As we walk past Foster, Aubri giggles.

"I wonder if Oberon knows about your father's plans to marry you off to him," she muses.

"If he thinks I'm going to marry that man, he had better think again. I already married the love of my life. That type of lightning doesn't strike twice in one lifetime."

Aubri looks worried. "Are you saying you'll never let yourself fall in love again?"

I look her straight in the eyes. "I don't think I have it in me to give my heart to someone else like that. When you lose someone you love as much as I did Mark, a part of your soul is lost forever. They take it with them, and the only way to get it back is to meet them on the other side."

Aubri abruptly stops, forcing me to stand and face her. "You're not thinking about killing yourself, are you?"

"Lower your voice," I admonish her as passersby give us curious glances. "Of course not. If I was going to do that, I would have done it years ago. Being fae has cursed me with a long life. One I have to live without Mark. I feel like it's my penance for lying to him for all those years. I should have told him the truth sooner, but I was frightened I would lose him if he knew what I really was."

"You never talk about him." She smiles wanly. "Why is that?"

"Because just thinking about him tears a new hole in my heart that will never mend." With a light hand, I rub my chest to ease the sudden ache there.

"Then don't think about him anymore tonight," she says with newfound purpose. "Let's find your father, meet Oberon, and get out of here."

I nod, hoping the night goes that smoothly, but I have a nagging suspicion it won't.

As we enter the ballroom, my attention is immediately drawn to my father. Even in a crowd, his aura grabs you like a whirlwind of energy, forcing you to acknowledge his presence. There's no denying his power or charisma, but none of that matters when you consider his cruelty. He's never been an overly loving father or husband, from what I can tell, but he's always been a fair king to his people. He kept his promise to save them, and he discovered a new home for us to not only live on but also thrive.

He cocks his head back slightly when he sees me. It's a silent order for me to come to him. I've seen it many times in my life, and each of those times I was forced to do something he expected of me.

"I'll catch up with you later," Aubri says, having seen the silent command my father gave me. "Try not to bite Oberon's head off, okay? He may not even know what your father has planned for his future."

"Oh, don't worry." I lift my chin in defiance. "I will make it quite plain that I won't marry someone I don't even know."

"Good luck with that," she says before walking off in the direction of a group of our friends.

With a deep breath to center myself, I walk through the throng of partygoers to stand by my father's side.

"Where's mother?" I ask him. "I thought she would be here to greet her guests."

"I'm not your mother's keeper, Emily," he says, clearly irritated by my question. "She's a grown woman who doesn't feel the need to tell me every little thing she does." He looks me up and down with a critical eye. "Black again? Aren't you tired of wearing that color?"

"I'm a widow. Remember? It was your selfishness that made me one."

"If you hadn't been stupid enough to fall in love with a human," he says with a menacing sideways glance in my direction, "you wouldn't have been made one so young. It's time for you to put away your widow garb and think about your future."

"Oh? Are you referring to the one you see me having with King Oberon?"

For the first time in my life, I seem to have caught my father off guard. He noticeably flinched when I mentioned Oberon's name. My guess is that he's disappointed I ruined his horrible surprise for my future.

"How did you find out he was here?" His voice might sound natural, but I've seen him like this before. He's furious beyond words, but he would never allow me to gain the upper hand on him. I am, after all, his wayward daughter who allowed herself to get impregnated by a lowly human. I know how little he thinks of me. I'm sure it's one of the reasons he's willing to marry me off to someone like Oberon.

"Good gossip like that can't be contained." I let that thought simmer for a moment before I continue. "I won't marry him. You can't force me."

"For once in your life," he says in a low growl, "think about what's good for our people and stop being such a selfish little bitch."

I gasp in surprise at his display of viciousness. When I turn my head to look into his eyes, I see anger, but I also see fear.

"What are you afraid of?" The question comes out of my mouth before I can stop myself. "Has he threatened to do something to us if I don't marry him?"

My father grabs me by the arm and pulls me past the open doors and onto the veranda.

"Leave!" he gruffly orders the few unlucky guests who have wandered outside.

Some of them scamper back into the ballroom while others give my father scathing looks of disapproval.

He lets go of my arm and turns on me with a ferocity I haven't seen in years. Not since he confronted me about marrying a human.

"You will marry Oberon for the good of your people and not fight me about it. Is that understood?"

I grab his arm before he can avert his gaze.

"Why are you so scared?" The fear in his eyes frightens me more than his demand. "Has he threatened you?"

My father grows still and silent. His gaze slides to the white marble at our feet before lifting his eyes to meet mine.

"He said he would take this world away from us if you don't marry him."

My heart drops a beat. "Does he have the power to do that?"

"From what my spies have told me, the dark fae have become extremely powerful since they left us. They reached a world that was ripe with magic and somehow harvested it to make themselves more powerful than anything we've ever seen. I have no doubt he will take what he wants by force if we don't freely give it to him, and I refuse to lose our new home. We've spent too much of our own magic here to make it livable again. We have nowhere else to go, so I need you to put your people first and do what's right."

I let go of my father's arm and start to laugh at the irony.

"Are you serious?" I ask in disbelief. "You want me to sacrifice myself and my future because Oberon wants to do the same thing to us that you did to humanity? You have some nerve expecting me to help you."

"I'm not asking you to help me. I'm asking you to help your people!" My father's outburst makes him look like he's on the brink of insanity. Maybe he is going crazy, but I lack the power to care.

"My people sat back and let you do anything you wanted to the humans to make them comply with your demands," I remind him. "Why should I care what happens to them? If you ask me, we're getting what we deserve. The humans had a saying for situations like this. Karma is a bitch. It looks like it's time for us all to pay for what we did to this planet."

"I don't know why you're being this way, Emily. I get it that you're angry with me for not saving your husband, but he was human. He would have died years ago regardless of my interference."

"But you stole years from me and my son with him! You've never understood how devastated I was after losing my husband. He was my world, and you took him away from me!"

My father looks toward the open doors as a commotion inside the room draws his attention. His lips tighten, and his expression turns to one that is cold and hard.

"Oberon is here." He looks me straight in the eyes. "Is your final answer no then?"

I straighten my back and look at him with a sense of just retribution.

"Yes. I will not marry Oberon. I would rather die."

"Oh, it won't be you who dies," he says harshly. "But it will be people you care about. Just remember that you had a chance to save them, but in this moment, you doomed their future."

My father walks back into the castle with a brisk pace.

What did he mean by that? Who was he talking about?

My chest begins to ache. The night has only begun, and I fear my father's words will come back to haunt me before it's over.

CHAPTER 17

When my people first discovered Earth, the dark fae left us to venture through the universe on their own. At the time, it seemed strange that they would leave a planet so plentiful and perfect for our needs. Not much was said about their departure, and I always assumed that was because many fear the dark fae and their sordid past.

A thousand years ago, there was no such thing as light and dark fae. It wasn't until a faction of the fae began dabbling in the dark arts that such a distinction was made. Those who became known as the dark fae followed Oberon's father down a path of no return. They used their magic to raise the dead for selfish reasons.

Oberon's father, King Oneidas, lost his wife and daughter in a tragic accident. Their deaths sent him spiraling into a tailspin of unimaginable grief and spurred him on a quest to uncover the secrets of black magic. The power he sought was forbidden and caused a permanent rift, dividing the fae into light and dark. Even though Oneidas was able to resurrect his wife and daughter, necromancy became taboo, even among the dark fae. Those who returned from the dead were soulless creatures good for nothing more than servitude. They were proficient at fighting and killing. In order to make the most out of their special talents, an elite fighting force known as the shadow knights was formed.

As I follow my father back inside, I can feel the shift of energy in the room now that the dark fae are among us. King Oberon stands just over six feet, towering over most men, even my father. His rugged good looks earned him quite the reputation of a ladies' man before the dark fae left us. With long brown hair and striking blue eyes, the king of the dark fae draws attention to himself wherever he goes. He always has.

"King Oberon!" My father's tone is welcoming, almost jubilant. He's always been able to hide his emotions from others well, but I didn't know how good of an actor he truly is until this moment. He shows zero fear as he shakes hands with our guest.

"It's good to see you Elrod," Oberon says with a congenial smile, but his verbal slight doesn't go unnoticed. He intentionally left off my father's title as king. If I noted his disrespect, I'm sure others in the room did too.

While my father and Oberon make polite chit chat, I study the other dark fae in the room.

Standing to the right of Oberon is a man I don't recognize. His face is slim and handsome, reminding me of a fox. He appears young but in the world of the fae, looks can be deceiving. With gray hair streaked with black, his pale blue eyes stand out. When our gazes cross, something unholy happens to his face. I gasp in surprise when three slits open on his forehead. Each one conceals an eye of a different color. One yellow, one purple, and one black. As quickly as they opened, they close again, making me wonder if they were actually there at all or simply a figment of my imagination.

"Oberon," my father says, having also decided to dispose of the other king's title, "I would like you to meet my daughter, Emily."

Oberon bows his head in my direction. "It's a pleasure to finally meet you, Princess. I'm sorry it's taken this long for us to make each other's acquaintance."

"From what I remember, you were too busy chasing the fair maidens of Aos into your bed."

"*Emily*," my father admonishes.

I briefly glance in his direction before returning my full attention to Oberon.

"Well, she has you there, brother. At least she's not a whimpering fool like most of your conquests."

With these words, I have to look Oberon's sister in the eyes. I was avoiding it, but can't any longer.

The eyes of the resurrected are completely white except for a pale black circle that wraps around the pupil.

"Hello, Iris, it's good to see you again."

Iris laughs harshly. "Oh, please don't start lying, Emily. I was just beginning to like you."

I smile grimly. "As you wish. If you value honesty, then I'm not happy to see any of you back here. Why have you returned? I thought exploring the universe was more important to you than building a new home. Or have you returned now that all the work to restore this planet has been done by us?"

"Our explorations were just as important as your work here. We've returned to replenish the magic you spent on this planet. We're not as selfish as some would have you believe." She briefly glances in my father's direction. "Besides, it was time for Oberon to start making babies, and we couldn't think of anyone better than you to help him make that happen. Not only will you be able to provide my brother with an heir, but the two of you will inherit the throne and bring our people back together after your father passes away."

"That won't be anytime soon, I assure you." My father's tight-lipped smile tells me that he's doing everything in his power to keep his anger under control. The unsubtle reminder of his mortality has definitely set him on edge.

"You can never be too sure about such things," the man with five-eyes says with a cocky grin.

"And who are you?" My father can't seem to contain his contempt for the man.

"This is my trusted advisor, Uri," Oberon says. "You would do well to heed his words, Elrod. He's a seer."

Several gasps can be heard from the crowd.

My father scoffs. "There hasn't been a seer born in a thousand years, and you're telling me this freak is one?"

The eyes on Uri's forehead open and target my father with an eerie gaze. Are they judging him or simply displaying their contempt for his remark? Either way, it's unsettling.

"We see straight through you, King Elrod," Uri says. "You would be well advised to not anger us."

"Oh?" My father lets go of the restraint on his anger as he peers at Uri with unmitigated hatred. "Are you threatening me, boy?"

Uri starts to take a step forward, but Oberon places a restraining hand on his chest and shakes his head at his friend.

"This isn't the place or the time," he whispers to Uri. "Leave if you must, but do not lose your temper here. Understood?"

Uri doesn't look pleased with Oberon's order, but he backs down and nods to his king.

Oberon drops his hand away from Uri before returning his attention to my father and me.

"Princess Emily," Oberon holds out his hand to me, "would you grant me the honor of a dance?"

"There's no music playing," I point out.

"Well, I'm sure your father can fix that for us." Oberon looks my father's way and grins.

"Of course." When my father waves his hand at the quartet in the corner of the room, they lift their instruments to fill the air with music.

With no other excuse to give, I place my hand on Oberon's and allow him to escort me to the dancefloor. Those gathered move out of the way and give us a wide birth. When Oberon lifts the hand he holds and places his other hand on my waist, we make our way around the ballroom with every eye watching us.

"I take it you're not too keen on marrying me." Oberon peers down at me with a look of amusement.

"I'm already married," I inform him curtly.

"No. You're not. You're a woman who lost her first husband. I think you simply use him as an excuse to stop living."

"If you had ever experienced true love, you wouldn't say that. You would mourn the loss until the day you die."

Oberon remains silent while he mulls over my words.

"If your late husband could see you now, do you think he would want you to live like a hermit and turn your back on living your life to the fullest?" he asks.

"He would want me to be happy," I snap.

"Well, you certainly sound happy," he says sarcastically.

"I would be a lot happier alone than married to a buffoon like you."

"Please, feel free to tell me what you really think of me," he snorts.

"I know you're someone who would threaten a whole planet of his own people to get what he wants. That's all I need to know about you."

"Then you don't know me at all, but if you would give me a chance, maybe you wouldn't find me so repulsive."

"You're not denying it," I say in triumph. "What makes you think I could ever care about a man who puts so little value on innocent lives?"

"Innocent," he says under his breath like a curse word. "Do you truly believe anyone in this room is innocent? You *do* remember what destroyed this planet, right?"

"The humans destroyed it so our people couldn't have it."

Oberon narrows his eyes. "But what drove them to make such a devastating decision?"

I remember that time all too well, and I hate Oberon for making me think about it.

"Fear," I finally answer. "They were scared of us after the transformations began happening."

"We turned them into animals, Emily. Did you honestly think that showed humanity that we came here in peace? If anything, it proved how cruel we could be." Oberon sighs, unable to hide his irritation. "Didn't you ever wonder why we left so abruptly to explore the universe?"

"I assumed you didn't want to work to rebuild this planet."

"I've never been afraid to roll up my sleeves and work. We left because we didn't agree with your father's way of handling the humans. Contrary to popular belief, dark fae simply dabble in magic that others are too frightened to use. We aren't monsters."

I want to point out that his friend, Uri, and his sister certainly look like monsters, but I can't bring myself to voice my opinion on their outward appearance.

"Are you trying to tell me you're the good guys?"

Oberon tilts his head. "Haven't you learned that there are no good or bad guys in real life? We're all shades of gray when it comes down to it. All of us do what's in our best interest, whether we like to admit it or not. Very few people in this world are selfless."

"That seems to be a rather bleak opinion about the people around you, or maybe it was formed because of the company you keep."

The music stops and so does Oberon.

"And maybe you still have some growing up to do, Princess. Not everything you've been told is the truth and not everything you see is real."

"Ladies and gentlemen, can I have your attention for a moment please?"

Oberon drops his hands away from me as we both turn to face my father.

"This evening, I have a rare demonstration to share with you all." When he looks at me, I notice a mischievous glint in his eyes. "If you will all follow me, I believe you'll find what I have in store worthy of your time."

Everyone follows my father out of the ballroom.

"Would you allow me to escort you?" Oberon offers me his arm.

It would be bad manners not to accept his offer without good reason. As soon as I slip my arm through his, I notice two people watching us closely: Uri and Iris.

"Do they always watch every move you make?" I ask.

Oberon chuckles. "Only when they think I'm in danger."

This time it's my turn to laugh. "Do they honestly think I'm dangerous?"

"Of killing me? No. Of hurting me? Well, that's been a rather contentious argument between Uri and Iris lately."

"Which one of them thinks I will hurt you?"

"My sister, but to be fair, she's always been rather protective of me. It's one reason she's the captain of my guards. There's no one else she trusts more than herself to keep me safe."

When we pass them, both Uri and Iris follow in our footsteps. Oberon doesn't say a word as we follow my father out of the room and down the hallway to the back of the house.

"We're going to the Room of Choosing," I say in surprise. "Why is he taking us there?"

"He said he wanted to demonstrate something to us. What do you think that means?"

My pulse begins to race as I consider all the possible answers to that question. One answer stands out among all the rest, but it can't be the right one. My father likes to hold things over people's heads to make them do what he wants. There's no reason why he would purposely destroy the one thing keeping me in line.

"Welcome to the Room of Choosing," my father says as we walk into a room that's twice as big as the ballroom. Floating in the air behind him are three clear spheres small enough to fit in the palm of your hand comfortably. Each sphere contains a miniature version of Earth, and on each of these worlds, what remains of the human race live out their daily lives like nothing is out of place. All of them, including Ivy, have always believed the lie that they live on what remains of the real Earth, but the reality of the situation is that none of them have ever stepped foot on their home world. Their world is a lie, but it's that lie that's kept them safe for the last five hundred years.

"Long ago," my father says like he's about to recite a fairy tale, "we set out from Aos seeking a new home. When we came across this planet, we thought our luck had changed for the better, but the humans saw us as their enemy. Their hatred for us led them down a path of destruction, proving they never should have been made the caretakers of this planet in the first place.

"I believe that's why we were drawn here. The powers that be in the universe led us straight to this world because they knew we would take care of it. They knew we would appreciate its bountiful treasures and bring her back to her former glory. Humanity was bleeding this world dry with their greed. If we hadn't come along, Earth would have eventually become uninhabitable.

"The loss of Aos hurt all of us, but it also provided us the wisdom to not make the same mistakes twice."

My father looks directly at me as if he wants to make sure I hear his next words.

"There are those among you who believe humanity should be given a second chance. To prove their worth and join us in the paradise we returned Earth to. When the Choosing first began, there were over two hundred spheres in this room, and one by one, all but these three proved their unworthiness. Unfortunately, one of these worlds must be destroyed due to an unfair advantage."

When he walks directly behind the world Ivy and Jack are living in, I push my way through the crowd.

"That was not their fault!" I shout to my father. The people around me take two wary steps back. "I went there on my own."

"And it's because of you that this world must be taken out of the Choosing." He breaks eye contact with me to address the crowd. "The rules of this contest were set long ago, and my daughter was part of the committee who made them. Let it be known that I do not choose favorites. Not even when it means hurting someone I treasure more than my own life."

I watch in horror as my father places his hand underneath Earth 104 and uses his magic to transform it into dust. As the final grains slip through his fingers, my world suddenly begins to go dark. Before I hit the floor, I feel a pair of strong arms catch me.

"I've got you, Emily," Oberon says as he holds me, but his voice sounds distant like we're worlds apart instead of close. "Everything will be all right."

CHAPTER 18

"Oh, Emily. I'm so very sorry. So so sorry."

My mother's voice pulls me out of the darkness and back into the light. Before I open my eyes, I wonder why she's apologizing to me. Did we have a fight I don't remember?

Then it hits me. The floodgates of my memories crash open, releasing a tidal wave of anguish, loss, and despair. When I open my eyes, I see my mother sitting beside me. A quick glance behind her shows that I'm lying on my bed in my old room in the castle.

The look of sorrow on her face confirms what I remember my father doing. I quickly sit up and wrap my arms around her, burying my face against the side of her neck as she hugs me tight.

"I'm so sorry, Emily." She sobs against my shoulder, making the nightmare I've woken up to all too real. "I should have found you sooner."

"He killed them." The words come out as a strained whisper through my tears. "He kills everyone I love."

My mother places her lips next to my ear, keeping me close. "Listen to me very carefully. If you want to see Jack and your granddaughter again, you have to keep crying. They're alive, but your father can never know. Do you understand?"

What is she talking about? How can Jack and Ivy still be alive? I watched my father destroy the sphere they were living inside of.

"How can they still be alive?" I whisper back. It's obvious my mother thinks we're being watched. I don't doubt it. My father probably *is* spying on us. I wouldn't put anything past him. Not after what he did, or at least, what I thought I saw him do.

"In times like this," my mother says in her full voice, "you need to lean on those who offer you support." She pulls back and wipes away my tears with a gentle touch. "I know he's a veritable stranger, but I believe it would do you good to spend some time with Oberon."

I almost blurt out the word "no" but think better of it. My mother's expression tells me that I need to be careful with what I say next.

"I barely know the man, and I'm not sure I want to get to know him any better. How will spending time with him help me?"

My mother takes hold of my hands, squeezing them firmly. "You need to trust me, Emily. Whether you like it or not, your father will demand that you marry Oberon. Ever since we left Aos, all he's cared about is securing a future for our people. You know that better than anyone. Your father became so obsessed with it that he found himself doing horrible, unimaginable things. Things that the man I married never would have even considered. I know you're hurting right now, but I also think you need to prepare yourself. Oberon is not a patient man. He'll expect the two of you to be wed sooner rather than later, and perhaps it's for the best."

"But—"

My mother holds up a hand to stop my objection. "You know I'm right. In fact, Oberon asked me to send you to him once you were awake and refreshened. His ship is still in orbit, and the change of scenery is exactly what you need *right now*."

The earnest expression on her face tells me that I need to do what she says. Maybe Oberon has the answers to my questions. Ones my mother doesn't feel comfortable voicing in her own home.

"I need some time to get myself together."

After my mother stands from her spot, she offers me a hand to help me off the bed. Once I'm standing, she hugs me close to her one more time.

"Trust Oberon," she whispers before kissing me on the cheek and walking toward the bedroom door. Before she opens it, she turns back to look at me like it might be for the very last time. "I love you more than life itself. You know that, don't you?"

"I've always felt it. I love you too, Mom."

With a wan smile, she places her hand on the doorknob. "Oberon left his sister here to escort you to his ship. She's downstairs waiting."

As I watch my mother leave, I almost call her back.

Why do I feel like this might be the last time I ever see her?

I shake my head to get rid of such thoughts and make my way to the bathroom to freshen up. I have no idea what's going on, but I do know Oberon has the answers.

Trust him, my mother said.

How does she expect me to trust a man I barely know? Especially one who is trying to blackmail me into a marriage I don't want. It'll take a miracle for me to place any faith in him. I just hope my mother knows what she's talking about.

By the time I make it down to the grand foyer, my nerves are on edge and my heart feels like it's about to race out of my chest. If Oberon knows where Jack and Ivy are, I can stand his company for a little while, but if he somehow tricked my mother into trusting him, he can forget about a marriage to join our people together again.

Iris paces back and forth in front of the glass doors in the entry way. The guards stationed in every corner of the room keep a close eye on the undead fae within their midst. I wonder if Oberon understands what has to be overcome to heal the rift between the light and dark fae. There are thousands of years of mistrust between us. The only time we ever worked together is when Aos could no longer support life. We needed each other then to keep our people alive.

When Iris notices me walk down the staircase, she stops pacing. The look in her strange, unsettling eyes and the tapping of her right booted foot against the marble floor shows clear impatience.

"It's about time you woke up," she complains. "Have a nice sleep did you?"

"I fainted because I just saw my father kill my son and grand-daughter," I remind her curtly. "I think you can cut me some slack for that, Iris."

She rolls her eyes without an ounce of pity in her expression. Is her heart still dead or is she capable of feeling compassion for others? Considering her reaction, I would have to vote the latter.

"Whatever, Princess. We need to get going. My brother doesn't like to be kept waiting."

With an abrupt about face, she walks determinedly toward the front doors. The guards on either side of the entrance pull the doors open before she reaches them.

Without much choice, I follow in her footsteps but find it hard to keep up with her brisque pace. Once we're outside, Iris roughly grabs one of my arms and pulls me down the street.

"Let go of me!" I attempt to pull my arm out of her grip, but I might as well be fighting a rabid tiger with steel jaws.

"Stop fighting me." She casts an annoyed glance at me over her shoulder. "Just follow and keep your mouth shut."

I do as she says only because my mother told me to trust Oberon. Although, she didn't say anything about trusting his sister. Under Iris's care, I hope I make it to his ship before his sister kills me with her strange brand of hospitality.

After Iris pulls me into an alley way, she finally let's go of my arm. While I rub the sting of her touch away, she gives me a peculiar order.

"Take all your clothes off."

I feel sure I misunderstood her words. "Excuse me?"

"You heard me." She crosses her arms and spreads her feet apart. "Take all your clothes off. Your father may have placed a listening device on your clothing for all we know. Oberon doesn't want to take any chances."

"I am *not* taking my clothes off!"

"Then you're *not* going to Oberon's ship. Either strip naked or be left here always wondering."

I don't have to ask her what she's referring to. If I don't comply with her demands, I may never learn the fate of Jack and Ivy. There's only one thing I can do.

I quickly strip down to my underwear, praying no one happens to come into the alley. At this time of night, the odds are in my favor that we'll be left alone, but there's always a chance fate will step in and turn your world upside down.

"All your clothes," Iris orders, waving a hand at my underwear.

"Can't you leave me at least a smidge of dignity?"

"The longer you take to do this the more time you waste. Both yours and mine."

I grit my teeth. "Fine!"

I slip off my underwear and toss them to the ground. Not wanting to give her any satisfaction, I stand straight and proud.

"Now can we go?"

Iris presses a silver skull pin on her lapel. "We're ready."

We're suddenly teleported to Oberon's ship. A woman who looks to be around the same age as my mother is the only one present to greet us in the stark gray room. A pale blue dress is draped over one of her arms. She is dressed in a long-sleeved white gown that compliments her gray hair and flows as she walks toward me.

"Hello Princess Emily, my name is Winn. I'll be your escort while you're on King Oberon's ship."

Winn holds the dress up for me like it's a robe. After I slip my arms through the holes, she pulls the bottom together and ties the sash into a bow at the side of my waist. The fit is perfect. She walks back the way she came and retrieves a pair of translucent high heeled shoes from a counter near the control panel in the room. When she bends down to place them on my feet, I feel slightly uncomfortable having her serve me in such a manner. Even as a child, I always dressed myself, never wanting to act the part of the spoiled princess.

Winn stands and turns to Iris. "You may leave us now. I have her from here."

Iris raises her hands in the air. "Fine by me."

Winn and I watch Oberon's sister storm out of the room grumbling something about not wanting to be a princess's babysitter. She was a princess at one time, but that seems to have slipped her mind.

"I hope I'm not the one who put her such a foul mood," I say.

"Oh, don't worry about Iris," Winn says with a melancholy smile. "She's been grumpy ever since she was brought back from the dead. I wish I could say she was better tempered as a child, but I'm afraid she was exactly the same."

Winn starts toward the door, leaving me no other option but to follow her.

"Are you a friend of the family?" I ask.

"I was governess to Oberon and Iris when they were children. Sometimes I still feel like I'm teaching them how to behave properly around others." Winn laughs.

As we walk through the gray halls of the ship, the few people we pass on the way to our destination bow their heads to us in greeting.

"Where exactly are we going?" I ask Winn.

"Oberon's private chambers. I believe he wants to talk about the terms of your marriage agreement."

"Well, that's strange. I haven't agreed to marry him yet."

Winn looks at me in surprise. "Oh? I could have sworn his exact words were that it was a done deal."

"No. It most certainly isn't a *done deal.*" I instantly regret the irritation in my voice. It's not Winn's fault that Oberon didn't make himself clear.

"My apologies then." Winn bows her head to me. "Perhaps he invited you up here to start the courtship process then."

He had better plan to tell me where my son and granddaughter are. That's the only reason I'm here and put up with Iris's insolence.

Winn stops in front of a door and turns to me.

"Oberon is waiting for you inside. I will remain out here while the two of you visit with one another." Winn clears her throat. "May I speak freely to you, Princess Emily?"

"Of course. I wouldn't have it any other way."

She grins, appearing pleased with my answer. "Oberon grew up in a loving but strict household. It's hard for him to share his feelings with others. If the two of you marry, I can promise that he will give himself wholly unto you. I have no idea if you will be able to fall in love with each other, but I do know he will honor you for the rest of his days. When he makes a vow, he never breaks it."

"Thank you for telling me that. I'll keep it in mind."

Winn bows her head in acceptance of my words. She turns and presses her hand on a screen in the wall. The door slides open revealing a room that looks like it should be in the mountains on Earth.

The room I enter is composed of wood from the high-pitched ceiling to the floors. The interior is cozy with a crackling stone fireplace, comfortable furnishings, including a brown leather couch with a gray fur blanket tossed along its back. There are even windows facing a holographic scene of snowcapped mountains in the distance.

"Not what you expected?"

Oberon appears from around a corner on the far side of the room. He's dressed more casually now in a long black vest and matching baggy pants. The expanse of his chest and arms are on full display. Does he expect me to be impressed with his physical appearance or intimidated? I'm neither.

"Where are my son and granddaughter?" My question may sound demanding, but it's the query of a desperate woman. I need to know my family is safe, and my mother seemed to believe Oberon knows where they are.

"Would you take my word that they're safe?"

"No," I answer truthfully. "I want to see them myself."

"I'm not so sure that's possible, but I do have proof."

Oberon walks over to the fireplace and grabs a metal box off the mantle.

"Come here," he turns to face me. "I think you'll find this interesting."

Without hesitation I walk over to him. He opens the box when I'm close enough to see what's hidden inside.

It's a sphere.

"Is that—" With a trembling hand, I cover my mouth, daring to hope the impossible.

"World 104?" Oberon asks, sounding amused. "Yes. It is."

I shake my head and drop my hand. "But how?"

"A few days ago, Uri had a vision about what your father had planned for this evening. We were able to get a message to your mother. You owe all your thanks to her for saving the world your son and granddaughter live on. She snuck into the Room of Choosing and replaced the sphere with an empty world."

"She's always been the brave one," I whisper, reaching out and lightly touching the top of the sphere with the tips of my fingers. "I'm surprised she trusted you with it."

"I'm not sure if it was trust or a lack of other options. When I told her about Uri's vision, she didn't even question it."

"That's because she knew my father was capable of something so cruel." I look Oberon in the eyes. "He was a fool to think killing my family would make me do anything but hate him more."

Oberon closes the box and places it back on his mantle for safe-keeping.

"I assume he planned to use the two remaining spheres as leverage over you. Even if your family had been killed, you seem like the kind of person who would save as many lives as possible. Would you say that's the type of person you are?"

"If I say yes, will you think me a fool?"

Oberon shakes his head. "On the contrary. I would consider you the perfect woman to have by my side while I drag the fae into the future, kicking and screaming if it comes to that. I think it's time we accepted humanity for all their faults and brought them back into the real world. Afterall, we're the reason their planet was practically destroyed. We couldn't save Aos with our magic, but we were lucky enough to find a planet that readily accepted it. I've heard some fae say Earth was starving for magic. It was like the planet once had its own form of magic but lost it somehow."

"I've heard that said too. Before we found Earth, I thought for sure our people would die out inside the spheres. They were the perfect blend of science and magic. Small enough to not waste any supplies while we travelled through space, but not sustainable enough to last us a lifetime."

"Would you allow me to show you something?" Oberon holds out his hand to me.

"*What* is it?" I learned long ago not to take the hand of a stranger without asking a few questions first. "And, *where* is it?"

"It's a view, and it's in the dining room. You have nothing to fear. I will remain a perfect gentleman while you're in my care, Emily. You have my word."

My gut tells me I can trust Oberon, but will my heart grow to regret that decision later?

I slip my hand into Oberon's warm palm. As he wraps his fingers around my hand in a firm grasp, I realize I miss the feel of a man. Since Mark's death, I haven't let another man touch me before today. My plan is to stay true to my marriage vows even though the human marriage vows I said gives me an out. Till death do we part, is what I vowed to Mark, but how do I let go of my love for him? How do I move on?

As Oberon leads me through the living room and around the corner he emerged from, I begin to wonder what it would be like to be his wife. He's handsome, and charming in his own way. He could have anyone he wanted as his wife, and he's chosen me. Why? Is it just because I'm the heir to the throne when my father dies? I get the distinct feeling that isn't the only reason.

As we turn at the corner in the room, I'm brought face to face with a large glass window that looks out over Earth. It's one of the most beautiful planets in the solar system. A floating blue and green orb floating in space as a safe haven for those who would call her home. The humans never seemed to realize how lucky they were to have her for their own. We, on the other hand, treasure all of her and marvel each day that we were able to bring her back from the brink of destruction.

"She's beautiful," I say, awed by my first glimpse of our new home world from this point of view in her rejuvenated state.

"Almost as beautiful as you."

I visibly cringe at his words. "I sincerely hope that's not the best you can do, Oberon. If you want me to be your wife, cliché statements like that will only earn you my pity."

Oberon laughs. It's deep and pleasant to hear. His mirth is genuine, and I find myself hoping to hear more of it in the future.

"I thought better of it after I said it," he admits, looking rather chagrined by his corniness. "But I only spoke the truth. If there is one thing I will never do to you, it's lie."

I retract my hand from his. "I was told dark fae are nothing but evil liars. Are you saying all the rumors are wrong?"

He shakes his head. "Not in the least. There are some among us who have used what my father taught them in despicable ways. He never intended to use dark magic as a weapon. All he ever wanted was use it to blur the line between life and death. I'm not sure he was thinking straight at the time. Maybe if he had been, he would have left it alone, but for better or worse, it's a part of our legacy now."

"Do you use it?"

Oberon clears his throat and suddenly looks uncomfortable. "I've been known to use it from time to time, but only for pleasurable pursuits."

The gleam in his eyes as he watches my reaction warns that I should drop the subject, but I've never been very good at heeding warnings.

"Are you implying that you use it during sex?"

I'm not sure if it was the question or the blunt way I asked it that causes Oberon to smile.

He narrows his eyes at me. "You say exactly what's on your mind, don't you?"

I shrug. "You brought it up. I'm simply curious about the answer."

He tilts his head. "Curious enough to feel a taste of it?" He holds his hands up. "I promise I won't touch you. If I did, you would never agree to marry me. In fact, I won't take you to my bed unless you beg me to. How is that for a deal?"

"Even if we're married?"

He nods. "Even after we're married. I've never had to force a woman to have sex, and I most definitely wouldn't set that precedent with my wife."

My curiosity is certainly piqued. How can magic arouse someone without the power of touch?

"Go on then," I challenge. "Show me what you've got."

Oberon moves until we're face to face. Our toes are barely two inches apart, and I can almost feel the warmth of his breath across my skin.

"Close your eyes," he instructs. "The sensation is more intense if you allow the illusion to feel real."

I close my eyes and wait. Even before he starts, my breathing becomes less steady from just the closeness of our bodies. When he begins to chant a spell I've never heard, I can feel the deep vibration of his voice inside my chest. The hairs on my arms begins to stand on end as he weaves his spell. Suddenly, phantom hands graze the sides of my neck.

I open my eyes to see if Oberon is touching me, but he isn't. He too has his eyes closed as he speaks his spell.

I lower my eyelids again, still feeling the warmth of hands I can't see. They make a leisurely path down my throat and over my chest, gently cupping my breast and eliciting a gasp from me. I want to tell him to stop, but there's a part of me that doesn't want his arousal of my body to end. One of the hands glides down the plains of my stomach and slides between my legs. With one stroke, I feel a sensation I thought was long lost to me. My legs spread wider of their own accord as my body yearns to feel the sweet sensation of a man touching my most sensitive part.

But it isn't a man touching me. It's only a spell. That realization breaks the illusion.

"Stop," I command, taking two steps back from Oberon. When I open my eyes, I see Oberon do the same.

"Is something wrong?" he asks, clearly confused. "Didn't you like it?"

"I don't need a spell to make love to me." I'm barely able to get the words out as I attempt to steady my breathing. "The next time I feel someone between my legs, I would rather it be a real man and not one you conjured with magic."

With a cocky grin, he asks, "Is that an invitation?"

"If you're lucky, I'll let you touch me one day but don't ever use that magic trick on me again. I won't lie and say it wasn't pleasurable, but when I lie with a man, it means something more than simple physical gratification."

"That's good to know." He takes two steps forward, placing us nose to nose again. "Because when I take you, I want all of you. Your heart, your mind, and your body, in that exact order. You may not realize it yet, but I'm the man you've been waiting your whole life for. The love you felt for your late husband was simply a prelude to the love you and I will share."

"Do you have some crystal ball that's told you that?" I scoff. "I would advise you to wipe it off and look again."

Oberon looks deeply into my eyes. My heart misses a beat.

"I have something better than a crystal ball," he whispers. "I have a seer who has told me about our future and about the children we'll have. My sister worries you'll break my heart one day, but Uri warns me that running away from you is futile. He says I'll never feel whole without you in my life." Oberon raises a hand and gently traces my cheekbone with the back of his knuckles. "The instant I saw you today, I knew he was right. No matter how long it takes, you will be mine, Emily. And when the time is right, I will be yours until the day I die. Uri has already seen it, and he's never steered me wrong."

The pull I feel to the man standing in front of me is undeniable. A part of me wants to wrap my arms around him and kiss that cocky grin off his face, but there's the part of my heart that will always belong to Mark. Do I have it in me to love again?

I don't know.

I simply don't know.

I part my lips to say something, but no words come to mind. What do I say? How should I react to what he's just told me?

That decision ends up not being mine to make.

The ship suddenly tilts violently to the right. Oberon reaches out and catches me before I have a chance to fall to the floor.

"What's happening?" I ask, fearing my trip here may end in cataclysm.

"I don't know." The worry in his voice and the lines that have suddenly appeared on his forehead tell me that none of this is natural.

The ship tilts sharply to the left, making it nearly impossible to keep my feet steady on the floor.

"Come on!" Oberon pulls me back toward the living room. "I need to get you off the ship!"

As we pass by the fireplace, I yank my hand out of his grasp and snatch the box with Earth 104 inside it. If this ship ends up going down, I'll be damned if I let Jack and Ivy perish with it.

CHAPTER 19

"Let's go!" Oberon grabs me roughly by the arm and yanks me toward the hallway. I almost lose my grip on the box. Frantically, I cradle it against my side before it has a chance to slip out of my hand.

When the chamber door slides open, we see Winn sprawled out on the floor unconscious.

"Hold onto something," Oberon orders. "I have to help her."

When he lets go of my hand, the ship tilts violently to the right again. I'm able to grab hold of the railing on the wall before the motion slams me against the other side of the hallway.

Oberon kneels beside Winn and checks her pulse. I assume he finds one because he lifts her from the floor in one fluid motion, cradling her to his chest before turning to me again.

"Grab ahold of me. We have to get to an escape pod."

Before the ship tilts again, I grab a fistful of his vest from the back and follow him. The sound of people screaming brings our jeopardy into full focus. What's happening obviously isn't a common occurrence aboard Oberon's ship, but at least there seems to be an emergency plan for such an event.

"Get to the escape pods!" Oberon shouts to everyone we pass. "We'll worry about the ship later!"

It's nice to know he's more concerned about the safety of his people than saving his ship. Maybe he does have some redeemable qualities. Only time will tell.

"Oberon!" Iris shouts.

I look over Oberon's shoulder and see his sister and Uri approaching us. All three of Uri's eyes are open on his forehead looking startled by what's happening around us. Strange that Oberon's seer didn't see this coming. Apparently, he isn't all knowing like the legends surrounding seers would suggest.

"What's happening?" Oberon asks as we approach them.

"The stabilizers aren't working," Iris reports. "If I didn't know any better, I would say they were sabotaged by someone."

When she looks accusingly at me, I instantly go on the defensive.

"I didn't do it," I state. "How could I? I don't even know where the stabilizers are. Besides, you made me come up here completely naked, so I obviously didn't bring any sort of remote control with me."

"Princess Emily didn't do it," Uri says. His words wipe away Iris's doubts about my innocence.

"Who did?" Oberon asks, his voice is filled with anger, and I would hate to be the person it's directed toward.

Uri shakes his head. "I'm not sure. Their identity is cloaked from me somehow, but I will find the culprit."

"Give me Winn," Iris says, not waiting for Oberon to react before reaching out to take her friend from his arms. "You take the princess in your pod, and we'll meet you on the surface."

"Hurry!" Oberon orders. "I don't know how much longer the ship will hold together under this strain!"

Iris nods before she and Uri turn around and make their way down to the other end of the ship.

Oberon grabs my hand, twining our fingers together. For some reason, I feel safe with him. I know I'll survive this nightmare and that he'll do whatever it takes to get me home. He pulls me a short distance down the hallway before opening a door that leads to a room with a single white pod inside. The door to it has already lifted in preparation for our arrival. It must be part of a fail-safe procedure to get people off the ship as quickly as possible.

The pod only has two seats which explains why Oberon let Iris take Winn without any argument.

Working quickly, Oberon gently pushes me into one of the seats and pulls the strap down from the ceiling to secure me into place.

"Hold onto the box as tightly as you can," he warns. "The pod's rockets will shoot us straight down to the surface. We're not supposed to bring loose items with us, but I know you'll never leave this ship without it."

"Never." I tighten my grip on the box.

"Didn't think so." His expression is mixed. On the one hand, he seems pleased by my stubbornness and on the other, he's worried. "Maybe I should hold it. Not to sound macho, but I am stronger than you."

"You obviously don't understand the strength of a mother," I state. "Get in your seat. The sooner we're safely on the ground the better."

Reluctantly, Oberon nods and takes his own seat. Once he's strapped in, the door of the pod lowers and snaps shut. Behind us, the sound of something mechanical moving draws my attention.

"Hold on," Oberon warns. "Things are about to get bumpy."

Only a few seconds later, the pod disengages from the ship and shoots to the earth. I instantly regret my decision to hold onto the box. The gravitational force as we plunge through space and into the atmosphere of the planet takes my breath away. With every ounce of strength I have, I hold onto the box containing my family, knowing I would happily die before ever letting it go.

Our freefall feels like it takes forever. In reality, our flight to the surface is only a few minutes long. I'm grateful the pod has no windows. It makes our descent less terrifying as the pod's entry into Earth's stratosphere shakes the pod so violently it feels like it will come apart at any moment.

"We're almost there!" Oberon's words give me the added strength I need to hold onto the box.

Only a few seconds more, I chant to myself over and over again.

The vibrating stops and the sound of metal being warped ends as we make it through the protective dome surrounding Earth.

I loosen my hold on the box to look at the wounds on both my arms where sharp metal corners punctured me.

"Don't let go of the box!" Oberon shouts, but his warning comes a second too late.

Something yanks us up and the box goes flying out of my lap.

"No!" My scream of despair echoes in the pod, but it does nothing to stop the box from slamming against the door and falling to the floor.

Desperately, I try to unbuckle my harness, but its lock refuses to disengage. I struggle against my restraints to reach for the box, but it's well out of my reach.

"There's nothing you can do. Just hold on. I'm sure the sphere is fine." Oberon's voice is calm and reassuring, but it can't stop the panic I feel.

What have I done? Did my foolishness kill my family? Is the sphere nothing but dust now?

I burst out in sobs, fearing the worst. Tears blur my vision and burn my eyes. How could I have been so careless? How could I have been so stupid?

Oberon's hand grabs one of mine. "It'll be all right, Emily."

"You don't know that. Why did you have to put it in a metal box? You should have stored it in something better!"

Even though my heart is breaking, I can still reason despite my anguish.

"I'm sorry." I look over at him expecting to see anger on his face considering my words, but all I see is pity. "It's not your fault. It's mine. I shouldn't have let go. I never should have thought we were safe. We'll never be safe. Not as long as my father lives."

Oberon squeezes my hand. "I will keep you and those you love safe or die trying. That is my vow to you. Whether you believe me or not doesn't matter. My word is my bond, and I will never break it."

Hope threatens to shine in a part of my heart that's laid dark and cold. I want to believe Oberon, but even he has to admit my father is a formidable adversary. If he's the one responsible for sabotaging Oberon's ship, there's nothing he isn't capable of doing.

Did my father discover Oberon had the real Earth 104? Or was it simply a powerplay to get rid of the dark fae king before he had a chance to woo the light fae to his side? Or did he do it for an even more unthinkable reason? Did he want to get rid of me before I had a chance to form an alliance with Oberon and claim the throne for myself?

I wouldn't put anything past my father. He's as cruel as he is selfish, and he'll do whatever it takes to maintain his power and control over our people.

His reign of terror must come to an end.

Whatever happens next, I'll make sure he doesn't keep the crown.

The pod hits something hard, jarring our hands apart as we both hold onto our seats. When the pod stops moving, water begins to stream in and the straps keeping us in place suddenly retract. The door automatically opens and water rushes inside.

Oberon is faster than I am and scoops up the metal box into one of his arms.

"Come on," he says, grabbing me by the arm and pulling me upward.

By the time I stand, the pod is already sinking into the depths of the water we're in. If Oberon didn't have a hold of me, the suction of its descent would have taken me down with it. The water around us gurgles as the pod sinks, never to be seen again.

A quick look at our surroundings shows that we landed in a large lake. Thankfully, the shoreline is less than thirty yards away.

"Can you make it to shore?" Oberon asks as we paddle in the water.

"Yes. Do you still have the box?"

Oberon lifts it above the lake's surface and the pressure in my chest vanishes.

"Let's get out of the water before we open it."

Even with the box, Oberon swims to shore faster than I do. The dress I'm wearing does nothing but hinder my progress, making it hard to kick since it seems determined to keep wrapping around my legs. Once Oberon reaches the shore, he sets the box down and wades back through the water to help me the rest of the way.

"Thank you." I'm breathless after my swim and accept his help with true gratitude.

Once the water is only ankle deep, Oberon lets go of my arm, allowing me the dignity to walk the rest of the way with my own strength. With every step, I feel my heart sink with the heaviness of guilt.

What will I find in the box?

A shattered world or a whole one?

The chances are fifty-fifty at this point. I either kept my family safe, or I killed them with my carelessness. Either way, I decide to sit down on the grass before opening the box. If I killed them, sitting down is preferable to falling. Oberon has already had to catch me once today. I don't need to make a habit of relying on him to save me.

Oberon sits down on the other side of me with a grunt.

"Do you want me to open it?" he offers.

"No." With a deep, steeling breath, I grab the box with both hands and set it on my lap. "I'll do it."

Slowly, I lift the lid.

The sphere is intact but not undamaged. A tiny crack runs along its surface. It's no larger than my thumbnail, but it could be causing havoc on the planet inside.

"We have to get them out of there." I look over at Oberon in desperation.

"How do we do that?" he asks. "I've never dealt with this type of magic before."

"It's not just magic. It's also science." With the orb in hand, I stand to my feet. "I need to find a Geomancer, and the only one I know of is in New Aos. We have to find our way back there."

Oberon jumps to his feet and looks around at the valley we're in.

"Do you have any idea where we are?" he asks.

"Not a clue, unfortunately. We'll need to find the closest town and get help."

He points to the snowcapped mountains that circle us from north to south on the right-hand side. "It would take us days to traverse those monsters. Besides, we don't have the equipment to make it across safely. We're going to have to go west and hope we run into people who can help us."

"Do you know where the other pods have landed?"

"It's hard to say. Some could be close. Some could be a continent away. It all depends on when they left the ship and the position of the planet at the time." Oberon pulls his hair to the side and twists it to squeeze out the excess water.

"Hold this," I say, carefully handing him the sphere. Oberon cups his hands together and waits for me to place it in the safety of his palms. "I want to gather some of these pine needles to make a bed for it in the box. I'm not sure how long that crack will hold before it completely splits the sphere in half, but I do know it doesn't need to rattle around in a metal box while we travel."

"You were right earlier," he says, looking slightly chagrined. "I should have planned better and placed it in something more secure."

With a shake of my head, I reach out and place a comforting hand on his arm. "Don't blame yourself. I don't. What I said to you in the pod was just my way of deflecting blame from my own guilt. Besides, it's not either of our faults. All the blame lays solely at my father's feet. He's the one who did all of this to us, and one day, he'll pay the price for what he's done."

"He won't get away with this," Oberon promises. "We won't let him."

In a strange sort of way, I realize my father has achieved one of his goals from this disaster. He's brought Oberon and me together with his evil deeds. I'm even beginning to like the dark fae king. I respect him, which is saying a lot since I thought I would end up hating him.

"I'll be right back." I walk into the forest and gather up as many dry pine needles as I can. When I return, I stuff half of them in the bottom of the box. After Oberon lays the sphere back in the box, I cover the world carrying my loved ones with the rest of the needles. I then tear off a layer of my dress to design a makeshift cross body sling to carry it in. With the box safe and secure, I feel ready to meet any challenges we might face.

Oberon and I are both startled by the guttural howling of wolves.

"Those are close," he says uneasily, "and they don't sound friendly."

"The only wolves on this planet are the ones my father made."

Oberon raises his eyebrows. "Are you telling me those are what's left of the human race on this planet?"

"Yes. After we placed humans in the spheres for the Choosing, my father tried to perfect his transmutation spell on what was left of humanity on Earth. These wolves still change forms, but they've lost their humanity. They become something different now." I test my sling to make sure the knots are tight. "We need to go before they get any closer. Those wolves are smart, strong, and hunt in large packs. If they corner us, we won't be able to escape them."

Oberon looks around the area. Presumably finding what he was looking for, he jogs over to a tree and picks up two fallen branches.

"Not the best weapons but better than nothing," he says, handing me one of the branches. "Let's go. Maybe we can find Uri, Iris, and Winn. Their pod shouldn't have been too far behind ours."

As we walk into the dark forest, I feel an uneasiness overcome me. My eyes drift to the star filled sky. Is my father watching me with one of his spy satellites? If he is, I want to give him a message. Hopefully, it's one he remembers from our time with the humans.

I stick my middle finger up in the air and hope he understands exactly what I'm saying to him.

CHAPTER 20

(Vamir's Point of View)

My daughter looks lost.

I've shattered her world so many times during her short life that I'm not sure she'll ever be able to forgive me. Yet, what I just told her about us living inside a sphere isn't my doing. It's the fae's weird sense of justice that's placed us in this mess. My mother told me she didn't realize what her father and the others had planned for the humans, and so far, none of the people inside the spheres have been able to meet their expectations. When I left New Aos, only three spheres remained out of the two hundred that were made by the Geomancers. For all I know, this sphere, Earth 104, could be the last sphere left, and humanities only hope for survival.

"Can you explain this sphere world concept to me one more time?" Ivy asks. "You're telling me that everything here was made by fae magic? That we're not on the real Earth but some replica of it?"

"Yes." With a quick look around, I find a small rock and pick it up. "Imagine this rock is the world we are on right now," I ball my hand up into a fist to enclose the rock, "and that my hand is the sphere protecting it. Everything outside the sphere is the real Earth. That's where my mother and the other fae are now, on the real planet."

"What do we have to do to get out of this sphere world?" she asks. "How do we get back to the real world where Emily is?"

Her eyes glaze over. I fear I may have blown her mind with my explanation about the world she thought was real.

As her father, I wish I could whisk her away from all the pain she's suffered on this fake Earth, but I can't. All I can do is act as her guide and hope the humans traveling with us have the fortitude to survive what they'll have to endure next.

"All I know is that your friends will face a series of trials here in the Barrens. There's a very good reason why most humans don't dare to venture out this way. The air we're breathing is filled with a chemical that activates human fear responses. Some people are more resistant to it, and it's those people who will have the best chance of surviving the challenges."

"*Surviving*?" she asks worriedly.

She looks like I just slapped her hard on the face. Immediately, she shakes her head and throws her arms up in the air.

"This is too much. Too much!"

With swift strides, she walks away from me but not in the direction of the cave. She obviously wants to be alone for a while, and who am I to dissuade her from that? I'm a nobody to her. I've failed her as a father, and I don't see us becoming friends anytime soon. All I can do is wait to see if she returns to me with more questions.

Weariness from the day's events overcomes me. Ivy isn't the only one who's gone through a lot today. I walk over to one of the trees, sit down, and lean my back against it. The next thing I know I'm being woken up by my daughter.

"Hey," she says shaking my shoulders, "wake up, Vamir. I need to ask you something."

My eyelids feel like sandpaper against my eyeballs as I lift them to look at her.

I clear my throat and rub my face to chase away the haze of sleep still clouding my thoughts.

"Sorry," I say, wiping at a trail of drool from a corner of my mouth,

"I guess I was more tired than I thought. How long have I been asleep?"

Ivy sits cross-legged in front of me. "I have no idea, but I've been gone for a couple of hours. It's been a tough day for both of us. I'm not surprised you needed some rest."

"Trying, yes, but also exhilarating for me. I wasn't sure I would ever be able to meet you in person, but fate decided to place us together."

"Fate," she scoffs. "Do you really believe our lives are preplanned by some greater force?"

"I do. There are people born among the fae who can see the future. They're called seers."

Ivy strokes a blade of grass thoughtfully before yanking it out of the ground.

"Do you think fate made me do that?" she asks, tossing the piece of grass away. "Did a seer predict I would end its life so abruptly?"

I shrug. "I have no idea. What a seer is able to predict is different for each of them, or, at least, that's what I've been told. Some of them see the future of others through the future of their own lives, and others see major events in fae history."

Ivy tilts her head as she mulls over my words. "Then the ones who see the future of those around them are only seeing their own future through various perspectives?"

"Sort of. Every life affects others. I've never actually met a seer. The last one died before I was old enough to understand what a seer was, but my mother was good friends with her."

Ivy pulls out the handkerchief with the diamond from her pants pocket. "Do you think it was the seer who told your mom to place this in the Queen's Circlet because she knew I would find it one day?"

"It's possible."

Ivy sighs and places the diamond back in her pocket for safekeeping. A tense silence falls between us, and I know she has more questions for me. Is she having trouble stringing together the right words or is she afraid to hear my answers?

"When you learned I was still alive, why didn't you come to me? You could have saved me a lot of self-doubt if you had just told me what I was and why my touch killed people. You don't seem to understand how horrible it was to grow up thinking I was a freak of nature."

"If I could go back and change one thing in my life, I would change that decision. At the time, I thought keeping my bad luck out of your life was the best thing I could do for you. I'm sorry I didn't come to you. I'm sorry I let you down like that. All I can do is ask for your forgiveness, but I don't expect it. In fact, I don't expect anything from you, Ivy. After I help you and your friends through the trials, I'll cut myself out of your life forever, if that's what you want."

"I don't know what I want," she says, looking torn. "A part of me wants to get to know you and a part of me wants to hit you so hard you see stars."

I chuckle. "There is so much of your mother and grandmother in you. It makes me proud to see that. They were always stronger than me."

"I had to develop a tough skin growing up. No one wanted to be friends with the freak who could kill them with one touch. I faced a lot of taunts and thrown objects in my day."

I grimace. "That sounds awful, but it seems to have shaped you into a strong woman."

"Is that how you're going to justify leaving me to fend for myself?" Her anger tightens her lips and brightens her eyes.

"No. There's no way I can justify what I did to you. All I can do is hope you have room in your heart to forgive me, but if you don't, I'll understand."

Ivy looks away, unable to meet my gaze as she thinks. Finally, she looks back at me with a new sense of purpose.

"So, these trials we'll have to face here. Do you happen to know what any of them are?"

Regretfully, I shake my head. "I honestly have no idea."

"What do you know that will help us pass them?"

"I know you'll only be given one chance to pass them all. If you fail even one, this world will be reduced to dust."

She whistles. "Wow. I was hoping we would be given some slack. Maybe the best three out of five or something."

"Zero slack. That's the way your grandfather designed the tests."

"I've seen him in Emily's memories." She leans forward and whispers, "Is he really that evil?"

"I've had a hard time believing he's completely evil. I think he just wants to do what's best for the fae no matter who it hurts. He doesn't believe humanity should be given a second chance. The people who follow his way of thinking are against humans joining them in the real world. The worry is that humanity will want to disrupt the paradise they've built, but what they consider to be paradise was actually built on the almost complete genocide of the human race."

Ivy leans back. "I'm not sure I want to live with the fae. They sound like horrible people."

"They're not all bad. My grandmother is one of the sweetest people I know. My grandfather's ideas are antiquated. It's really my mother who should be leading the fae."

"If Emily was in charge, I could see us all getting along, but from what I've seen of your grandfather, it doesn't seem likely he would willingly hand over his crown."

"I would have to agree. Something very drastic would have to happen before he abdicates the throne."

Another moment of silence falls between us as Ivy picks at the grass in front of her again. I can tell she wants to say something else, so I wait. Whatever she needs of me I will do. No questions asked.

"I don't hate you," she blurts out before lifting her gaze to meet mine. "I would have to know you better to feel that deep of an emotion."

"Totally understandable." Her words hurt. In fact, they cut me to the quick like a sharp blade slicing into my heart, but I'll never burden her with my pain. I made the decision to stay out of her life. It was the wrong choice. I'm man enough to own up to that, but I will never make her feel guilty for not caring about me.

"What's weird is that I do care about Emily." She leans back on the palms of her hands. "Having experienced everything she stored on the diamond makes me feel like I know her."

"In a sense, you know my parents better than I do." It's a hard truth to admit, but it's the truth, nonetheless. "She never talks about my father. I think it causes her too much pain, even after all these years."

"Their love was special." Ivy leans slightly forward again. "You should know that your father loved you very much. You and Emily were the most important people in his life. Now that I know who you are, I can see some of his features in your face."

"Really?" I sit up straighter. "I've never seen him. I don't even know what he looked like."

"Emily never described him to you? She never drew you a picture?"

"Nothing." My shoulders slump. "Anytime I brought him up, she would look sad, so I eventually stopped asking her questions. It wasn't worth causing her so much pain."

"I guess I could watch the sex memory again," she says with a grimace, "and then give you the diamond so you can see him in the rest of her memories. You know the first time the sex was kind of enjoyable, but now that I know they're my grandmother and grandfather, it's a little creepy."

I laugh. Ivy starts to laugh too.

"You don't have to watch it again," I say. "You shouldn't do anything that makes you feel uncomfortable for my sake."

"I've already seen it once. Watching it a second time isn't going to kill me. You need to know what your father looked like. It's time."

"Speaking of relationships," I say, feeling uneasy as I attempt to get to know my daughter better, "you and Damon . . . do you like him? Is he the right man for you or just the better of two evils considering Simon wants you too?"

Ivy shivers. "Ugh. Simon. He is not going to be happy when he learns that I'm his half-sister. We obviously can't marry one another now. We would probably have mutant children with two heads or four arms."

I laugh at her joke, but she might not be too far off the mark with her assumption.

"At least the truth gets you out of any entanglement with him. I see a lot of his father in how he acts."

"That's not surprising," she snorts. "His mother died when she had me, so his father was all he had for a role model."

"True, but there comes a time when we all make our own decisions in life. You can't keep placing the blame on someone else when you discover for yourself what's right and wrong."

"I'm not sure I agree with that." Ivy leans forward with her elbows propped on her knees. "If you're raised by someone whose right and wrong compass is skewed, can you ever truly tell right from wrong?"

"I see what you're saying, but I don't agree with it. I think everyone has the innate ability to distinguish what they should do versus what isn't acceptable once they reach a certain age. Social cues are everywhere unless the person raising you does so in a bubble of isolation. Maybe if they're the only one you have contact with, it could be true, but Simon grew up in a palace full of people. He would have been exposed to hundreds of situations where people did the right thing versus the wrong thing."

"So you're saying the way someone is nurtured doesn't matter?" she asks incredulously. "I don't believe that. Boris raised me to know the difference between right and wrong. If I had been left to live on the streets and ridiculed by everyone in town, I'm not sure I would have turned out so well. I would have been filled with hate and killed anyone who dared to approach me."

"I'm sorry you had to go through that. If I had known what people were doing to you, I would have gone to you."

"It doesn't matter now. I am who I am because of Boris's love, and I've made my peace with people being scared of me."

"The fae can take the poison out of your system."

Ivy sits up straight and I can see the wheels in her mind rapidly turning.

"Like they did for you?" she asks. "When you became a scout?"

"Yes. It's a painless procedure. All we have to do is make it through the trials and get out of the sphere."

Ivy scrambles to her feet. "Let's go get the others then. We need to tell them everything."

I stand up with a heavy heart because Ivy isn't going to like what I say next.

"We can't tell them anything." Her reaction is just what I expected.

"What do you mean we can't tell them anything?" she demands. "We have to tell them."

I shake my head. "If we tell them, this world will be forfeit. They have to face the trials on their own without any interference from us. All of the decisions have to be made by the humans. *Pure* humans."

Ivy kicks a nearby tree out of irritation. She automatically regrets her decision when she lets out a yelp in pain and hops around on one foot.

I refrain from laughing at her little temper tantrum. I'm certain it wouldn't earn me any favorable points in her eyes.

"Then what *can* I tell Damon?" she asks, testing her foot gingerly on the ground before placing her full weight on it again.

"You can tell him about me and my mother, but nothing about the upcoming challenges here and nothing about us being inside a sphere. If you do, we're all dead."

Ivy's hands form fists at her sides. She looks like she wants to hit something, probably me.

"Then why did you tell me about the trials?" she shouts. "Now I have to lie to everyone."

"I'm sorry. I thought you would want to know."

She growls in frustration. "It would have been simpler if I didn't."

I can't seem to do anything right with my daughter. How will she ever learn to trust me if I keep making mistakes like this?

"Let's go," she grumbles, leading the way back to the cave. "We've been away for too long. Hopefully, everyone is awake by now."

I walk behind her in silence, not wanting to vex her any more than I already have.

The ground beneath our feet begins to tremble violently. Ivy loses her footing and falls to the grass. I run to her side.

"Are you all right?" Even as I ask the question, I see her grimace in pain. A small gash on her left temple is bleeding after falling onto a small sharp rock on the ground.

She nods and touches the wound on her head. The trees around us sway violently and the wind thrashes us from all sides.

"What's happening?" she shouts over the roar of the gale.

"I don't know!"

A loud grinding sound draws our attention to the mountain. Large and small boulders begin to careen down its side. I grab Ivy by the arm and haul her up as quickly as possible.

"Run!" I order, dragging her with me before we're buried alive underneath the rubble.

We just make it out of the way, only being battered in the back with a few small rocks. An unholy whine fills the air, drawing our attention to the star filled sky.

A jagged luminescent line appears directly overhead, stretching from one edge of the sky to the other as far as we can see.

The wind settles, making it possible to speak without having to scream.

"What is that?" Ivy asks apprehensively as we both continue to stare at the line in the sky.

"I have no idea. I've never seen anything like it before."

Ivy whirls around to look behind us. She begins to tremble and her breathing becomes unsteady.

"Damon. Boris . . ."

I see tears stream down her face before she runs to where the cave opening should be. I follow after her, already suspecting the same thing she does.

When we reach the spot where the cave was, all we find is a pile of rubble at least twenty feet high. Boulders of all sizes block the entrance to the cave, leaving us helpless to save the people trapped inside.

"No!" Ivy falls to her knees in a wailing sob.

I consider consoling her, but I'm not sure she would welcome it. The best thing I can do is try to figure out a way to dig through this mess and save the man she cares for and the man she considers to be her real father.

How will I work that small miracle?

I have no idea, but if I'm ever going to have a real relationship with my daughter, I have to at least try.

EPILOGUE

(Emily's Mother's Point of View)

My husband growls at the screen when he sees our daughter lift her middle finger at him. We watched as she and Oberon crash landed into the lake. I had no doubt she would survive such a catastrophe, but Elrod had his reservations.

If I remember correctly, I believe the hand gesture our daughter just used meant a sign of disrespect. Inwardly, I laugh at her obstinate behavior.

"She's always been rather stubborn," I muse as Elrod turns the hologram off. "Would you expect anything less from our daughter?"

"A little loyalty wouldn't hurt," he rails while pacing back and forth in the sitting room of the castle.

"Calm down, Elrod. You're going to give yourself a heart attack and do exactly what she wants—die."

Elrod stops pacing and points an accusing finger at me. "I know it was you, Carina. I know you're the one who switched out the sphere."

"Well, of course it was me." I wave off his accusation. "Who else would have access to the room? You and I are the only ones who can go in there. It doesn't take a genius to figure that out."

"Why?" He crosses his arms over his chest. "Why do you under-mine me every chance you get? It's like you want to make sure Emily only trusts you."

"She'll never trust you, Elrod. You killed the only man she loved and turned her son into a pariah to the rest of the fae. Emily should be able to trust at least one of her parents, don't you agree?"

"Why is it that I have to be the villain?"

I stand from the couch and sashay to my husband. "Because you're so good at it, dear. With your brooding brow and thunderous voice. You make a very convincing antihero."

"You always know how to sweet talk me." He leans over and kisses me on the lips.

I pat him on the arm. "Just trust me. I know how to handle this situation. I've been preparing for just this moment."

"Oh?" Elrod's interest is piqued. "Is it time for you to unleash this super weapon you keep hinting at?"

I can't help but smile. "It's not a weapon, dear. Just a tool to make things the way they should be."

"Hmph." Elrod doesn't look convinced. "Well, I hope you know what you're doing, Carina. If you don't, we might find ourselves trapped inside a sphere of our own one of these days."

"You worry too much." I make my way to the doors leading out to the foyer of the castle. "Leave everything up to me."

After I step into the entryway, I greet the guards I pass with polite hellos while heading straight for my private elevator. Once inside, I push the button to take me a hundred feet below the surface to my chambers. Palace life has never suited me well. I enjoy the solitude of my rooms. There I can surround myself with almost everything I love in the world. I'm only missing two pieces—Emily and my grand-daughter. They'll be joining me soon though. I have no doubt about that.

Once the elevator doors open, I walk into my chambers.

"Music." A melodic tune composed by one of the most famous fae composers begins to play, filling my space with just the right amount of noise. Walking through the mostly white living room, I make my way down one of the hallways to a door only I can open. Once inside, I hum as I glide down the staircase.

The sound of a baby gurgling welcomes me well before I see my little boy and his nanny.

"How is my little man today?" I ask Gertrude.

Gertrude stands from the blanket she and Kiah were playing blocks on.

"He's been doing well, my queen." Her voice always quavers when she speaks to me. You would think after spending all day with Kiah that she would appreciate my company more. With her gaze glued to the floor, she continues. "Happy as can be, as always."

With a gentle touch, I place my index finger underneath her chin and force her head to tilt upwards until we're eye to eye.

"Don't be ashamed of the way you look, Gertrude. Take pride in what you are. Not everyone gets a second chance at life."

Gertrude's undead eyes finally meet my gaze. I notice tears begin to form in them but I choose to ignore her open display of emotion.

Kiah gurgles from his blanket, raising his arms to me.

"Oh, my sweet, gentle boy." In only a few seconds, I have my son propped up on one hip as he reaches out to play with my long white hair. His eyes, just like Gertrude's, hold the mark of the undead. I pull him closer to my chest to hug him. "Mommy's eternal angel. What would I ever do without you?"

Kiah giggles like he understands me, but his mind will always process things like an eight-month-old baby.

When Oberon's father began to dabble in dark magic, I begged him to return my son to me after he fell down a flight of stairs and broke his neck. It took a lot of cajoling, but he finally relented and showed me how to bring the dead back to life. He said that if I wanted to do it to my son, I would have to be the one who cast the spell, not him. I was fine with that. As long as I had my Kiah back, I didn't care.

After all these years I've only used my knowledge a few times.

"Did you do what I asked you to do today?" I ask Gertrude.

"Yes, my queen, I did exactly what you said. Things seem to be going well as far as I can tell."

"Good." I hand Kiah over to her. "I'll go see to our guest myself just to make sure everything is as it should be."

I walk down a dark hallway leading to a spiral staircase that goes another twenty feet down. Once there, I enter a stark chamber and see that the glass suspension pod my guest was in for so many years is now empty.

My guest lies naked on an examination table in the middle of the room. It took quite a long time to heal all his wounds, but the moment has finally come for him to emerge from this room and serve his true purpose.

Of course, he's been dead for so many years, I'm not sure what he'll end up remembering from his first life, but it almost doesn't matter.

I walk over and begin to cast my resurrection spell. It's taken me quite some time to perfect it, but now I can bring someone back to life within a few short minutes.

As the music around us continues to play, I feel like the strings of the violin section are playing within my own heart. Once the spell is complete, my new minion opens his eyes and looks straight ahead with a vacant expression.

I peer at him, bringing our faces so close together I can feel the coldness of his breath.

"Do you know who I am?" I ask him.

"My master," he replies in a croaked voice.

I can't help but smile at his answer. "Yes, I am, Mark. Now be a sweet boy and sit up for me so I can have a good look at you."

Mark sits up and remains perfectly still.

Perfection. I can see why my daughter loved him so much. He is quite delicious to look at. Even more so now that I control not only his mind but also his body. What fun I can have with what I see.

"Mark," I say, looking into his undead eyes, "do you remember someone named Emily?"

His brow furrows in confusion. "No."

Such a simple answer, but one that just won't do.

"That's all right, my sweets. I'll tell you all about her, and when I'm through, it'll be almost like you have your own memories of her back. She's very important to us, Mark. Very important indeed. We must protect her. Is that understood?"

"Yes."

Not much of a talker, but I'll soon have that sorted out. It always takes some time for the newly resurrected to act natural, but this is the first time I've ever performed the spell on a human. I'm not sure their minds were made for such a thing.

Oh well, it doesn't matter.

Once Emily sees her husband, she'll forget all about Oberon and come running back home. Once she brings me my granddaughter and I change her too, we'll all be one big happy family.

The End

AUTHOR'S NOTE

Thank you so much for reading *Unwavering, Wolf Kings of Twilight, Book 2*. If you have enjoyed this book, please take a moment to leave a review.

Just visit: Unwavering
https://amzn.to/3QGZVjp

As always, thank you for reading my stories! I hope you will join me on a brand-new adventure and discover interesting new characters along the way.

To receive the latest news about new releases, exclusive teasers, sales, upcoming books, and giveaways, join my newsletter today.
https://bit.ly/SJWestsnewsletter

Sincerely,
S. J. West

WOLF KINGS OF TWILIGHT

NEXT FROM S.J. WEST

Undeniable,

Wolf Kings of Twilight, Book 3

Exclusively on Amazon! FREE on KU!

https://amzn.to/3HLCAcl

WOLF KINGS OF TWILIGHT

ABOUT THE AUTHOR

Once upon a time, a little girl was born on a cold winter morning in the heart of Seoul, Korea. She was brought to America by her parents and raised in the Deep South where the words ma'am and y'all became an integrated part of her lexicon. She wrote her first novel at the age of eight and continued writing on and off during her teenage years. In college she studied biology and chemistry and finally combined the two by earning a master's degree in biochemistry.

After that she moved to Yankee land where she lived for four years working in a laboratory at Cornell University. Homesickness and snow aversion forced her back South where she lives in the land, which spawned Jim Henson, Elvis Presley, Oprah Winfrey, John Grisham and B.B. King.

After finding her Prince Charming, she gave birth to a wondrous baby girl and they all lived happily ever after.

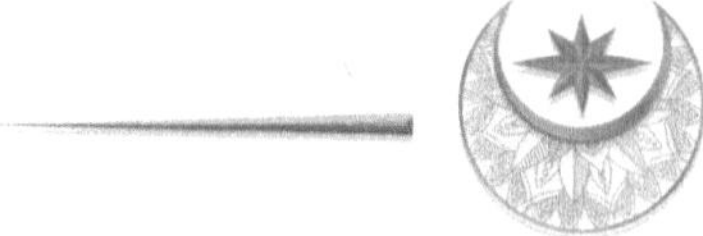

As always, you can learn about the progress on my books, get news about new releases, new projects and participate on amazing give-aways by signing up for my newsletter:

FB Book Page: www.facebook.com/ReadTheWatchersTrilogy
FB Author Page: https://www.facebook.com/sandra.west.585112
Website: www.sjwest.com
Amazon: author.to/SJWest-Amazon
Goodreads: https://www.goodreads.com/author/show/6561395.S_J_West
Bookbub: https://www.bookbub.com/authors/s-j-west
Newsletter Sign-up: https://bit.ly/SJWestsnewsletter
Instagram: @authorsjwest
Twitter: @SJWest2013

If you'd like to contact the author, you can email her to: sandrawest481@gmail.com